Accl

The Master of Seacliff

"Max Pierce skillfully walks a difficult tightrope of tone in this delightfully sexy gothic pastiche. He's able to both honor the wildly romantic nineteenth-century novel as well as bringing it up-to-date with its nod to contemporary sexual honesty. He mixes into his stew dashes of *Rebecca, Jane Eyre, Wuthering Heights, The Turn of The Screw,* and comes up with a surprisingly original and wholly entertaining work of his own."

—Charles Busch
Author, *The Tale of the Allergist's Wife*;
Author and Star, *Psycho Beach Party* and *Die Mommie Die*

"In the tradition of Charlotte Brontë's *Jane Eyre,* Emily Brontë's *Wuthering Heights,* Vincent Virga's *Gaywyck,* and the classic TV show *Dark Shadows,* Max Pierce's delightful suspense novel gives us all the rich and romantic elements of the gothic, but with a welcome queer twist. Here are a mysterious mansion above the sea, an innocent tutor, a troubled child, and a series of unsolved murders. And, in the dark character of brooding Duncan Stewart, Pierce gives us the sort of handsome, hirsute, tormented Byronic hero that gay male fans of the gothic either will want to become or will want to ravish."

—Jeff Mann, MA
Assistant Professor of Creative Writing,
English Department, Virginia Tech

"Max Pierce has reinvigorated the gothic novel. Everything you'd expect is there—the handsome, brooding, lord of the manor; the isolated seafront mansion, haunted by tragedy; the naïve young tutor who is determined to solve the mysteries that surround him. Yet by giving this old story a gay twist, Pierce has created something totally new and fascinating. Filled with extravagant writing, dark secrets, and deep passions, *The Master of Seacliff* is a great read."

—Neil Plakcy
Author, *Mahu*

"Five stars. *The Master of Seacliff* is a finely wrought Gothic thriller with a contemporary twist. Max Pierce understands the fine art of mystery story-telling, finding that magic of the past great writers who doted on dark old mansions that held their secrets of murder and mayhem much like an old spinster creaking in her attic rocking chair. But Pierce introduces a taboo subject of the time in which he sets this intriguing tale (1899 in America) and in doing so refreshes his story for a new audience of Romance aficionados. He populates his engrossing yarn with handsome men (yes, and women) most of whom appear connected by their closeted sexuality! Pierce writes with such uncanny attention to detail and to keeping the language and atmosphere of 1899 in place that he creates a page-turning thriller that keeps the reader guessing up to the final page. Gothic horror, interrelated murders and suicides, past and present gay relationships, and exploration of a time when a staff of servants underlined the intrigue of the old mansions all make this book an absorbing new novel. Pierce's elegant prose puts it all into perspective, keeping the sensual aspects alive but related in the tenor of the times. By the end of the novel, closing the covers, the reader satisfyingly reflects on the forbidden love affairs the walls of Seacliff had seen and how those gay trysts opened such strange events that made the discoveries of perpetrators so fascinating."

—Grady Harp
Author, *War Songs*;
Art Essayist; Curator

"I tried to resist, but could not. By the time I had finished the first chapter of this delightful pastiche of a Gothic novel, the seduction had begun and I could not turn away. *The Master of Seacliff* drew me in with its clever plot, brooding hero, dark secrets, and innocent, yet plucky narrator. This isn't your mother's typical Gothic mystery novel, though. Max Pierce weaves gay love into the tapestry of windswept cliffs, family tragedies, mysterious figures in the fog, and murder. The result is both tongue-in-cheek and deliciously romantic, but also a love story simmering with forbidden desires to which no proper gentleman would admit. It's a terrifically entertaining book that you can't afford to pass up."

—Jim Tushinski
Author, *Van Allen's Ecstasy*

"This book has all the page-turning elements of a gothic tale in place—mysterious keys to hidden boxes and locked rooms, vanishing former lovers, sly servants, letters gone awry, friends who may be enemies, and mysteries of sound and smell that confound the senses. Even more, it offers a tantalizing love story that may be doomed if Andrew and Duncan can't stop past treachery from engulfing their lives like the fog at Seacliff. A delicious read to savor on a stormy night."

—Becky Cochrane
Author, *A Coventry Christmas*;
Co-author, *It Had To Be You,*
He's the One, I'm Your Man,
Someone Like You, The Deal,
and *Three Fortunes in One Cookie*

NOTES FOR PROFESSIONAL LIBRARIANS AND LIBRARY USERS

This is an original book title published by Southern Tier Editions™, Harrington Park Press®, the trade division of The Haworth Press, Inc. Unless otherwise noted in specific chapters with attribution, materials in this book have not been previously published elsewhere in any format or language.

CONSERVATION AND PRESERVATION NOTES

All books published by The Haworth Press, Inc., and its imprints are printed on certified pH neutral, acid-free book grade paper. This paper meets the minimum requirements of American National Standard for Information Sciences-Permanence of Paper for Printed Material, ANSI Z39.48-1984.

DIGITAL OBJECT IDENTIFIER (DOI) LINKING

The Haworth Press is participating in reference linking for elements of our original books. (For more information on reference linking initiatives, please consult the CrossRef Web site at www.crossref.org.) When citing an element of this book such as a chapter, include the element's Digital Object Identifier (DOI) as the last item of the reference. A Digital Object Identifier is a persistent, authoritative, and unique identifier that a publisher assigns to each element of a book. Because of its persistence, DOIs will enable The Haworth Press and other publishers to link to the element referenced, and the link will not break over time. This will be a great resource in scholarly research.

The Master of Seacliff

HARRINGTON PARK PRESS®
Southern Tier Editions™
Gay Men's Fiction

The Master of Seacliff

Max Pierce

Southern Tier Editions™
Harrington Park Press®
The Trade Division of The Haworth Press, Inc.
New York • London • Oxford

For more information on this book or to order, visit
http://www.haworthpress.com/store/product.asp?sku=5778

or call 1-800-HAWORTH (800-429-6784) in the United States and Canada
or (607) 722-5857 outside the United States and Canada

or contact orders@HaworthPress.com

Published by

Southern Tier Editions™, Harrington Park Press®, the trade division of The Haworth Press,
Inc., 10 Alice Street, Binghamton, NY 13904–1580.

PUBLISHER'S NOTE
The development, preparation, and publication of this work has been undertaken with great care.
However, the Publisher, employees, editors, and agents of The Haworth Press are not responsible
for any errors contained herein or for consequences that may ensue from use of materials or information contained in this work. The Haworth Press is committed to the dissemination of ideas and
information according to the highest standards of intellectual freedom and the free exchange of
ideas. Statements made and opinions expressed in this publication do not necessarily reflect the
views of the Publisher, Directors, management, or staff of The Haworth Press, Inc., or an
endorsement by them.

This is a work of fiction. Names, characters, places, and incidents either are the products of the
author's imagination or are used fictitiously, and any resemblance to actual persons, living or
dead, business establishments, events, or locales is entirely coincidental.

Cover design/photography by Anthony A. G. Kluck.
Cover model: Steven Mason, Jr.

Author Photo by Stathis Orphanos.

Library of Congress Cataloging-in-Publication Data

Pierce, Max.
    The master of Seacliff / Max Pierce.
        p. cm.
    ISBN-13: 978-1-56023-636-8 (soft : alk. paper)
    ISBN-10: 1-56023-636-1 (soft : alk. paper)
    I. Title.
    PS3616.I356M37 2007
    813'.6—dc22

                                                                    2006010633

For my parents. Also Patricia and Ed Lippman, Sr.:
until we meet on the Island of the Blue Dolphins

Acknowledgments

Craig Hamrick told me I could write this book, and it is to him that I offer this humble product, the realization of a dream. Ayofemi Folayan and Barbara Ankrum provided light in the early drafts, and Terry Wolverton, Cara Chow, Marcella Greening, Matthew Knight, Dan Luckenbill, Trish Nickles, and David Vernon gave me invaluable insight into making the story better. Ed Lippman Jr. puts up with me, despite myself.

The Master of Seacliff
Published by The Haworth Press, Inc., 2007. All rights reserved.
doi:10.1300/5778_a

Chapter One

I often wonder what direction my life would have taken had I never discovered Seacliff. Leaving the simple world where I was raised, one as predictable as sunrise, had been easy. I raced onward—blind but blissful—to what I knew would be a more vibrant and vital future. Looking back, I laugh at my innocence and complete lack of clarity that such a prospect could also hold deceit, temptation, and extreme danger.

On a muggy May afternoon in 1899, I peered out a beveled window, the only passenger of a private railcar, watching the scenery grow more and more remote. My right hand held a sketchbook fashioned from scraps of paper I had saved; in my left, a worn charcoal pencil. But on this day I could not focus. From the sights and sounds of New York City, which had always been my home, with its tall buildings and thousands of people, I now traveled north to a coastal area as remote and foreign to me as Robinson Crusoe's world.

I headed toward a new life, on the crest of a new century, the twentieth century, and to Seacliff, where people who were only names without faces awaited me. Responsible for and to myself for the first time; this fact excited and frightened me. The engine and the wheels of the train sensed my fear; I could hear its metallic voice urge, "Go back, go back. Go back, go back." But I had no place else to go.

"Andrew Wyndham, you're upsetting yourself over nothing," I said aloud, thankful no one was around to overhear. "What's done is done."

Until last week, the pattern of my life, at the ripe old age of twenty, appeared set in stone. My life was committed to forever working for my aunt and uncle in their dry goods store on Tenth Street in Manhattan. I had been there since the age of nine, when my parents were lost at sea. At that time, my mother's sister and her husband appeared quite pleased to have me in their home. As I grew older, they saw me as a continuation of their legacy: the store. But as I developed into adulthood, I knew in my heart that a life as a shopkeeper was not my calling. I dreamed of escaping the store and becoming an artist. Having been inspired at age twelve by an exhibit of up-

The Master of Seacliff
Published by The Haworth Press, Inc., 2007. All rights reserved.
doi:10.1300/5778_01

and-coming French Independent painters at the Metropolitan Museum, I wanted to move to France, live in a small vine-covered country cottage, and paint from morning to midnight.

"There are two ways to acquire wealth," my aunt said. "Marry into it, or find a position serving those who do, and hope for the best." Getting to France required money, a commodity I did not possess. Thus, when an old friend presented me an opportunity to work among the affluent, I seized it.

I had known Michael Betancourt for years. A physician, about ten years older than I, he possessed an inner strength I hoped to acquire when older. He worked for my uncle while in school. He remained friendly, although he had moved beyond our social level years ago and now had an office on fashionable Fourteenth Street, overlooking Union Square. Michael had always taken an interest in my life, especially in my art. I substituted him for the older brother I always wanted. I hoped he thought about me in a similar fashion.

"Andrew, I have spoken to your uncle about the possibility of employment outside of their shop. I know it would be most difficult to persuade you to leave, but I have a situation in need of your services." A mischievous curl came to the corner of his lip.

"What? Please tell me."

"Duncan Stewart is an old friend, and his son requires a tutor. At their estate: up the coast about two hundred miles."

"I know nothing about tutoring a child." I pictured myself in a stern black suit, my sandy blond hair plastered in a most severe manner to my head and my blue eyes hidden behind unnecessary glasses. Rapping a ruler on a desk I saw myself dry and wrinkled, inside as well as out. It was a marked contrast to how I envisioned my life as an artist: letting my hair grow full and long and wearing loose pastel clothing as I sketched beside the Seine.

He put his arm around my shoulder, drawing me in. "You have a solid education. Why not put it to use?"

Michael's voice reassured so, as did the lightness of his forearm across my back. He transmitted energy into me, so different from the draining feeling my family evoked. My body began to tingle, and I became embarrassed at the emotions I often had to wrangle into submission.

Unaware of my discomfort—as always—my friend continued. "You will receive a monthly salary, in addition to your room and board. This could be an excellent avenue to pay your passage to France, Andrew."

Freedom! I could begin a new life. Tears of happiness welled up, and the overflow streamed down my cheeks. Michael pulled me close, and the scent of his jacket, the same spiced fragrance I once associated with my father, comforted me. He handed me his handkerchief, pulled me up squarely by the shoulders, and his hazel eyes looked at me through his silver-rimmed spectacles.

"The Stewart's private railcar leaves Battery Park on Friday. I am going ahead but will meet you at the Fosterstown station, the last stop on the railway. We can ride to Seacliff together."

The direction of my life changed with these statements.

My relatives showed no sadness at the news of my impending departure. My aunt, yet again offering her opinion on acquiring money, had stated, "Andy, such a stroke of luck! You'll be hobnobbing with the Astors and Vanderbilts in no time. Don't forget about those who raised you." My uncle, who prided himself on his knowledge of genealogy of the East Coast's more prominent families, was less enthusiastic.

"Old man Stewart was a fine person as long as he didn't think you were cheating him. Shot dead in his own house, he was. Crazy Scots."

"Murdered!"

"Talk was, Duncan Stewart murdered his father to get control of his business. But they pinned it on someone else. Make sure you keep on your Bible studies while there." He paused. "And don't be sticking your nose in their problems either. They're a cursed lot, those folks."

I ignored his remark about minding my business. "Cursed? That only happens in Mr. Poe's tales, Uncle."

"All that money can't buy them God's blessing."

I learned no more from my uncle. He always concluded his stories with a moral of some sort, and this was no exception. But no longer would I have to listen to his parables or his derisive remarks about my art. Paris would become a reality, now temporarily postponed until I earned the money. And earn it I would, as an employee of Duncan Stewart, the master of Seacliff. Although shocked by the news of a murder, I was eager to get to any house and employer far away from my own.

A whoosh of steam announced the train's arrival, and I looked out upon a rather lackluster group of buildings. I picked up my traveling bag, and as I stepped onto the platform, the strong smell of the Atlantic washed over me. It was much cooler than muggy Manhattan, and I was glad I had carried and not packed my brown cloth overcoat. I took an extended breath and exhaled. My life began anew today, with a new home, employer, and his young son, who would be my responsibility to educate.

Although my anticipation grew, I pulled my thoughts back to the immediate. Michael was not there to greet me; the platform remained deserted. Walking over to a flat bench against the ticket office, which was closed, I sat down to wait.

I pulled some paper out of my makeshift sketchbook and started a study of the mighty train that brought me here. Lost in thought, I had completed one drawing when a slurred voice came from my left.

"Want some advice? Get back on that train. There's nothin' but death and despair at Seacliff."

Jolted, the papers fell from my lap and scattered along the ground. The wind picked up a few pieces and began tossing them in the air. A grizzled man stood at the west edge of the platform. He was short, tanned like oil paper, and wearing dried out, wrinkled clothing. Staring ahead as he limped toward me, the lenses of his glasses made his eyes look larger than normal. Without waiting for me to respond or acknowledge him, he continued, rasping.

"Take it from one who's seen the devil's wrath. They'll all join Satan in hell. You too, unless you leave. Run!"

I wanted to run; this was true. Away from this man who reeked of an overwhelming mix of hay, horses, and, most prominent of all, liquor. Seacliff polarized people's opinions; this was certain. First my uncle's, and now this man.

"What do you mean, sir?"

"No time to talk. Board the train, now. It leaves again tonight. Hide where they can't find you, till you get home." He extended a wiry arm for my bag, then jerked his craggy face to the east and narrowed his gaze. A cloud of dust swirled around a team of coal-black horses coming up the road. Straining my eyes, I saw Michael sitting next to the driver and waving his hat at me.

"Seacliff is my home," I answered with forced confidence. But as I turned, the stranger had evaporated.

I collected my scattered papers as the coach pulled up. Michael, his cheeks pink from wind, beamed as he hopped off the seat. He looked elegant in a camel-colored overcoat and matching hat.

"My apologies for not escorting you from Manhattan and for this unexpected delay." His resonant voice and firm handshake calmed me in an instant. He gave me a quick hug, which made me glow inward as well as out.

Picking up my valise, he directed me to the waiting carriage. Made of polished ebony, with silver appointments that added contrast, and red velvet curtains at each window, I had never seen one more opulent. It was led by two black stallions, with two smaller horses behind. The coachman was an older man, as round as he was tall, and about my uncle's age, with a full beard and dancing gray eyes below a bowler hat. Beside him on the seat was an unusual-looking boy, about six years old. His eyes were the same gray, but enormous. His hair fascinated me: it was as white as chimney smoke. Staring at me with an expressionless look, he cowered next to the older man. This boy was not dressed well enough to be my new pupil.

"Andrew Wyndham: Mr. Johnson. Seacliff wouldn't function without him and his wife."

Mr. Johnson tipped his black hat to me. "Welcome, Mister Andrew. This is me grandson, Asher. Just call him Ash." He nudged the boy, who responded by doffing his cap to me as well.

"Hello, Ash." There was a sweet quality to this wraithlike child, and I hoped my own charge would be as endearing. Eyeing me, Ash dove further into the recesses of his grandfather's coat. As Michael and I got in, I noticed the scripted DS on the door. My employer's personal monogram; I belonged to him now as well.

The proud stallions began their trot home. As we passed the tavern, the stranger with the pronounced limp emerged and shook his fist at the carriage. Mr. Johnson shouted back, but I couldn't make out his words. I thought about mentioning it to Michael, but pushed the unpleasant experience from my mind. In seconds, the landscape changed from the wooden sidewalk of the town to open countryside. The springtime air was pleasant, but I could see in the distance a looming fog. We headed toward that fog, the coast and Seacliff. Before I could contemplate further, Michael's voice interrupted.

"We have about a half-hour ride. Sit back while I tell you about life here."

"Uncle told me a little about Duncan Stewart."

"I have no doubt." Michael's face creased into a comical grimace.

"But you know how he exaggerates everything."

"Perhaps. What did he tell you?"

Michael's expression intrigued me more than Uncle's stories had last night. Now was the time to ask questions, for Michael would never lie to me.

"Mr. Stewart's father was murdered—"

"And Duncan was suspected, that is true. However, it was concluded that Gordon Stewart's assistant, a man named Albert Brown, killed Gordon and then himself."

"If that is the case, then why does such a rumor continue?" I said, thinking of the stranger at the station.

Michael avoided looking at me. "People are naturally suspicious of Duncan."

"Do he and Mrs. Stewart have other children?"

"Duncan has never married," Michael began, and then continued, not acknowledging my shocked reaction. "He is considered by many to be the most eligible bachelor in the East, but tends to let the Stewart interests completely absorb his attention. At one time he was betrothed but headed off to Europe against his father's wishes, returning with his son."

Michael's voice faded, and the horses' clip-clop was the only sound we heard for several minutes. I decided it best not to ask how my employer acquired a son.

After a while, my friend continued. "Duncan may surprise us all by marrying."

My family often made the same comment about me, a proclamation I found irritating. Having long ago pushed thoughts of love away, I believed that to be a true artist meant my predetermined fate was one of solitude. Perhaps Mr. Stewart's commitment to work rivaled my own dedication to art. I pledged to befriend this kindred spirit whose own success and generosity allowed me to realize my dream.

"Please tell me about his son . . . Timothy, is it?"

"Tim is a typical eight-year-old, into all sorts of mischief. Unfortunately, he enjoys enacting his pranks out on others. His last governess remained only two months. Duncan felt that a man was needed, and I recommended you."

It made me proud that Michael thought of me as a man. Too often I had heard my passion for art was that of one weak and effeminate. I added, "Mr. Stewart supports my plan to go to France."

"Duncan is a great patron of the arts. Until recently, he . . . uh . . . he sponsored the acclaimed pianist Steven Charles."

The name meant nothing, and I shook my head. Michael was always abreast of well-known people. I would have to pay more attention in this new life. I might be in the presence of my idol Mr. Claude Monet without realizing.

"Steven is an incredibly talented individual. They met at a recital in the London home of a mutual friend. When Duncan returned to Seacliff from his holiday, Steven had joined him," he paused. "I'd never seen Duncan so happy. But about eight months ago, Steven abruptly left without saying farewell. He took the late train back to Manhattan and hasn't bothered to contact Duncan about his whereabouts."

I thought of the limping stranger at the station, urging me to leave on that same train.

"Duncan went in search of him, but to no avail. He returned about three weeks ago from London but hasn't been quite the same since Steven left. In the meantime, there were some issues . . . with the governess. And that's where you come in, my friend."

The complications of my new life settled in. Gaining the funds I needed to leave came with a price. The carriage picked up speed, now that I had learned my future.

"Michael, this sounds difficult. I'm only a tutor. An inexperienced one at that."

"Ah, Andrew, that's where you're mistaken. You're such a bright, cheerful lad. This house needs you. Tim has no mother, and with Steven gone, Duncan concentrates solely on business at the expense of his son. Tim needs a mentor who can provide a structure to his young life. An authority figure who can teach him not just history, grammar, and mathematics, but lessons of life. In time, you can encourage Duncan to take a more active part in his son's upbringing. You've triumphed over personal adversity, and I know you will succeed. Duncan is quite eager to have your services, even on a temporary basis."

"Michael, I'm flattered by your faith in me, but I . . ." I didn't know what to say. My bravado faltered.

"You can agree to stay the next three months. At the end of summer, if you are truly unhappy, I promise I will find you a position in Manhattan."

I nodded my head. I could not disappoint Michael. And I had no other option. I felt I traded bondage to my aunt and uncle for a home that sounded even unhappier than my old one.

Looking out the window, I watched as the dense fog enveloped the carriage and the sunlight faded with rapidity. A chill skipped down my spine, one not caused by the obvious drop in temperature. I no longer wanted to know details about the murder, or how Duncan Stewart produced a child without a proper marriage.

I heard a command from Mr. Johnson to the horses, and the carriage came to an abrupt halt. His proud voice directed itself to Michael and me.

"We've arrived at Seacliff, gents."

I shall never forget my initial glimpse of Seacliff. It is as impressive today as the first time I saw it, long ago, arriving in that ebony carriage.

Peering out the square window of the black coach, we had stopped at a large set of bronze gates. The sound of the sea grew steadily stronger as we approached, but now the sound of high tide made it almost difficult to hear Mr. Johnson's voice.

My eyes followed a slope, up and up acres of lawn, shrubbery, and tall evergreens to the top of a hill. An impressive and graceful gray mansion rambled along the crest. I could not determine whether there were two or three stories, but the setting sun made it glow with the fading rays of daylight.

Had Michael and my uncle not spoke of the tragic history of Seacliff, I would have sensed it regardless. It looked too grand, too smug in its position. Designed to look as if it had stood atop the hill for centuries, I knew that was a façade, much like its serene demeanor. I knew passion lay behind those stone walls.

I thought of a man being murdered either by his son or his business partner. The same son: producing an heir without marriage. Steven Charles: repaying his benefactor's kindness by fleeing in the middle of the night. I, Andrew Wyndham, had just consented to live amid this setting for three months. Tutor to a neglected child, and answering to his father, a broken, obsessed man, still a suspect in his father's death.

Mr. Johnson pointed to a small cottage inside the gate. "This is me and the missus' house, Mister Andrew. But anythin' you need, just tell us." The boy, Ash, scampered off the driver's seat and ran away like a spooked animal.

The carriage jerked and the stallions resumed their steady trot up a winding road. As we climbed higher, I glimpsed a beachfront and the Atlantic out the opposite window. The fog decided I had seen enough and again surrounded us. The temperature continued to drop as well, and I drew my cloth coat a little tighter around my body. The carriage turned, and we were now behind the house.

"The entrance is at the back, so all the main rooms have the best view of the ocean," Michael explained.

The sound of the horses' gait changed; we now traveled on a paved flagstone driveway. I surmised we would be at the front door soon. My pulse quickened and my throat tightened. In moments, I would be face to face with Duncan Stewart. I rehearsed my planned greeting in my mind again.

The carriage stopped a final time. Michael opened the door and I stepped out. Before me were two massive iron gates which covered doors made of leaded glass. Large gas lanterns flanked them, and their light cast an eerie glow onto the fog. The sun had almost completely withdrawn. To my left was a large courtyard with a white marble fountain in its center. The water babbled and four carved stone heads squirted water into a vase in the center. I imagined they laughed at the newest member of the Stewart household, who traded his life of oppression only to live among others' misery.

The massive doors swung open, and a tall, distinguished man with a full head of black hair streaked with white stood before us. Unlike the jovial Mr. Johnson, this man exuded grimness.

"Good evening, Dr. Michael. Mr. Wyndham." The man punctuated his welcome with a short, curt bow, which did nothing to lessen his height before me.

"Fellowes, has Duncan returned from his ride?" Michael said.

"Yes, sir. And he requests that you wait in the drawing room. Miss Elena arrived, and is there."

I was breathless, not only because of the size of the estate, but of the grandeur of it all. Walking in the front door and seeing the opulence did nothing to assuage my feelings of inadequacy, either. I also got the feeling Mr. Fellowes didn't approve of me.

Beyond the entrance, black and white marble stretched down two short flights of steps, then opened into a larger room—the Great Hall, I would later learn it was called—which resembled a giant chessboard. Ahead were twin staircases, with carved mahogany banisters that led to an upper floor. A massive bronze and crystal chandelier hung from the center. Led by Fellowes, we walked down the steps into the hall. I thought this odd until realizing the house was built into the hillside.

Michael whispered, "Fellowes has worked for the Stewarts for over forty years. He was Gordon Stewart's valet and now Duncan's."

At the bottom, we entered a smaller room, furnished with exquisite pieces I had only seen when sneaking through the lobby of the Waldorf-Astoria Hotel. A roaring fireplace warmed a welcome, and at a piano that dominated the center of the room, sat a striking woman.

"Elena," Michael said, embracing her, and bringing me over. "May I present Mr. Andrew Wyndham. Elena Van Horne is one of Duncan's dearest friends, and your neighbor at the adjoining estate."

Elena Van Horne looked as if she had been fashioned from a statue of Venus, or a Botticelli painting. She had bright blonde hair, pulled into a tight bun that rested on the nape of her slender neck. She wore an emerald green velvet gown that matched the color of her expressive eyes. Had Michael not cited Duncan Stewart's bachelor status, I would have taken Elena Van Horne to be the mistress of Seacliff.

"Welcome, Mr. Wyndham. May I please call you Andrew?" Her voice was clear and well modulated, just like the women whose conversations I would overhear at the Metropolitan Museum or outside Delmonico's restaurant.

Fellowes interrupted, "Excuse me, Miss Elena. Mr. Stewart requests I show Mr. Wyndham to his quarters. He wishes to meet with you and Dr. Michael. Alone." The valet regarded me with a cold look as he accented the word *alone*.

Elena dropped her chin. "Duncan is in one of his moods, Michael." But turning to me, she exuded warmth.

"Please excuse us, Andrew. Fellowes will take you to the kitchen, where Mrs. Johnson will serve your supper. You must be exhausted after your travels. I'm sure Duncan will want to see you at your best, in the morning." Her personality and the coziness of the fireplace made me feel a little less hesitant. I nodded and said my goodnights.

Michael said, "I shall write, Andrew; if you need me urgently, there is a telephone. Otherwise I expect to see you at the end of the summer." As he hugged me, I felt a tinge of sadness, realizing I was entirely on my own. Alone in a house where the master that I expected to welcome me remained distant and faceless for another night. At least Elena Van Horne seemed unaffected by the frostiness of Seacliff and genuine in her welcome.

As I trailed behind Fellowes through the Great Hall, I heard Michael's gentle voice.

"You mean at *Duncan's* best, don't you, Elena? Damn it, I will not have him frighten Andrew on his first night here."

Elena's rippling laugh echoed as the valet led me down a corridor lined with marble statuary of cherubs holding grapes and flutes. I would save every nickel I earned and would count the days until three months' time had passed and I could be free from my promise to my friend.

My room was off the hallway across from an oak door. Peeking through the small square window, I saw the fountain in the driveway.

"This service door is the one you should use. The front door is for the family and their guests," Fellowes ordered, his look reinforcing the fact that I was a mere employee.

I walked into the simple and clean-smelling bedroom: smaller than the one I left in New York. A narrow bed with an iron frame was tucked against the western wall. A small dresser made of pine stood opposite, with a washbowl and pitcher on it. In the center was a window that looked onto the dark hedges and trees of the front lawn.

Fellowes deposited my bag on the bed and made a great display of wiping his hands. "The kitchen is up the hall on your left. Should you require anything, please communicate through Mrs. Johnson and the appropriate arrangements will be made. Good night, Mr. Wyndham." He closed the door, leaving me alone.

I unpacked my few possessions, placing my treasured volumes of Shakespeare and Oscar Wilde on the dresser, and my homemade sketchbook beside my bed. Although small, the room was mine alone, and this pleased me. I scribbled a short letter to my aunt and uncle, informing them of my safe arrival. I scrubbed my face and walked to the kitchen.

In the distance, a grandfather clock, probably the towering one we passed in the Great Hall, chimed the eighth hour. Other chimes resonated through the house, then silence. I could sense the house's stillness, as if it studied my every movement. The master of Seacliff could not be bothered with me, but his house might communicate its position.

The smell of fresh cornbread and of beef led me to a heavy door. I pushed and entered into the largest kitchen I had ever seen. I was reminded of last spring when my cousin and I dined at the Kensington Garden restaurant on Fourteenth Street. We enjoyed a sumptuous meal but found ourselves short of cash. We washed dishes in the kitchen that evening to compensate for our feast. But the kitchen of that grand establishment was nothing compared to this.

On the wall directly in front of me was a massive stove, easily twice the size of my aunt's. Several kettles were on the burners, and a hypnotic blue flame peeked out from underneath. Next to it was a large metal door with a chrome handle. To the right, paned windows ran the entire twenty or thirty feet of the wall, with more cabinets and an enameled countertop underneath. On the wall beside me were blond wood cabinets, each filled with the most beautiful dishes. I estimated at least six different patterns.

An older woman bustled through another swinging door opposite from me. She wore a steel-gray cotton dress with a bib apron over it. Her hair was the same color as her dress, but unlike Elena Van Horne's sleek perfection in grooming, wisps sprung out in a haphazard fashion from this woman's bun.

She wrung her hands on the apron but dropped them when she saw me. Her round face had a pinkish glow and exuded the same warmth of the kitchen.

"Glory be, there's a boy with a hungry look in his eye. Sit down here and I'll fix ye up with me beef stew," she said, trundling over to the black stove and stirring the contents of a large pot. "I'm Mrs. Johnson, but I bet you guessed that already." She clucked as she sliced a generous portion of cornbread. "Me husband told me you'd arrived. You'll be needin' some food after that all that traveling. I remember me own trip over from Ireland like it was yesterday. It's been quite a long journey now, hasn't it?"

Looking around the giant kitchen and then out the window at the tall trees blowing in the wind across the acres of the estate, surrounded in the night fog, I nodded. "Yes, I have come a long way."

She placed a blue crock of stew and a plate of the cornbread before me. Disappearing through the large metal door, in an instant she returned with a yellow pitcher and a lump of butter the size of my fist. Pouring milk into a tall glass before me, she said, "Refrigerated room for all the perishables. Mister Albert thought of everything. Designed this entire house, he did."

Albert Brown: the architect of Seacliff and murderer of Gordon Stewart. I made a mental note to bring this subject up when I knew Mrs. Johnson better.

I closed my eyes and gave thanks for being delivered to Seacliff. When I opened them, Mrs. Johnson was beaming at me. She looked to the ceiling and said aloud, "'Tis He above from whom all blessings come. Thank you Lord, for bringing Mister Andrew to us."

She had brought a bowl for herself and sat down. The food was piping hot, and rich with vegetables. I had become so accustomed to my aunt's watery, lukewarm soup that this was a pleasure indeed. The milk was as cold as a winter's frost, and the cornbread and butter were a delicious combination of the two temperatures. Mrs. Johnson refilled my bowl and glass, and had a generous second helping also.

"Yer ma and pa must have been sad to see you leave their nest."

"My parents died when I was nine." I had answered this question so often, I no longer registered emotion. But the look on Mrs. Johnson's face was as identical to anyone who heard my matter-of-fact answer.

"Oh, Lordy be. I'm so sorry." She lowered her voice, "How did it happen?"

"They were lost at sea, returning from France." When I was younger, I dreamed I would find them again, their deaths having been a mistake.

"Ash's father was lost at sea, too."

"He seems like a nice boy."

Mrs. Johnson began clearing the dishes. "Yes, he's a good lad. Me husband and me are raising him."

"His mother . . ." I began.

Mrs. Johnson stopped washing the dishes and looked out the windows that lined the wall. I followed her gaze, noticing the wind had picked up considerable strength, and the fog had gotten much heavier.

"A parent should never have to bury their child. T'would give me great peace if I could know. Gwennie was such a good girl." She turned to me. "Gwendolyn: me daughter."

"Her death was sudden?"

The housekeeper looked back toward the ocean. The cheer had drained from her plump face.

"Ash's father and she planned to marry, but he shipped out before the weddin'. Lost at sea, he was, just like your own parents. Gwennie was destroyed when she got the news. Then the baby came early, and there were problems. We prayed, and for a while I thought the Lord had answered us. Then six weeks after Asher was born she jumped from the top o' Whispering Hill. We didn't know how heartbroken Gwennie was. Too absorbed in our own problems, I suppose."

Tragedy was a way of life here. No wonder the stranger at the station implored me to leave. Mrs. Johnson continued to look out the window, and instinct told me she stared at the sea that had claimed her daughter's life.

I carried my empty dishes over to the sink. Refusing my offer to clean up, and appearing to have her good nature restored, Mrs. Johnson ordered me off to bed with a shove. Feeling more exhausted and not wanting to press the woman further lest I learn more bad news, I complied.

Dressing for bed, the various images I saw and the stories I was told flooded over me. It was almost too much to absorb, and outside, the rural silence made me long for the perennial noise of Tenth Street to invade my thoughts. I stretched out upon the bed and concentrated on the money I would earn toward France. Three months. Only three months. At the least, this house, although steeped in tragedy and scandal, would provide that future. And regardless, how could events of Seacliff's past affect me?

Chapter Two

I awoke, and raising my body from its new bed, warm and comfortable, I was hesitant to leave. Sleeping undisturbed through the night, I adjusted to the firm mattress and felt protected under stacks of quilts. I dreamt of sketching the palace at Versailles, which faded into the bronze gates of Seacliff. Today I would begin earning the funds for my future, and I was eager for the challenge.

Turning to stretch, I looked to the window, when a weird scream, short and repetitive, from the lawn, almost sent me soaring out of my safe bed into the ceiling. It was high pitched and reminded me of the noise my aunt would make as she leapt upon the counter to escape the tiniest of mice. It sounded like a cry for help. I strained my ears to determine its source but heard only the sea and a stillness that was deafening compared to the sounds I left behind in New York. My heart pounded, but the house and grounds remained silent.

Hearing nothing else, I decided my mind had played a trick on me and I climbed out of bed. Above the tops of the sculpted hedges a heavy fog blanketed the grounds like a smoke-gray cloak. I would learn that every day at Seacliff started this way. Thick and moist, the air filled the area from the beach to the top of the hill, and would hang, sometimes heavy, sometimes translucent, but always present, until noon. Then, as if Merlin waved his wand, the fog disappeared, but only for a precious few hours. During this time, sunlight worked in earnest to warm the grounds, never quite succeeding. Often a brief yet furious rain pounded the property. The afternoon fog rolled in around teatime and gathered in strength until late at night. At that point, the moon broke through, casting its nocturnal beam across the coast and giving the symmetrical lawn an otherworldly pallor. More often than not, a storm passed to complement the earlier one, but the evening version was accompanied by thunder, lightning, and all the appropriate dramatics as it passed across the sixty-five acres that comprised Seacliff.

With care, I washed my face, tackled my unruly hair to obtain a more subdued style, and inspected my clothing. I dressed in the brown suit that I

The Master of Seacliff
Published by The Haworth Press, Inc., 2007. All rights reserved.
doi:10.1300/5778_02

had hung with care in the wardrobe last evening. After reviewing my appearance over and over, I heard the grandfather clock chime the hour, and I could no longer postpone the day's agenda.

I was most curious about my new charge, and more so, his father. Would they like me? I must make them, I thought. My artist's life depended on their acceptance.

Managing to find my way out of the cavernous servants' wing, I retraced my steps back to the kitchen, where I could hear a hymn sung by an alto voice. Mrs. Johnson greeted me with a wide smile as she directed me through the swinging door.

"This be the morning room. I'll have breakfast up in a jiffy."

"Mrs. Johnson, did you hear an unusual sound earlier?"

"What kind of sound, child?"

"A scream?" The silliness of it registered in my voice.

"Most likely it was me singin'. When I'm baking, me voice could keep the gulls out at sea for hours!" she said, rolling back into the kitchen.

Three large arched windows formed a half circle around the morning room, but even with dense fog surrounding the outside like somber sentinels, it stayed cheery. The wallpaper was a vertical pattern of large roses and yellow jonquil, and the floor was tiled the color of fresh cream, with an intricate pattern of interlocking cornflower stars. A large circular table was set with gleaming silver, and the pattern of the china was identical to the rose wallpaper. In its center, a crystal vase brimmed with orchids and lilies. The floral scent was delicious and overpowering, and I studied them as I drew a long, deep breath. What an interesting still life they would make; I so wanted to draw them now.

Mrs. Johnson scuttled back in. "Beautiful flowers, aren't they? Miss Elena arranges them for us, but 'tis the good Lord's providence that we have them at all."

The grandeur that overwhelmed my senses since my arrival began to settle. I thought of the simple meals in my old home, the clean but plain pine table, and the absence of conversation. A long sideboard to the right of the doorway was laden with food, and Mrs. Johnson brought out more. The choices seemed endless, and it appeared the entire pantry of my uncle's store had been purchased for my initial breakfast at Seacliff. The wonderful smells of cinnamon, bacon, and fresh bread filled the room, and a gurgle in my stomach emphasized I was quite hungry and how completely my life had changed in the past twenty-four hours. Mrs. Johnson pointed to one of the chairs, inviting with its plump beige cushions, and as I sat down, I sunk two inches into the cozy fabric and noticed a second and third place setting.

Mrs. Johnson clucked with a nod at the plates, "That'll be for Master Tim and Mister Duncan; when he shows. House full o' clocks and that one never knows the time. He's out for a ride, so take my advice and eat up. Mr. Fellowes has gone to get Master Tim." She deposited a heavy beige linen napkin in my lap, and exited through the swinging door, singing another hymn. Although familiar, her rendition of it made me giggle.

Duncan Stewart. My fate resided in his hands. I was relieved he was out, and perhaps I wouldn't have to face him and his son at the same time. The thought of meeting him unsettled me. Trembling, my hand grasped a delicate porcelain pot, and as I filled my rose-decorated teacup, a young boy, with tousled black hair that covered his ears and fell over his forehead, burst in from the dining room door. This must be eight-year-old Tim, heir to Seacliff, and my responsibility.

"I want to ride with my father!" he yelled, shattering the quiet air. The child's appearance matched the tone of his voice: rumpled, unmatched clothing, unlaced boots. His black eyes were "full of the devil," as my aunt would say.

"Master Tim!" Mrs. Johnson shouted, flying in from behind him and brandishing a ladle. "Now 'tis a fine way to be actin' in front of your new teacher." The speed with which the large woman moved amazed me.

"I don't want a teacher." His voice became more strident, and he stamped his small feet, scuffing the pristine floor tiles.

Rising from my chair, I mustered all the calm and reserve in my body and extended my hand, smiling. My charge was not the gentle lamb I'd dreamed of.

"Good morning, Tim. My name is Andrew. I don't think your father would like your tone of voice, do you?"

"You don't know nothin'!" The child's eyes glared as he flopped into one of the overstuffed brocade chairs, as far away from me as the circular seating allowed.

Mrs. Johnson managed a weak smile and retreated into the kitchen. I longed to join her. My memory raced as I looked for some point of reference from my own youth. With despair, I remembered I had been a well-mannered child, and my cousin was the consistent recipient of discipline. How I wished I had paid more attention to the various scoldings my uncle had given him. But having been hired to educate this child, my success depended on our amiable relationship.

"You may be correct; however, young gentlemen should use proper grammar. In this case, the correct word usage should be 'anything. You don't know anything.' Now let's . . ."

He left me in midsentence, grabbing a piece of toast from its silver stand and racing into the kitchen, where I heard a crash of glass, and Mrs. Johnson responding with words not found in any hymnal. A moment later, Tim galloped by and headed toward the Great Hall, all the while making loud and obnoxious sounds.

Mrs. Johnson shook her head as she came back into the room with an enormous ham decorated with rings of fruit, which she placed in the center of the teak sideboard.

"That's our Master Tim. Chock full o' temper even since Mister Duncan brought him home!" She gave a tired laugh while ladling steaming oatmeal into a large white bowl.

Not knowing whether to go after the child or eat, I sampled the oatmeal. The feeling of warm food traveling down my throat gave me a sense of courage and renewed energy.

Little Ash had followed his grandmother out from the kitchen and helped her arrange the breakfast dishes.

"Hello, Asher," I ventured. Perhaps I would have better luck with him.

He regarded me with the same silent, wide-eyed expression as the night before. Mrs. Johnson put her hand on his shoulder and he slouched into her like a young kitten.

"Ash don't say much." She looked toward the windows and the sea, the same direction she had looked last night. I knew she thought of her daughter.

"Silence might be a blessing, Mrs. Johnson."

The housekeeper burst into jolly laughter, and even the white-haired child seemed to understand my wry tone. I detected a hint of a shy grin, before his grandmother nudged him toward the kitchen.

"Run along now and help yer grandpa, Asher."

She watched the window until the child passed by, down the hill toward their cottage.

I could no longer postpone the confrontation between my new pupil and myself, and with no sign of his father, I needed to get to work. I finished my breakfast amid the serene beauty of the morning room. First, I would find the library to pick up some additional books before I ventured into the schoolroom. Mrs. Johnson pointed through the dining room to a closed door.

"The library's through there. All the public rooms connect this way or by the hall. 'Twas Mister Albert's efficiency at work. Get a nice breeze between them all in the summer."

I thanked her for my breakfast, accepted her shocked refusal to assist in clearing my plates, and walked down the hall.

The library was magnificent in every aspect. The walls and ceiling were painted a deep red. On the left was an enormous ivory marble fireplace that connected to the one in the dining room. A blazing fire and a large leather ottoman positioned nearby invited me to share its warmth, and I stood before it as I absorbed the details of the room. Large French doors, framed by ecru panels and sapphire draperies, fronted a terrace which ran the length of the house. The panels and draperies were identical in color to the carpeting and its border.

Above the fireplace hung a British hunting scene of several horses and riders chasing an elusive fox, which had jumped a river to safety and appeared to be laughing. In this house, no doubt young Tim Stewart was the fox, and I had been cast in the role of the hapless hunter. Turning away from the painting, I became lost in the rows and rows of books. I estimated over a thousand volumes alone, a Joseph's coat of many-colored spectrums of height, width, and bindings. I wanted to read them all, at once, and then capture them forever in a painting.

A large brocade sofa stretched the length of the fireplace that it faced. Two marble-topped end tables, each with an oriental vase filled with beautiful spring flowers, gave a different fragrance than those in the morning room. Guarding one table on a walnut pedestal was a bust of Shakespeare, almost hidden by an exotic palm tree. Several oxblood-red leather chairs were clustered around small mahogany tables. Near the French doors was a small square table covered with green felt, with two decks of cards atop it. I thought of how my family would be scandalized to see evidence of card playing, and laughed. Life with them seemed long ago and small compared to the extravagance and personalities I now lived among.

I didn't know what books I needed, but I wouldn't walk into the schoolroom empty-handed. Staring at them, I pulled ones that had interesting bindings. One was an art book, and I had chosen two volumes of applied science and mathematical applications when a brusque male voice, with the slightest hint of a British accent, questioned from the hall door.

"*You're* the tutor?"

I whirled in his direction, trying to cover the fact that I had been surprised half out of my wits. I did not expect to meet Duncan Stewart like this.

He rested one hand on the doorframe above his head, and the other curled into a fist at his waist. He strode tall and proud into his library, but with his tight black cloth pants, a blue velvet shirt that needed to be buttoned, and scuffed boots, he more resembled a horse trainer than the master of Seacliff. He regarded me up and down, and to my dismay, narrowed his eyes and frowned.

"You're no more than a child yourself!"

"Sir, I am twenty, and most capable of tutoring your son." I did not hide my annoyance at this outlandish statement.

His eyes were black as his stallions and the coach that had brought me from the station to his estate. They flashed as he looked down. He had a classical nose over a thick moustache that expanded into a full beard. Unusual, as most men of the upper class I knew of were clean shaven. I thought of the tales of Blackbeard and the rumor of murder that swirled around this man. Duncan Stewart would have looked comfortable with a sword and eye patch.

I remembered overhearing Elena Van Horne's comment about his moodiness. My uncle's voice echoed in my mind that I should be quiet and deferential to my employer, but I was angry. Calling me a child, indeed.

He shoved his hands in his pockets and stood there in silence, studying me from head to toe. No doubt he sensed my dislike of him and that opinion must change. Extending my hand toward him, I took a deep breath. I'd start over. I could only improve what had not begun as ideal. I began speaking as I walked; the greeting I had practiced over and over since I boarded the train yesterday.

"Andrew Wyndham, sir, I am most pleased . . ."

Duncan Stewart passed me as if I were invisible, walking through the connecting door into the dining room. "We'll talk over breakfast."

Books still clutched in my hand, I was perturbed he didn't follow my preconceived ideal of our first meeting. In that scenario, the master welcomed me heartily, pledging his support, to which I accepted his largesse with magnificent grace. Now I had no choice but to go back where I began the day.

Following him, I deduced he stood over six feet tall. He had a full head of unruly black hair like his son's that brushed back from his forehead and stopped at the bottom of his neck. An aroma of tobacco, musk cologne, and liquor wafted in his wake, and my eyes observed how he walked, so confident and masculine, yet as graceful as a panther.

This was the man who produced a child out of wedlock. A man some speculated had killed his father to seize control of that business. A man who dressed and wore his hair as he wished. He was unlike anyone I had ever seen.

He drew a chair from the table facing the bay window, and directed me to sit, his first display of politeness. He began helping himself from the sideboard to a private banquet of scrambled eggs, the ham, toast, and fruit. A newspaper was folded at his place, and a large glass of grapefruit juice awaited him.

He overfilled his plate, and sat down to my left. His shirt was open almost to his middle, and a patch of dark olive skin separated his facial hair from that on his broad chest. Without really looking at me, he fingered through a thick patch of black hair for a silver medallion that hung below his throat. For one so wealthy, he lacked proper manners.

"Serve yourself, breakfast is informal at Seacliff," he said, waving his hand at the bounty of food.

"Yes . . . no, sir," I fumbled. "It's just that I've already had breakfast, thank you."

He stopped in midbite, and looking at me for the second time, his onyx eyes narrowed.

"I'd *prefer* that you and my son *join* me for breakfast. I am a very busy man. At this table, I shall expect a daily progress report from you on my son's scholastic strengths and weaknesses." Tapping the table with his fingers to punctuate each remark, he added, "Where is my child?"

"I . . . I don't know, sir. I—"

He stopped me by raising a large open palm. A silver ring the size of my thumb encircled his third finger. "I'm not surprised. Timothy is a most precocious child. Infractions or lapses in manners should be reported to me immediately. We have had . . . instances . . . and his behavior will not be tolerated."

His face had flushed and the volume increased by the time he finished, and I could see that Duncan Stewart was indeed hotheaded. Then in a heartbeat, he became silent, turning back to his plate and eating while perusing his newspaper, ignoring me.

His businesslike, unfeeling demeanor confirmed my initial impression of Seacliff. The warmth and serenity I experienced since my arrival was vanquished, replaced by the master's distance and loud behavior. As Duncan

Stewart buttered another piece of toast, he looked toward the expansive lawn, yawned, and scratched his chest. How could this beast be Michael's friend? Kind, sensitive, well-dressed Michael who never raised his voice: a perfect role model. Now I was indentured to this . . . hairy pirate.

"There has been some lapse in Timothy's schooling, and I want my son ahead of his peers, not behind. It is, unacceptable. I trust you are up to the challenge."

Hearing the tiniest squeak behind him, I could see a sliver of light from the swinging door to the kitchen, revealing a swatch of green skirt, and a tinge of gray hair. Mrs. Johnson must have her ear to the door and this thought made me chuckle.

"Are you amused by my son's inferiority?" he growled.

"No, sir." I leaned in on the edge of my seat, growing agitated that he assumed the worst about me. "I'm just grateful—"

"No gratitude is expected. I . . . trust Michael's judgment. You provide a service: my son has a need. Supply and demand; rather simplistic," he said, sounding annoyed again. He added, "You needn't grovel," and turned his attention back to his newspaper.

I opened my mouth to retort when a scream rang out from near the window.

"What was that?" I said, exasperation evident in my voice.

Duncan Stewart remained unfazed. "My peacocks." He lowered his paper and glowered. "I hope you're not the skittish sort. There are all kinds of unusual noises out this way. A prior governess was forever shrieking about some nonsense."

"I don't shriek," I replied with firmness, but he had already raised the newspaper back up to hide his face.

In the distance, a clock chimed with a light, merry sound, followed by the booming voice of the grandfather clock in the Great Hall, who began his solemn drone seconds later. Then, after a pause, the morning room mantel clock continued the chorus with a faint tinkling sound, like cubed ice in a glass.

Duncan Stewart rested his silverware across his cleaned plate and pushed it back. Having whetted his appetite, he focused on me with the same intensity as he had his newspaper. I had never seen such black eyes. Looking at the clock, he pushed back in his chair and frowned again.

"If you've already eaten, shouldn't you find my son and get to the schoolroom? I know *I* have much work to attend to."

I didn't know whether to burst into tears in exasperation or throw the heavy volume of *Scientific Theory and Practice* at him. He enjoyed taunting me, pounding his dominance over me. I rose from the plush beige chair and spoke, matching his brusqueness with precision.

"As you have no specific instructions for me Mr. Stewart, I shall begin Tim's lessons without further delay. My time is as valuable as yours. Good day."

He acted surprised at my curt tone, and not waiting to be subjected to another condescending remark, I picked up stride as I passed back through the library. His clipped voice carried from the morning room into my ears.

"Awfully glad you're here, Andrew."

The fact that he acknowledged me by name did nothing to balance his horrible first impression. If he was as abrupt with his own child as with me, it was no wonder that Tim was a savage! How I would answer to such a father, I was not sure. The solution would be simple: avoid him unless necessary. If I endured the daily breakfast report I could be free after that.

As I rounded the corner into the hall, I was almost knocked over by Fellowes, who seemed to be lying in wait for me beside the grandfather clock.

"I shall take you to the schoolroom, Mr. Wyndham. Master Tim has been waiting for over a half hour." His voice echoed in the stillness and I was certain not only Duncan Stewart, but also my uncle in Manhattan heard the reprimand. It was clear no support from the valet would be forthcoming.

We entered the Great Hall. In the morning sun, it remained as opulent as last night, but as cold and impersonal as Duncan Stewart was at the table. The black and white marble glistened like a placid lake, and I saw through the wall of glass doors that the fog remained thick. At the top of the stairs we turned again and Fellowes stopped.

"These are the portraits of Mr. and Mrs. Stewart, Mister Duncan's parents." His voice changed, sounding similar to the guides I heard in the Metropolitan Museum, and his tone was as one lecturing to dozens of earnest schoolchildren.

I looked up at a large oil painting of Gordon Stewart, resplendent in tartans and a kilt. His eyes were as intense and black as his son and grandson's, but there was a softness I had not seen in the subsequent generations. The portrait of Duncan Stewart's mother hung to his right. Wearing a voluminous white gown and green slippers, her red hair was upswept onto her head and a delicate green ribbon was woven through it. A faint smile rested on her full lips, but her emerald eyes were cold, even in oil.

"Janina Foster Stewart, the most beautiful and generous woman I have ever seen. At one time the name Foster was more important than that of Stewart. I served her family before she met Mister Gordon." Fellowes crinkled his brow and I realized he was far away from the present time. Gesturing to his left, we faced a large set of double doors with what appeared to be a small hallway connecting two opposing rooms.

"Mister Duncan's quarters are to the left, although you must never disturb him there. He takes appointments in his study at the other end of the hall."

"Who has the other room?"

"No one . . . now." Fellowes looked down his nose at me. "When Mrs. Stewart was alive, it was her bedroom."

"When did she die?" I asked, praying no horrific event played a factor.

"Three years after Mister Gordon. Her heart was as large as this estate, but it was also weak."

"Mr. Stewart's death must have been a great shock to her."

My statement brought Fellowes back from the past. His imperious look expressed that the history lesson had ended and to probe no further.

It was really none of my business. But I couldn't get the thought of the master of Seacliff, murdered, out of my mind. And probably by Duncan Stewart himself. With that personality, it was easy to see why he'd be suspected.

"Master Tim's bedroom is the second door, and the schoolroom is this way."

We walked down another long walnut-paneled hall lined with windows. I realized we had passed into another wing of Seacliff. I wondered if I ever could learn my way around the house.

"The schoolroom is the first door, and the children's library is adjacent."

"A second library, how convenient," I commented, feeling the need to interact somehow with the valet.

"The Stewart family has always placed a great emphasis on education and the arts. Mrs. Stewart served as a trustee at several prestigious schools. I trust you won't disappoint as the previous tutors and governesses have." His look underscored the feeling that I was far from suitable to teach the heir of Seacliff.

"Thank you for escorting me," I replied, not allowing his gaze to disconcert me further. Between him and Duncan Stewart, there had been enough frost for one spring day. I was eager to establish my own ground, and the

schoolroom would be my domain. Intending to shut both the master and
the valet out of this new sanctuary, I clutched the crystal knob on the door.

Fellowes added, "Mrs. Johnson will bring lunch promptly at eleven.
There is a small table where you may eat. Should there be any problem regarding Master Tim, Mr. Wyndham, advise me at once."

I nodded, not intending to advise him of anything, closed the door, and
sighed as I leaned my back against it. Tim sat at a desk in the far corner, occupied with paper and colored pencils. As I walked in, my attention was
drawn to the wall of windows that looked across the eastern side of the
grounds and onto the ocean. The sun was breaking through and it had the
room well lit. An enchanting stencil of exotic lands bordered the ceiling
around the top, which was paneled in a knotted pine. There were several
desks, but they were all askew, as if tossed in random fashion by a harsh
storm. A door was ajar, and I guessed this led to the children's library.

Dozens of books were open and scattered on the shelves and floor. I
looked to the front of the room at an imposing desk, which was in complete
disarray; the oversized chair turned over onto the floor behind it. It dawned
on me that large desk was mine: I was the tutor.

"Good morning again, Tim. I hope you haven't waited too long," I said
with cheer. Best to start fresh here as well.

The raven-haired child remained engrossed in his drawing.

"Perhaps we can come here together tomorrow," I offered.

"Didn't Fellowes show you the way? That's his job."

His father's child for sure, I thought.

"Yes, but it would be nice if we came together, don't you agree?"

"I suppose," Tim said, sullen, and his eyes remained focused on his drawing.

"I like to draw also." Walking over to where he was seated, I glanced
down. "What have you created?"

He held up his picture. A charcoal rendering of a graveyard; complete
with headstones and winged creatures I gathered were bats. I shuddered at
the subject, but perhaps this was a talent I could explore.

"That's quite well done."

Hearing this, he broke into a grin.

"It's Whispering Hill, where Ash and I play. Up there."

Looking through the windows to the far edge of the grounds, on the horizon I discerned a low spiked fence and the faint outline of some headstones
and statuary. Even in daylight, it seemed as foreboding as Tim's rendering.

"Perhaps you can take me there," I replied, looking at Tim square and calm in the eyes.

Now it was the child's turn to register surprise. A small victory won, I hoped.

"All right," he said in a matter-of-fact tone. "Miss Jones would never go."

"Miss Jones?"

"My last governess. She said it was haunted. She said Seacliff was horrible and we were all crazy. I hated her. She's gone now." His mischievous smile and the inference in his black eyes were not lost on me.

"I don't believe in haunted graveyards or ghosts, Tim," I said, squeezing into the desk beside him.

"You will. Then you'll leave too. No one stays here long," Tim said, staring at his morbid drawing.

For all his loud and unruly behavior, I recognized that Tim was a lonely child and I identified with that. His cold father paid little attention to him, and what interest there was focused on his academic skills. From what I had gathered at the breakfast table, as long as the child was ahead of his studies, nothing more was required. It would be paramount to my success at Seacliff that I befriend this child. We were all each other had.

I got up, surveyed the room and announced in my best authoritative tone, "We can't get any schoolwork done without straightening up in here first. You can help me."

"Can't we go to Whispering Hill?" Tim said, a sly look on his face.

"I shall consider that after we tidy up. I would actually like you to show me the entire grounds."

That placated him and we cleaned and organized the schoolroom in silence. It seemed only minutes had passed when Mrs. Johnson appeared in the doorway holding a large silver tray containing our lunch.

"My lands, the place is lookin' as neat as a pin!"

I finished stacking the last of the books to return to the library next door. The dusty cover of *Aesop's Fables* fell open and my eye caught a childish scrawl:

Property of Miss Elena Van Horne

The books in this room must have been used by the last generation of children of Seacliff, and it appeared Elena had studied with Duncan. I thought of her, no doubt a beautiful blonde doll of a child, and next tried to imagine a young Duncan Stewart, becoming queasy with the thought. I turned the page. Across the table of contents, in bolder block letters of black charcoal were printed the words:

DUNCAN LOVES LEO

Wondering who Leo was, I closed the book and sat down to a quiet and uninterrupted lunch. Trying to engage my student in conversation, I found I talked more to myself. I could tell from the sharpness in Tim's black eyes that the child was intelligent, and I was curious how to gain his trust.

The afternoon went smooth and at its end I felt Tim and I developed at least a mutual understanding. I concentrated on only the most rudimentary studies to gauge where he was, and while we cleaned I discovered a lesson planner left by my predecessor, Miss Jones. At least I had a starting point. Tim appeared eager to show he was a bright student, but in reality lacked focus and discipline.

By three o'clock the schoolroom and library were transformed from places of neglect into rooms that would provide the foundation for teaching this child who had been entrusted to me, and whose care in turn provided for my future. Feeling drained, I announced our lessons were concluded for the day. Having survived this initial test, as long as I kept distance from Duncan Stewart, I could mark the days until I left.

Chapter Three

"Can we go now? You promised."

I faced my young charge. With his face creased into a disapproving frown, he was a tiny replica of his father at the breakfast table this morning. I sensed the child expected me to back out of our agreement to tour the grounds, so I smiled, throwing him off guard.

"Yes, let's away."

The sun disappeared behind the clouds and the landscape reflected the despair attached to the cliff. In the distance, a figure in a gray cloak weaved toward the entrance of the cemetery.

"Who is that at the top of the path?"

"No one's there. Let's go."

I looked back out the window but the figure had vanished. Perhaps like the peacocks, whose screams I mistook for human, I was wrong again.

I followed Tim as he ducked down a back staircase. At the bottom, he opened a heavy oak door, and I found myself on the paved driveway.

"How many entrances does Seacliff have, Tim?"

"Too many."

I laughed at his reply, and he joined me. We walked along the paved drive, and took a footpath that directed us toward the cliffs. The grounds in this area were simple but not as manicured as the immediate area by the house. The number of trees increased until we were surrounded by dozens, obscuring our view of Seacliff. Emerging from the grove and standing at the summit of Whispering Hill, I turned back to see the mansion and the schoolroom window. I expected to encounter the person I had seen from that window, but no one was around.

"Listen and you'll hear how the hill got its name," Tim said.

Indeed the rustle of the tree branches emitted a sound that could be interpreted as whispers. The child widened his eyes.

"Scary, isn't it?'

"Not really," I said, pleased that my statement diffused his intensity.

The Master of Seacliff
Published by The Haworth Press, Inc., 2007. All rights reserved.
doi:10.1300/5778_03

The salty smell of the sea air was so heavy I tasted it on my lips. Pulling my coat around me, I wished I owned a heavier one. The waves below crashed onto the rocks with an impulsiveness that Seacliff lacked. For all the passion and drama played out between its stone walls, Seacliff hid its emotions behind a cold, aloof, and crisp demeanor. My cheeks reddened as I thought of Duncan Stewart. Why would I expect him to be kind and polite? As he pointed out, he was a businessman: I was his employee. A servant paid to do a job.

I watched Tim studying the ocean. He danced with excitement. It was as if he drew energy from the tempestuous water. Then pointing, and yelling something I couldn't understand due to the wind, he grabbed my hand and pulled me toward the top of the hill.

A wider path of white gravel led up from the cliff to a weathered wrought-iron fence that marked the graveyard entrance. It was a large burial ground; portions of it were as neglected as the schoolroom. Many of the headstones dating back to the last century were listing or toppled over. At the center, almost hidden by gnarled oaks, stood a marble mausoleum, almost the size of my uncle's shop in Manhattan.

Tim pushed on the iron gates, which responded with a predictable moan, and we entered. As we walked ahead, I could see the Stewart name carved above the weathered bronze entrance to the mausoleum. To my surprise, little Ash sat outside atop a stone lion.

"What are you doing here by yourself?" I asked, concerned the strange child chose this as a playground.

Ash gave me a shy smile, but did not answer.

Tim replied, "He's always here. He's an oddball."

"And I believe it was you, Tim Stewart, who insisted on bringing me, so who is more odd?"

He stuck his tongue out at me, but I was convinced I had won another round.

"Come inside. My grandfather is buried here He was shot dead in our house." Tim bounded up the steps and disappeared into the darkness with Ash tailing behind.

It was chilly inside the mausoleum, which was as grand as the main house. The interior appeared to be constructed out of the whitest marble, almost like sculpted snow. There were corridors to either side, and I was drawn to a large stained glass window depicting Jesus on the cross. The cloudiness outside gave the rainbow-colored glass an eerie effect, casting shadows onto the floor. To either side of an empty pedestal stood brass candelabrum, and burning brilliantly were a dozen white tapers that gave the room a surreal glow. The absence of wax on the floor told me that they were just lit, but by whom? There was one answer; the cloaked figure I saw from the window. My eyes had not played tricks on me.

I turned but the children were nowhere to be seen. I called out and got no response. I should have guessed this was their plan. I called to the empty air.

"I'm sorry to disappoint you, but I'm not frightened." In truth, I was irritated I hadn't foreseen this scheme. I started to leave and stopped, realizing Tim was my responsibility and I would be the one looking foolish if I returned to Seacliff alone.

I walked down the corridor. Each section of wall was adorned with intricately carved marble animals and figures: lambs, lions, and cherubs. There were a half-dozen markers for various Stewart ancestors, some dating back over fifty years. Gordon Stewart's name leapt out at me, and next to his, chiseled into marble was Janina Foster Stewart's name. My mind's eye flashed to the two portraits above the staircase. Gordon Stewart: murdered. Had Albert Brown designed this mausoleum, knowing his employer would die at his hand? Or had Duncan Stewart indeed murdered them both?

My nose twitched and I detected the faintest scent in the air. I couldn't quite discern what it was, or where it came from. There were no arrangements of flowers in this mausoleum, only the dozens of candles.

I heard a giggle and the squeak of the gate. I darted down the hall to find Tim and Ash sitting on the steps outside.

"We've been waiting for you," Tim said, with a petulant but insincere smile.

"It's a shame you didn't remain inside. The architecture of this mausoleum is incredible. Notice the symmetrical lines throughout the building. You would find these classical columns in Athens. How the sunlight filters through the windows, providing not only illumination, but color as well."

The two children gaped at me, speechless. My digression to the design of the building dissolved any attempt to frighten me. Trying to mirror Tim's own false sweetness, I added, "I think tomorrow we shall study the designs of Ancient Greece, and you can do a recitation for me."

He scowled, but said nothing and I thought how much like his father he was. After a moment, he lifted his eyebrows.

"Would you like to see the zoo?"

"All right; then back to the house. Will you join us, Ash?"

The white-haired child had vanished.

Tim caught the questioning look in my eye. "He does that a lot."

"Shouldn't we find him?"

"Would you like to go back in and look for him?" Tim said, grinning similar to one of the carved gargoyles.

"Let's go on to the zoo."

Walking together, I half expected to see Ash, or the cloaked figure, but this was not to be. I tried quizzing Tim, who offered no answers to any of my questions, only shrugging and pointing out various trails that led up and down the hillside. He stayed beside me most of the way, but at one point he took my hand in his, which pleased me. As we passed the formal gardens on the western side of the house, I sighed and again yearned for my sketch pad. I would make time to sit in that garden and paint the magnificent flowers that would be in full bloom by summer. I hated postponing my art for other matters, but in this case it could not be helped.

Along another unkempt stretch of path, Tim looked up at me. "I forgot to tell you, the zoo has no animals in it."

It occupied the desolate edge of the property, and consisted of seven iron cages arranged in a semicircular fashion. The neglect and abandonment of this area was greater than the cemetery. Weeds grew tall from cracks in the foundations and the paths were littered with broken branches and rocks. The faintest remnants of animal smells were in the air, but more pervasive was an odor of decay. The fog shrouded everything. Releasing my hand, Tim did a cartwheel: his eyes wide with excitement as he puffed out his tiny chest.

"My grandfather collected animals from all over the world. The lion cage is the biggest and has a secret cave where the big cats would sleep. Right about now, you can hear their ghosts roaring!"

"You like ghosts, don't you, Tim?"

With my query, he ran into the cage and disappeared into the back. Not wanting a repeat of the mausoleum episode, I followed right behind. The large cave was dark and it took my eyes a moment to adjust. As I called to Tim, I heard the clang of the cage door outside, and my heart dropped.

Running back into the now empty main area, I pulled on the gate; confirming what I knew: I was locked in. How foolish to fall for the child's prank.

I shook the gate and yelled, but to no avail. The sunlight dwindled and the peacocks announced their arrival; four of their shrieks punctuated the still air. When I called out, they replied; mocking me.

The wind swirled and the events of the day caught up with me. I leaned against the rusted iron bars feeling tired and wondering how long I would be imprisoned before anyone came searching. Mrs. Johnson might question my whereabouts at supper—I hoped. Or would my absence go unnoticed until Duncan Stewart called for me at tomorrow's breakfast? His reaction at finding his new tutor duped by his eight-year-old son would not be a pleasant one.

The peacocks continued screeching and I wanted to scream as well, not from sadness at my plight, but of anger from being outsmarted by this little hellion. I sunk down to the cold ground of the ancient cage to try and devise a way out of this mess, when a voice called.

"Hullo!"

I scrambled up and peered through the bars. Almost obscured by the fog, a man tied a proud pale-blond horse with a white mane to the remnant of an iron hitching post.

"I'm locked in!" I called, hoping I didn't sound frantic.

In a calm manner, he strolled up the path. Tall and slender, he looked about Duncan Stewart's age. His tousled blond hair bounced as he moved. As he approached the cage he eyed me with curiosity.

"You're certainly unlike any wildlife I've seen. What species are you?"

"Will you please let me out?"

The stranger examined me up and down with an intent gaze, making me more than a little uncomfortable. There was a familiarity about his green eyes, and he folded his arms and put his left hand under his chin, letting one long finger caress his clean-shaven face.

"Perhaps you are here to plunder the Stewart fortune. I should leave and let the ghosts of this estate, of which there are many, get you." Turning on his heel, he walked away.

"I'm not in the mood to play games," I snapped. "I am Andrew Wyndham, and I am the tutor here."

"Here? A tutor of animals? But these cages have been empty for years. How unusual." The stranger broke into a wide smile, revealing the whitest teeth, between sensual lips.

I had more than my fill of this teasing. I took a deep breath. Regarding my expression, the stranger came back to the gate.

"Now, now, no hysterics. Let's see, a swift jerk here . . ." With deftness he twisted the iron handle and I was freed from my prison. "It unlocks from the outside, but it can be difficult. May I suggest if you plan to explore these cages again you block the gate with this rock, perhaps?"

As I emerged from the cage he handed me a handkerchief and added, "There now, blow your nose like a good boy."

The handkerchief, which had a pleasant smell of lemon was monogrammed with the initials "LVH". He bowed.

"Leo Van Horne, at your service. I'm the black sheep of an otherwise illustrious family. My sister, Elena, told me you'd arrived. Welcome."

I regained my composure, but was compelled to explain the situation. "Thank you, sir. Tim was showing me the grounds; and I . . . was locked in."

Leo gave a loud laugh. "I passed Tim on the pathway running as only the guilty can. But not to fret, in fact, congratulations, you're just the newest victim of another of his famous schemes. A Seacliff tradition, I'm afraid. We were the same when we were children, Elena, Duncan, and I. We grew up together; taking classes in the same room where you now teach."

My mind flashed to the old book and its inscription: *Duncan loves Leo.*

"Come along, I'll take you back to Seacliff, that is, unless you're ready to flee as Miss Jones and her predecessors. But I hope not, for you've just gotten started. And, may I warn you, so has Tim. Here, take my cloak, I'm sure you are chilled."

As he wrapped the heavy wool around me, I wondered if Leo Van Horne had been the figure I saw from the schoolroom window.

"Were you near Whispering Hill earlier, Mr. Van Horne?"

"No, I try and avoid death wherever possible. Up you go." He swept me onto his horse and then climbed on. It was my first time on a horse, but I didn't want to admit this. Instead, I held onto Leo's slender waist with a firm grasp.

We rode in silence to the main house. The fog was so thick I couldn't see my hand before my face, but Leo's horse maneuvered through the brush with expert ease to the driveway, where the lights from the windows cut through the fog and greeted us in its austere way. Shivering, I now preferred the coldness of the house over that of the outdoors.

"Thank you again, Mr. Van Horne," I said, not so skillfully sliding off his horse.

"If you don't call me Leo, I shall be forced to take you back to the zoo and leave you there." The green eyes danced, and his lips twisted into a sly smile. A tingle ran up my spine from where his hand held my waist, and I noticed he kept it there. "And don't think you are dismissing me so readily. I'm coming in."

I stammered, unable to produce an intelligible word.

"You'll need to knock that chill off or you'll catch a cold and then you'll be of no use to anyone except Mrs. Johnson and her homemade cure-alls, which are mostly alcohol anyway. Come, I know where Duncan keeps his liquor."

He hitched his horse and entered through the front door without knocking. Wondering if Fellowes watched from some secret place and would reprimand me for not using the service entrance, I followed.

Leo walked down the tiled stairs and headed for the drawing room. The room where I met Elena Van Horne: now I stood in the company of her brother. How graceful and sleek they both were. They complemented the grand house more than the brusque masculinity of Duncan Stewart.

Leo poured two glasses of brandy from a crystal decanter on a mahogany sideboard to the right of the piano, and handed me a glass.

"Brandy. Doctors orders. You've had a fright I'm afraid, whether you admit it or not."

Never having liquor before, the thought of my family's expressions if they could see me brought a smile to my face. The sensation of the brandy rolling down my throat brought immediate warmth to my toes and began working its way up my legs.

Leo studied me as a cat would a mouse.

"What were you doing at that musty old cemetery anyway? It predates both our estate and Seacliff by a hundred or so years, but I don't think old George Washington really slept there." He winked.

"Tim wanted to show me the cemetery and mausoleum. I saw a person entering the grounds, but when we got there, no one was around. Tim took me to the zoo and locked me in that cage."

"You must have seen a tree branch blowing in the wind. I've been riding along the beach below Whispering Hill for a couple of hours, and no one walked along the cliffs. As for Tim locking you in, consider it an initiation."

"But who lit the candles in the mausoleum?"

"The boys probably did. You've met Asher? He's particularly fond of that place. Terrible tragedy. We loved Gwennie. She was like our baby sister."

Leo poured himself another drink and refilled mine, even though I had only taken a few sips. Replacing the decanter on the oak cart, he crossed his arms.

"And how do you find the estimable Duncan Stewart?" He displayed a crinkled smile, and I took his question to be a sarcastic one.

"I have only just met him this morning."

"No first impressions?"

"We spoke briefly while he ate breakfast."

Leo seemed too interested in learning my thoughts on my employer, and I didn't want to tell the truth. After all, the Van Hornes and Stewarts had been friends for years. I nodded at the magnificent rosewood piano that graced the center of the room.

"Do you play the piano, Leo?"

"No, although my parents were hell-bent on making me learn. Elena plays quite well. In fact, I think the only use this poor piece gets these days is when she is here."

"Did Mrs. Stewart play?"

"Janina? Probably," he paused. "But this piano was imported from Europe. The owner's initials are above the keyboard."

I sat on the bench. Above the keys, in a delicate gold script were the initials, 'S.C.'

"Oh," I said aloud, "Steven Charles."

Leo's lips curled. In a heartbeat I knew I opened a Pandora's Box and wished I could retract what I said.

"Michael Betancourt mentioned him, didn't he? Spoiling all the fun as only a doctor can. Well, what did he say?"

"That Mr. Stewart took Mr. Charles under his care."

"Much like a spider takes a fly."

"Mr. Stewart is a patron of the arts," I said.

"Tactfully put. In a sense of the word, indeed he is. What else?"

"That Mr. Charles left."

Leo got up from the couch and sat beside me on the piano bench.

"Duncan met Steven Charles on one of his crossings to or from Scotland: or maybe it was at Buckingham Palace. Steven is an accomplished pianist and had been touring England. You are correct in that one of Duncan's few good qualities is that he is supportive of the arts, probably because he's so naturally dull and entirely obsessed with his knack for turning straw into gold."

I thought about Mr. Stewart being an arts patron. After all, he agreed to fund my art career by allowing me to work at Seacliff. How interesting that he would take a pianist not only under his wing of financial support, but into his home as well. This didn't sound like the gruff man I met.

"Steven came to this house with Duncan, with some excuse about taking a brief holiday from performing. My guess is that his engagements were drying up. What we expected to be a six-week stay turned into six months, and then two years. Duncan set him up in Janina's old room, directly across from his own . . . you know."

"The room at the top of the landing. Fellowes told me—"

"Dear old Fellowes. Another case altogether. He and Janina were like Siamese twins." Leo's grin grew wider. "But Steven! Every bit as charming and outgoing as Duncan is not. Also stunningly attractive and quite well versed." He paused, "I imagine he grew bored of the manor life. Steven performed for heads of state and royalty. And as delightful as my sister and I are, well, out here it's just not the same." He laughed, but it was a bit too loud.

"And having to put up with Duncan continuously would be exhausting, even with the Stewart wealth as an inducement. Thus, at the end of last summer, Steven took off. In the middle of the night. Dramatic entrance, dramatic exit, that one."

"It all sounds so odd."

"Not if you know the master of Seacliff as we do. Disappearing was Steven's only recourse. When we were children, Duncan had a butterfly collection. He never understood that it was better to let them fly freely and live than to pin them inside a glass case. Steven was like that, a beautiful blond, sapphire-eyed butterfly. And Seacliff is a glass case . . . no, a glass coffin."

"That's a bit morbid," I said, moving away from him and back onto the couch.

"Give yourself time, Andrew," Leo said, following me to the couch and stretching his long arm across the back. Darker blond hairs poked out of his shirt cuff, and a delicate gold chain wrapped his wrist.

"Where do you think Steven Charles is now?" I asked.

"No one knows for sure. My sister saw him at the station in town boarding the evening train, but he didn't disclose his destination. Duncan followed as soon as he realized his handsome and talented butterfly had escaped, but it was too late. Steven made certain he would never be part of the glass coffin again. I'd like to fancy he's back in Europe. He was well connected with several of the titled nobility, and they would hide him with no questions asked. Duncan went overseas to drag him back, but Steven managed to elude him again." He took a drink. "I think that's the first time Duncan didn't get the last word." He now eyed me. "It was while he was hunting for Steven that Miss Jones was dismissed. You've heard that story, I hope?"

"Tim said she left because she hated Seacliff." I was feeling woozy from the brandy; it was warm in the drawing room and Leo's eyes were intense.

"And also the matter of a pair of missing heirloom earrings that turned up in her bureau—"

"She stole them?"

"Personally I didn't think so; the gems weren't her type, too gaudy, but Fellowes thought otherwise, and he and my sister exert a powerful influence on Duncan. Keep that in mind."

I said nothing.

"I trust you'll prove more resilient that she did."

I changed the subject. "You, your sister, and Duncan studied together as children."

"Gordon and Janina thought it vital to have the Van Horne children around their prized son, and my parents wanted our name associated with the high and mighty Stewarts. But we loved our governess. Had her for years and treated her like a queen. It was the lesser servants we deviled."

Leo's hand now rested on my shoulder. I thought about the departure of Steven Charles. Perhaps the combination of that and the looming suspicion over his father's murder had hardened Duncan Stewart into the cold man I met.

The contrast between my employer and Leo Van Horne was interesting. Two boys; raised together. Yet Leo was full of life, albeit a bit cruel, whereas Duncan Stewart acted downright dour.

"What are you doing here, Leo?" the clipped voice growled.

Duncan Stewart had changed clothes from our morning meeting and looked less feral. His black hair was tamer and he now wore a crisp linen shirt almost buttoned to the neck, with a green paisley cutaway. His gray trousers were pressed, and his shiny boots reflected the glow from the fire. A rumble outside forewarned an evening storm.

Leo returned a sly smile. "Delivering your tutor back to the house. Your son locked him in the lion cage at the zoo. I didn't want him to run off screaming. Not yet, anyway."

This confession made my heart sink. I hoped to forget about the episode and deal with Tim on my own. Now his father was involved.

Duncan Stewart marched into the room and placed his fists on his hips. The smell of tobacco and musk trailed in his wake. "Is this true?"

"It's nothing, Mr. Stewart. Best forgotten," I said, knowing I sounded too pleading.

"Nonsense. Look at your appearance! Fellowes!"

His comment on my clothing angered me. I knew nothing I ever did could appease him.

The valet appeared at the door within seconds. "Yes, Mister Duncan. Good evening Mister Leo." He did not acknowledge me.

"Where is my son? Bring him here immediately!" His eyes blazed, and I feared for my charge.

"Master Tim is in his room. He returned alone some time ago which concerned me, as it had gotten dark. I shall get him." I recalled what Leo said about the valet's influence and my leg began to tremble. I spoke up.

"Mr. Stewart, I think it best if I handle the situation. Your punishing the child will only make him misbehave more."

"Andrew is right, Duncan. Remember Jones!" Leo said.

"Leo, you have all the answers."

"Always."

Duncan Stewart absorbed this, and spoke in a calmer voice. "As you wish, Andrew. Fellowes, never mind."

I hoped my statement convinced him as much as Leo's comment, but I wasn't sure.

My employer gave Leo a curt nod. "Thank you for returning Andrew. Goodbye."

"Not so quickly old boy. Did you forget you asked Elena and me to supper?"

"I recall inviting your sister."

A clap of thunder almost made me jump. The temperature in the drawing room had plummeted between these men. Leo enjoyed taunting Duncan, who took the bait.

Leo continued, "I presumed supper was planned so we could meet Andrew. Perhaps your young tutor can fill in the country folks on life in Manhattan?" He gave me an expression that even I knew was overdramatic. "You are joining us aren't you? I hope Duncan isn't relegating you to a solemn dinner with the other servants."

I didn't know how or if I should respond. But Duncan Stewart did.

"Absolutely not!" He lowered his voice. "Andrew, supper shall be in one hour. Perhaps you'd like to wash up and change. I'll entertain Leo. We're old friends." He punctuated this last remark with sarcasm.

From the hall, Elena's voice floated through the air. Moments later she appeared in the door. As with last night, she looked stunning and her pale rose gown with lace collar brightened the space she occupied.

"Andrew, how nice to see you. Brother dear, I waited for you at the house. Thankfully, I've beaten the storm." She eyed the room, her head cocked to the side. "What have you three been up to?" She slid a slim bare arm around Duncan, who kissed her forehead. Her tiny wrist was heavy with a garnet and diamond bracelet.

"Sister, Andrew is joining us for supper."

"Well, naturally. Miss Jones dined with us during her time here." She smiled at me. "I hope we won't drive you away with our boring conversations."

Duncan Stewart addressed Fellowes. "Please make certain Mrs. Johnson has a place for Andrew and Timothy. I . . . I told her this morning, but she may have forgotten."

"She's gotten so absentminded lately," Leo observed.

"Excuse me," I said, slipping out. My exit was unnoticed by Duncan Stewart, as he crossed with Elena to the liquor cart, but Leo's green eyes followed me out the door.

Fellowes lay in wait by stairs as I walked to the corridor that led to my room.

"Master Tim is the sole heir to Seacliff. It's dangerous for a young boy to walk alone in the woods at dusk."

I wondered if his long throat had any other timbre to it than ice. "Yes, Fellowes. As I told Mr. Stewart, I will address Tim's behavior tomorrow." The valet's jaw froze in place, and only after I returned to my room was I amazed at my response to him. In truth, I was more excited at the prospect of dinner with the Van Hornes.

Chapter Four

My wardrobe was limited to two suits: the brown was my favorite but it had become rumpled and soiled from the experience in the zoo. That left the light gray, a far-from-desirable option for what I wanted to be an important evening. As I laid it upon the bed I questioned my interest in looking my best at a supper to which I had been invited more out of haste than desire.

As I dressed, I began feeling apprehensive. I was not relishing another encounter with Duncan Stewart.

I thought of Leo, and how excited yet disconcerted I felt in his presence. These feelings were not unusual, and as I straightened and restraightened my shirt and jacket I thought about him; handsome and with a humorous take on life. I liked that he had no qualms about speaking his thoughts, yet he seemed to read mine as well. I applauded anyone who was not afraid of Duncan Stewart.

I was as ready as I could be, but I gave myself one final check in the mirror before I went upstairs to collect Tim. Under no circumstances would I venture alone into the dining room.

Walking down the upstairs hallway with its lush green floral carpeting, I passed portrait upon gilded-framed portrait of stern Stewart ancestors, all registering their collective disapproval of me. One rendering of an elderly matron in colonial dress featured a large black cat whose eyes followed me. A nervous wind rattled against the windows, as the rumble of thunder rolled in the distance, which didn't help my own internal storm.

I knocked at Tim's door, but there was no reply. Hearing a noise inside, I walked in. The child lay sprawled across his unmade bed in the same clothing. He stared at the ceiling, arms crossed over his chest.

"Tim, you need to dress. I'd like you to accompany me downstairs."

"Leo let you out of the cage."

"Yes, and that is the final discussion of that incident. I trust you won't try such a trick again."

The grimace on his face made me certain he was trying to put a hex on me. When I didn't dissolve into dust, he chose to answer.

The Master of Seacliff
Published by The Haworth Press, Inc., 2007. All rights reserved.
doi:10.1300/5778_04

"I'll eat in here, alone. That's what I usually do."

"I'd rather eat alone also, but your father has invited us to join him and the Van Hornes, and we must go."

He perked up at the mention of his father, and I nodded my head. I think my frank admission about eating alone startled him also. He slid off the bed and began to wash up. There was some cheeriness to his face that hadn't been there all day.

"Don't you usually have supper with your father?"

"He's never home. Miss Jones and I ate together. After she left, I'd eat with Mr. and Mrs. Johnson and Ash. Or Fellowes. Many times I don't get any supper."

"If you've misbehaved, I take it?" I said as I straightened the part in his hair with an ivory comb.

Tim did not answer, and I just knew he planned some new act of terror against me. Until I could gain his respect, I should expect these challenges, and needed to keep my guard.

I helped him select fresh clothing. The sight of his extensive wardrobe made my eyes bulge: dozens of jackets, shirts, and short pants, all made from the finest fabrics. They were as jumbled as the schoolroom had been, and I told Tim that we would organize this room as well. "Tomorrow," I pronounced.

"Why? You may be gone tomorrow."

"And where am I going?"

"Away. Where the others go."

The child's loneliness burned through his face. But when I tried to hug him, he wriggled out of my grasp.

"Let me assure you Tim, I have no intention of going anywhere." *As long as I can avoid your father,* I added in my mind.

Tim took my hand as we walked down the staircase into the Great Hall. "Father's usually too busy to have supper with me. Or he's gone. He just came home from England."

"Yes," I answered, thinking about Steven Charles. Duncan Stewart had gone to England to bring him back. A louder roll of thunder echoed through the vast room. I looked at Tim, dressed in clothing I only dreamed of, but whose face reflected sadness. What a lonely life this child of privilege led.

We walked side by side into the library, where the fireplace's popping symphony welcomed us. Duncan Stewart chatted with Elena Van Horne by the glass doors that led outside, and neither acknowledged our entrance.

Tim's hand tightened on mine, and I did the same. Leo arose from one of the leather chairs: a glass in hand and clicked his heels.

"How nice you look Andrew; and you too, Tim. Trapped any wild animals lately?"

I wrinkled my face and put a finger to my lips. I didn't need Leo stirring up trouble. A glance toward Duncan Stewart revealed he hadn't heard this comment.

"Good evening, Tim. Andrew, you look refreshed," Elena said, crossing the room to greet us. I noticed Tim treated her with the same indifference as me when she tried to fuss over him.

At the same time, the compliments on my appearance from the brother and sister made me feel at ease. My face flushed, and I was glad the room was not bright. Duncan Stewart continued to ignore us. He tossed his cigar in the fireplace and stretched his arms.

"There's no need for Fellowes to announce supper. Let's eat." He walked off; Elena behind him, followed by Leo. Tim and I trailed last.

Tim stayed by my side and did not attempt to talk to his father. However, he eyed him with intensity, absorbing his every movement and word. It hadn't occurred to me this child could be as frightened of his parent as I was, and Duncan Stewart's lack of acknowledgment irritated me even more.

The dining room was spectacular with its cut-glass chandelier ablaze with electrical lighting, and the table laden with china, crystal, and a ransom of silver. Ornamental dishes of sliced fruit and candy were out and the napkins were starched and fashioned into what looked like little sailboats. Once again I found myself catching my breath at the haughty luxury of it all. For the past twenty-four hours, I had taken a trip into one of the magical tales my father read to me when I was a child. He always changed the name of the main character to my own. But this was not a tale. It was real: I was here, and I could only conjecture at what my beloved parents would have said about my good fortune.

Elena slid her slender arm around me. "Please sit next to me, Andrew."

"Perhaps I should sit next to Tim?" I offered, as I saw Elena sat to the immediate right of Duncan Stewart. A location far too close for my comfort.

"Nonsense, Tim's a big boy and he can feed himself, isn't he Duncan?"

Duncan Stewart remained oblivious as he surveyed his domain through the large window.

"Tim, sit across from Andrew," then, she added with her rippling laugh, "Such confusion for a mere five people. Perhaps next time we should have place cards."

I fretted over the thought of "next time." But if Elena Van Horne were here, it might not be so bad.

"Oh sister, you're so greedy," Leo said with false annoyance. "Timothy, I see it's you and I together again." He grabbed the child and tried tickling him, but Tim eluded his grasp, laughing.

I stole a glance at Duncan Stewart, unaffected by this display of affection between his only child and another man. He regarded us with the same aloofness I witnessed this morning. After drawing Elena's chair for her, he sat down at the head of the table. Behind him, through the open drapes, I could see the trees and bushes dancing in the wind.

I followed Leo and Elena's lead and lifted the sailboat-shaped napkin, discovering a small roll of warm white bread underneath. The smell of the bread was wonderful and heightened my anticipation and hunger.

Fellowes entered, taking pride in being in command of our meal. I learned later that he had assumed many of the duties of a butler. A young servant girl, who I met earlier, but whose name I had forgotten, followed through the swinging door carrying an ornate silver tray of individual soup bowls that she placed before us. I was served last.

Leo said, "Turtle. I see you're giving your tutor the royal treatment, Duncan. Can we expect a roasted pig, or just a fatted calf as our main course?"

Duncan Stewart ignored Leo and raised his wineglass toward me.

"Andrew. Welcome to Seacliff." Now his black eyes twinkled, and I wished he were more like this. Feeling his eyes and complete attention on me linger, if only for a moment, made me uncomfortable, and I dropped my head. "Thank you, sir."

I stared at the array of forks, knives, and spoons lined up before me, as well as multiple drinking glasses. I knew the wealthy used a variety of utensils for different courses of food, but I had no idea where to begin. My excitement reverted back to nervousness, and I longed to run into Mrs. Johnson's kitchen where life was simpler.

"Just start at the outside and work your way in," Elena said, turning her head so no one else could hear.

Fellowes stationed himself behind Duncan Stewart, and as we finished our soup, he pulled a cord dangling from the ceiling, which summoned the servant, who cleared the plates, and delivered the next course. The meal was somber, and although this was my first supper, I had the distinct feeling Duncan Stewart brooded more than usual tonight. Elena and Leo noticed it too, for in between their cheerful banter they glanced at Duncan, then at each other, and at one point, Elena shrugged her delicate shoulders. It was a long supper, with several courses of food, and I began to note each time the clocks in the various rooms chimed. The morning and dining room time-pieces were within seconds of each other, joined by the library, then a lapse before the drawing room, with the grandfather clock completing the sere-nade. I said little, speaking only when asked a question, but I listened with open ears. The conversation remained between Leo and Elena, and I could tell the two were close and caring. As the supper plates were cleared, Duncan Stewart appeared to lighten up, and joined their discussion.

"Aren't those the garnet clips I gave you last Christmas, Elena?" he said, twisting the corner of his moustache. His clipped accent was unusual, and when he wasn't addressing me, I enjoyed hearing it and watching him out of the corner of my eye much as Tim did.

"Yes, Duncan, but Arthur Upshaw would prefer I wear his ruby and dia-mond pendant. Do you remember the summer he trailed us all over Italy?" Her laughter was so light and contagious I wished I worked for her.

Mrs. Johnson served dessert: individual chocolate puddings in frosted crystal bowls. I saw an end to the tedious evening and began to relax.

Leo winked at me. "My stunning sister has an endless supply of suitors throughout the eastern United States and numerous foreign countries."

"Rivaled only by Duncan Stewart and his bevy of heiresses," Elena re-plied. "Speaking of Arthur, how is his sister, the horse-faced Miss Victoria Upshaw?" she said, batting her eyes in an exaggerated manner.

"You amuse me," Duncan Stewart answered, smiling at her, but looking preoccupied.

"Sister, have you heard from that Frenchman in New Orleans lately?"

Elena frowned with the same elegance that enhanced her laughter. "I may have an endless supply of suitors, but the quality of most is rather lack-ing. Andrew, the gentleman my brother refers to with wicked glee is a wid-ower old enough to be my father. And he has seven children; all monsters."

I laughed aloud at Elena's story when Duncan Stewart interrupted, slam-ming his fist onto the table.

"Tim, do you think that locking up your new tutor this afternoon was an intelligent decision?"

His personality had taken a complete transformation from the one shown moments before. The gaiety of the room ground to a halt.

I looked at Tim, holding his first spoonful of pudding in the air as if he were frozen, and shrinking back so that Leo blocked his father's view. Duncan Stewart had seldom acknowledged the child during supper, and while I hoped he would, it was not with an outburst like this. Tim peeked around Leo and stared at his father, but rather than fear, I saw defiance on the child's face. Fellowes mumbled something about the kitchen, and departed his post. Leo drank a generous gulp of his wine, and Elena's voice broke the uncomfortable silence.

"Duncan . . ."

"Do you, Tim? Is this what is to be expected of a Stewart? Ridiculous pranks?" His face was red and those cold black eyes were on the child. I spoke up.

"Mr. Stewart, it was nothing. Tim was just . . ." I started, sounding as soft and meek as I felt against the harsh loudness of Seacliff's owner.

He turned to me. "That is an idiotic response. I will not have my child behaving this way." Pointing at his son, he barked, "Put that spoon down; apologize to your tutor and our guests and go to your room. You shall have no dessert."

Tim held the spoon at his mouth, saying nothing. His expression matched his father's. A contest of wills was being played out. And my employer had just pronounced me an idiot.

"Timothy Foster Stewart, are you listening?"

Tim inched the spoon closer to his mouth. I prayed he would put it down. Looking at Elena and Leo, I saw similar pleading expressions on their faces.

"Drop that spoon, Timothy or I'll—" Duncan Stewart's voice boomed as he moved his chair back from the table. The prisms on the chandelier swayed from the sound of his voice.

Tim slipped the spoon of pudding in his mouth, removed it clean, took another generous scoop, held it in the air, and dropped it just as his father commanded. It clattered off the table onto the floor, spreading chocolate pudding across the white damask cloth, the beige chair cushions, and the carpet. The child scrambled out of his seat and rushed out. I heard his boots race across the marble and fade as he ran up the stairs.

Elena put her left hand over her eyes and Leo tossed his napkin down, his eyes blazing emerald fire.

"For God's sake, Duncan, he's a child, not a cadet!"

"You've forgotten the horrid tricks you played on . . . what was her name . . . Mary O'Flannery, the upstairs maid? I believe a snake in her chamber pot figured in one scheme," Elena added, as she folded her hands back in front of her.

Duncan's eyes blazed. "I'll thank you both to not tell me how to raise my son." He glared at me. "Nor you, young man."

I wanted to tell my employer to go to the devil, and was ready to bite my tongue in two. I knew the electric chandelier wasn't hiding the redness of my face. First being called an idiot: now "young man" in a most condescending tone. As if was the same age as Tim.

Elena touched his forearm. "Duncan, we know that this is a difficult day for you. But to humiliate the child—"

"I'll thank you, Elena Van Horne, to mind your own business. The child is out of control: has been for some time, and the firmest hand is needed. Andrew, there is no excuse for my son's behavior. He shall be duly punished."

I said, "Mr. Stewart, with all respect, I think he has already. Excuse me, please," I wanted to get as far away from this insensitive tyrant as I could. Elena smiled and nodded and I knew I had made the right decision, in her eyes, anyway.

"Duncan's not always the Janus-faced monster he appears to be, Andrew," Leo said. "However, you should know that today is the eighth anniversary of his father's murder, here in the house. Naturally, Duncan's a little edgy, for reasons unknown."

"I don't think Andrew needs to be concerned with past events. He is engaged as Tim's tutor, not the family historian."

"That's it, sweep everything under the rug. I think Andrew should know what's happened here, unlike the traditional Stewart path of conveniently forgotten memories," Leo said with complete calm, crossing his arms and pushing his chair back from the table.

Both men looked at me, and it seemed Duncan Stewart expected me to respond. And there was no doubt Leo dared me to. Well then, they would get a response. Calling me an idiot, indeed.

"Perhaps if feelings were discussed more openly there would be no need for such abrupt outbursts of emotion," I said. I couldn't face my employer, and I envisioned him lunging at me from across the table. At this point, if he strangled me I'd not be shocked. As for Leo, his mouth curled into a smile.

"Wisdom in youth, a blessing indeed," Elena said.

I released my grip on the heavy napkin I'd knotted during the evening. I didn't care any more about my feelings. I felt a protective instinct toward Tim. And I wanted out of that dining room.

"Excuse me. I am responsible for Tim." I stood up, as did Leo, who bowed in dramatic fashion as I walked out. I caught a brief glance of Duncan Stewart's face; his mouth open, the black eyes burning into me, but silent. Feeling pleased in some bizarre way, I walked into the Great Hall more confident than before as the sound of raindrops pelted the terrace.

No one wanted to cross or disagree with the master of the house, but if he were wrong it should be pointed out. I would not be bullied. I remembered a mean older boy from school that delighted in taunting a smaller, crippled child. I went to my friend's defense, returning home with two black eyes, but having made my point.

The portraits of Gordon and Janina Stewart observed me as I ascended the stairs. Gordon Stewart had been murdered eight years ago this evening, but that did not excuse the actions of his beast of a son. I rapped on Tim's door but received no answer. I tried the handle; it was locked.

"Tim, please let me in."

"Go away!"

"Your father acted out of turn. But he is sorry and you know he loves you very much."

This sounded false, even to me, but I tried to make the pretense as believable as possible. It angered me that I had to cover up for the insensitiveness of Duncan Stewart to his only child. No wonder Steven Charles ran away in the middle of the night, if this was how Duncan Stewart treated those under his roof.

I waited outside Tim's door for a few moments, hoping he would allow me in, yet knowing he wouldn't. The grandfather clock's heavy chime was almost drowned out by a clap of thunder and a flash of lightening that caused the electrical lights in the Great Hall to flicker. I walked back down the main stairs, intending to go to my room. Leo and Elena stood in the library watching the storm through the glass doors. I attempted to slip by, but Elena heard my footsteps.

"Andrew, please join us."

Her invitation was so warming after the moments of tension that I did. Leo put a glass in my right hand as he rubbed my arm. "Duncan's stomped off, probably to his study to boil some more. Good show, by the way. Here's a celebratory brandy."

"Yes," Elena agreed, "Miss Jones would have hid in the attic for a week with one of those outbursts. Ultimately, Duncan will respect you for standing up to him."

"Perhaps it would be best if I returned to New York." Much as I sympathized with Tim's plight, I did not think I could not do my job with an employer such as this.

"Nonsense!" both Van Hornes chorused, and Elena put her arm around me.

"Duncan is temperamental, but you seem to be able to hold your own. Tim so desperately needs you. This is not the first outburst of father-son conflict," Elena said with a sigh. "Really, Duncan's not this horrible."

"Sister, there's no need to sugarcoat things. Andrew, Duncan is horrible, but you'll do just fine. And it's about time someone put that old meany in his place. Everyone always tiptoes around him." Leo crossed and returned with the brandy decanter, and refilled our glasses.

"His father's death must have been a terrible blow," I offered, taking a grateful sip of the liquor. Perhaps I was too hasty to write my employer's demeanor off as an everyday occurrence.

The Van Hornes exchanged glances. Elena took my arm and led me to the long brocade sofa.

"Actually, Duncan and his father were rather estranged at the time of Gordon's death," Elena said.

"And there's that delicious theory about Duncan killing his father and Albert," Leo added, grinning.

"Dear brother, you know that's not true. Duncan was on his way to stop Albert. But it was too late."

Leo grabbed my hand. "Duncan was going to be cut out of the business entirely. Gordon was highly regimented about work, and back then, Duncan was as lazy as a mule."

"Duncan and Albert were extremely close, and if anything, I think Gordon resented that," Elena continued. "Albert always accepted Duncan just as he was. I think that's what Duncan takes so hard, the loss of Albert."

This was all confusing. But perhaps this explained, but not excused, why my employer was so hard on his own son.

Elena read my expression. "We were hosting a ball in Albert's honor. He was leaving. Gordon and Janina convinced him to seek medical treatment," she whispered. "Only those of us close to the family knew the real reason." Elena rubbed her temple to emphasize her point, and I understood what she meant. Albert Brown was mentally frail.

"And he agreed to go," Leo added.

"Initially, yes, Janina said the strain of the Stewart businesses had sapped Albert's physical and mental strength. He left the party early, then Gordon followed. There was no cause for alarm."

"But when Duncan got the word that his father was headed back here, he exploded out our door like a cannonball." Leo gestured behind him, "And tells the police he blacked out along the way. When he came to, they were dead."

Elena used a poker to stir the fire. "I think that's the most unusual thing about all of it. Yes, Albert had been under tremendous strain. But to kill Gordon? Those two men were like brothers. Their deaths are still so incredible to believe."

"That's why Albert couldn't have done it. And I wasn't the only one who thought that," Leo smirked. "Besides, who benefited from their deaths?"

"With both men dead, we'll never know why," I finalized, looking out at the storm. The rain pummeled the stone terrace, and the wind whirled the oak branches, scattering leaves everywhere.

"Dear Andrew, you may be wrong about that!"

Leo's eyes brightened as he crossed the room to a writing desk; he opened a drawer and began rummaging through it. I was amazed at how familiar Leo and his sister were with Seacliff. It was as if they lived here. After two disastrous encounters with Duncan Stewart, I wished they did.

"Brother, what are you up to?"

"Janina used to keep her tarot cards here, but now I can't find them. Tim or Asher probably squirreled them away. Never mind. A candle will do just as well, and we can use our hands."

Wondering what was going to happen next, I followed Elena over to Leo. He took a candle from the drawer and placed it in a delicate porcelain holder in the center of the card table.

"This is a little trick I picked up in Martinique ten years ago. I was there on holiday, and met the most fascinating native woman."

"That Martinique holiday cost Father a pretty penny, as I recall. Money we didn't have," Elena said, with more than a hint of sarcasm in her voice.

"Perhaps we can establish contact with Albert Brown and ask him just what he was up to that night. After all, it's said that the dead return on their anniversary to walk among us, unseen. Old Al might be listening in right now. Andrew, have you ever participated in a séance?"

I shook my head. I wasn't even sure of the word. I had heard stories of people who could communicate with the dead, but I thought they were just tales invented to frighten children into sleep. Leo's proclamation fascinated me.

"We'll need all three of us to make this work. Gather around the card table and place both your hands atop it. Our fingertips should be touching to form a circle."

I looked at Elena, who had a wry smile on her face.

"Indulge my brother, Andrew, or we shall never hear the end of it."

At that moment the lights in the chandelier overhead sputtered, and I wondered if it was a mere coincidence. I sat facing the French doors leading to the terrace. The wind was blowing wild and without direction, but the rain had slackened. Elena and Leo sat on either side of me. Leo wore a mischievous look; Elena accommodated her brother. I could just feel the tips of each of their fingers: Elena's slightly cool touch, and Leo's firm warmth pressing against mine. The green felt of the card table tickled my palms. With a flourish, Leo grew solemn.

"Now we must have absolute concentration. And do not break the circle for any reason or the furies of Hell may be released. I'll ask the questions."

Leo's oval face grew shadowy, and his green eyes reflected the flame of the candle in the center of the table.

"Close your eyes. Spirits of the dark, we ask for you to guide one who departed this life eight years ago. Spirits, release one from your world to return to ours."

The room and the entire house grew still. I could almost hear the grandfather clock ticking out in the hall.

"Albert Brown. Return to us from the valley of the shadows. Spirits, allow him to pass over the river Styx and into the realm of the living."

Listening to Leo, I cracked my right eye open. A glance at Elena reflected her boredom with it all.

"Keep your eyes closed, please," Leo said.

I sat silent, absorbing each detail. The warmth of the room, and the warmer feeling from the brandy. Two people I didn't know well, but trusted. I had wanted to leave the table, but now felt weighted to the chair.

A noticeable chill grew in the air, and the house seemed to come to a complete halt. The branches on the trees and the bushes grew still and the rain stopped. Leo continued his intonations.

"Albert Brown. Return to this house, Seacliff, you loved so very much."

A sudden clap of thunder with a shaft of lightening punctuated by a curse from Mrs. Johnson in the kitchen, told me through my closed eyes that the electrical power must be out all over the house.

Leo continued, "Albert. On this night, eight years ago, you murdered Gordon Stewart. Or so it has been written. But we who knew you do not believe these lies. Tell us the truth!" Leo's voice was stern, commanding, and hoarse, not at all the cynical man I met earlier.

Everything remained still, as if we were in the eye of a storm. I peeked and saw that the candle flame had lengthened into a tall, thin column. Something brushed against my right leg. I hadn't seen a cat in the house, but perhaps there was one. A moment later the brush happened again, but this time it began working its way up my trouser leg and rubbing firm against my ankle and calf. I didn't want to break the silence, but this was quite disturbing.

"Leo, remember, complete concentration," Elena said in a rather dry voice.

The mysterious sensation on my leg departed without further notice. But now a whisper of air brushed my neck, and a fragrance caressed my sense of smell, growing stronger. Soon the scent was overpowering. I recognized it, but unsure from where. The wind began picking up, moaning as if in pain.

Not understanding what was happening I opened my eyes and looked at Leo, who wrinkled his nose. He smelled it too. He sat up, opened his eyes, and said out loud, "Steven?"

At that precise moment the French doors blew outward, making a loud crashing sound as two of the panes shattered. Elena screamed and bolted up from her seat, her eyes on the library door. I jumped too, seeing a dark silhouette framed in the doorway, filling the space, with a curl of smoke rising from its head.

"What the Hell is going on in here?"

The lights came back on. Before us stood not a specter of death, but worse: Duncan Stewart. The look of anger on his face was enough to make me wish to brave Satan himself, rather than the master of Seacliff. Cigar smoke trailed around him.

Elena regained her composure and addressed him as she glided over.

"Playing parlor games. The wind and your entrance timed together frightened me and I lost myself." She pounded his broad chest with her tiny fist. "Why do you have to burst in like that?" she queried, a pleasant annoyance in her voice. It amazed me how she could reverse any difficult situation.

I looked outside. Despite what Elena had said, there was no wind now. The grounds were quiet. Thunder rolled away in the distance, the storm having passed. Duncan looked around, suspicion on his dark face, and then

I watched his nose wrinkle as he looked to the open terrace doors. Did he smell the same fragrance identified as Steven Charles'?

Leo's boot pressed on the top of my foot. I knew to let him and Elena handle the situation. He blew out the candle, and in a flash scrambled the playing cards.

"Old boy, come in. Or are you going to just continue barging in unannounced and frightening us all to death? There's no need to be so excited, lest you think my sister and I are corrupting your son's tutor. Not yet, anyway."

Duncan Stewart's mouth tightened and I believe he would have punched Leo had they been alone. Instead, he studied both of us, which made me unpleasant. Again, I appeared to be the source of friction between the men.

Elena floated over to the French doors and closed them. She returned to Duncan's side, a vision of calm and put her delicate arm around his waist.

"We were just being silly. Leo was amusing us with his usual tricks. You're upset over nothing Duncan, and you know how that delights my brother."

I chuckled under my breath. How wise she was.

"Let's adjourn to the drawing room, and Andrew and Leo will tidy up and join us momentarily." Looking over her shoulder at us, and nodding, she led Duncan, who eased under her voice, out of the library. I could hear the rustle of her satin and the sound of his boots as they moved across the hall. Leo watched them go.

"Steven wore sandalwood cologne. Too much, I might add. Even now."

"But Steven left Seacliff."

Leo looked at the fire. "And it appears he's returned, in a supernatural sense anyway."

"You think he's dead?"

"Yes. And that explains why Duncan didn't locate him although I was never convinced he looked that hard. And now things are making sense. Much more sense."

Leo glanced around the room, and I got the feeling he wasn't speaking to me.

"It's all falling into place. Hmm."

A shudder traveled from the base of my neck to my feet, and although I did not believe in ghosts, I had the feeling we were being watched.

"Should we tell Mr. Stewart?"

"No. It is best we should keep this between ourselves for now, in fact, let's not involve my sister. She's incredibly protective of Duncan." He put his arm around me and pulled me to the door. "Come, Elena has soothed him by now, let's join them." The thought of facing Duncan Stewart, soothed or not, for a third time in one day was too much. I broke away from Leo.

"I'll tell Mrs. Johnson about the broken pane, and go to my room. It's been quite an exhausting day. But I thank you for all your kindness."

"Kindness means nothing at Seacliff."

Before I knew what was happening, Leo pulled me into his arms and kissed me on the lips. His mouth was warm and his tight grasp held me captive. I forgot about the sandalwood I had smelled as I breathed in Leo's lemon scent. He released his mouth and looked at me, his green eyes dancing.

"I've wanted to do that since I saw you in the zoo." With that, he released me, bowed in his grand manner, and added, "Forgive my impulsiveness," as he dashed away.

I stood alone in this comfortable room, with its blazing fire, cozy furniture, rows of books and the lingering scent of lemon upon my mouth and jacket. I didn't know whether to be shocked, insulted, or amused by Leo Van Horne's actions. This was all some peculiar dream, and I would wake up in my old bed in Manhattan at any moment.

The French doors blew open again and I rushed to close them. The wind had picked up and I took a deep breath to clear my head of the past few hours. Looking down across the lawn of Seacliff, the trees shook their limbs like an angry crowd in the moonlight. Standing in the doorway the sandalwood fragrance brushed across my nostrils, and I whirled around to locate its source, seeing none. I dismissed the smell as my overactive imagination. It had to be.

Chapter Five

Memories of the evening filled my dreams, and as I awoke, most prominent was that of Leo Van Horne's mouth on mine. The fact my first serious kiss came from another man was the least of my concerns. I flashed through the years of developing yearnings I had been fearful to discuss, knowing on instinct such a revelation would result in misunderstanding or outrage. Having read with interest the newspaper accounts of Oscar Wilde's travails had only pushed these desires further in the dark.

I foresaw my life as a solitary artist, assuring myself that my lack of interest in women other than as friends and the intense desire to pattern myself after men I admired was a queer but personal trait. Dear, kind Michael came to mind. My stomach turned as I saw with sudden clarity the true motivation behind my furtive glances, the quick embraces. How I thrived on the limited physical contact we shared. How silly he must have thought me, hounding after him like some stray dog in search of the crumbs of affection. Michael knew Leo was here. I contemplated his guidance to Seacliff as a gentle nudge toward a declaration I hadn't comprehended before. After all I had experienced in twenty-four hours, an impromptu kiss from Leo seemed a usual event in a most unusual house.

I decided that the simplest thing was to begin the day as I had the one before; I resolved to make no errors. Having no idea what time Duncan Stewart arrived at his breakfast table, I planned to be there with Tim first. One of the maids had been most gracious in the mending and cleaning of my soiled suit, and it awaited me, fresh and crisp in the wardrobe. I finished dressing as a solemn knock echoed on the door. It was Fellowes; cheerless as usual. I didn't think it was possible anyone could be so dour all the time.

"Mister Duncan wishes to see you in his study. Now."

With regret, I recalled my insubordinate comments to my employer last night. In trying to defend my student, I had insulted his father. I'd be sent back to New York, a failure. My dreams had been crushed, like a dry twig under the heavy boot of Duncan Stewart. I brought this upon myself by not keeping my mouth shut and minding my own business.

The Master of Seacliff
Published by The Haworth Press, Inc., 2007. All rights reserved.
doi:10.1300/5778_05

Following the valet to the back spiral stairs, I thought of my school studies of the French Revolution. I now empathized with those led to the guillotine. Only in this case, the aristocracy had triumphed over the commoner. Climbing what seemed like endless circular steps, my sweating hand became chilled by the railing; a cylinder of ice to my touch. The coldness of the house had defeated me in a matter of two days.

At the top of the stairs, we faced a large oak door and Fellowes entered. At the opposite was the corridor to the schoolroom, a place I would not see again. Deciding it was better to face the inevitable; I lifted my chin and entered.

Duncan Stewart's study, as the other rooms at Seacliff, was massive, but its lower ceiling, paneled walls, and fireplace gave it a warmer personality than the others. His mahogany desk was at the far end from where I now stood. Along the walls, one mounted wild animal head after another stared out, teeth bared: creatures I'd only seen drawings of and read about, were interspersed between walnut display cases that housed a collection of antique weapons, from Revolutionary War muskets to small pistols and bejeweled daggers. In the room's center, a rug made from the hide of a gigantic white bear covered the floor. Walking across it, I saw that the animal's front teeth were missing, which gave the beast an almost laughing countenance. As we grew closer, the smell of leather, tobacco, and musk permeated the room. Without a doubt, it was Duncan Stewart's domain.

He ignored our entrance into his lair. A tray of empty dishes had been deposited on a leather ottoman to his left and I held my stomach to silence its gurgling. Based on his conversation the prior morning, and seeing his discarded tray, only confirmed my worst suspicions. My departure was imminent. It would be a matter of seconds now.

"Mister Duncan, Andrew Wyndham is here," Fellowes intoned. I wondered how few generations removed the valet was from the executioners of France.

Duncan Stewart nodded, a cigar sticking straight out of his mouth, yet he continued writing, not looking at me.

Leaving me to my fate, the valet collected the tray of dishes without so much as a rattle of china against crystal, turned, and departed, giving me an expressionless nod as he left. I remained standing, though my knees signaled they might buckle at any moment. Waiting for him to speak, my eyes wandered around. I felt so small and insignificant in his vast, masculine den. I envisioned my head joining those of the conquered on the wall. There was just enough room between the lion and the rhinoceros to accommodate me.

Duncan Stewart motioned for me to come forward, never once looking up. Looking down at his desk, I saw Michael's name scrawled atop the letter he was composing. He must be denouncing his friend for bringing such an incorrigible youth into his home in the guise of a tutor.

He pointed at one of the two enormous blood-red leather chairs that faced his desk and I sat. The leather was cold, biting me through my brown wool trousers. I positioned myself on the edge and dug my feet into the bear rug to keep from sliding off the slick hide. I clasped my nervous hands in my lap to keep them from shaking.

My mind gyrated with a thousand scenes. Should I throw myself on Duncan Stewart's mercy or tell him how horrid I thought he was and depart Seacliff with my pride intact? He appeared more domesticated than yesterday morning; his mane of hair had been combed and he dressed in a charcoal gray morning suit. A red cravat accented his handsome black beard, which looked trimmed. Ready for the kill but well groomed to do so.

The dark eyes turned upward, and I met them head on. I knew he sensed my fear. I prayed the end would be swift, painless. His mouth opened: my breath stopped. The master of Seacliff was ready to pronounce final sentencing upon me.

"Last evening, I was wrong regarding Tim. My behavior was reprehensible."

I choked on the air in my throat, not believing these words.

"Do you not accept my apology, Andrew?"

"It is not to me that you need apologize, Mr. Stewart, but to your son." At once I wanted to retract that; but only bit my lip in the process. I was appalled at my lack of respect for my employer. Perhaps in my subconscious, I wanted him to dismiss me. I disliked so much about Seacliff, and he topped my list.

He responded as if I accepted his request with consummate grace. "I have made amends to my son," he said, scrutinizing me. "You think me a cruel tyrant." It was not a question, but a statement.

"No, sir. I do not," I lied.

"You intimated at much at supper. What has changed your mind in the last ten hours?"

I thought of Leo. If I was banished from Seacliff I might not see him again, and I would certainly never get to France. "I was out of turn, Mr. Stewart," I offered. "I forgot my place." I dug my feet farther into the thick white fur of the bear's hide. Perhaps if I could be more recalcitrant about my actions he would not send me away.

He chewed his cigar and nodded his head. "My first impressions of you were entirely correct."

"That I am too young for the position, sir?" He had tricked me. I would be fired anyway.

"No, that what you lack in years, is made up for by common sense."

Stunned, I managed to keep my jaw from dropping. Perhaps my nerves were playing tricks with my hearing.

"Would you like a glass of water, Andrew? You're pale as parchment."

I shook my head.

"Whiskey, then?"

"Of course not, sir."

He poured one for himself and keeping his eye on me, put his bearded chin into his left hand. "I think you're afraid of me, Andrew." He leaned back in his chair. It made a squeak, and I jumped a bit.

"No, sir. I am not afraid of you." I hoped that sounded convincing, but I wasn't sure.

"Andrew, for one so young, you are far too rigid."

I'd had enough of his denigrations. I grabbed the desk and pulled myself up. "If you are going to dismiss me, why don't you get it over with? Must you taunt me as well?"

"Sit down," he growled. "Things are not always as they appear, my fine young man." He pointed to the chair. "Sit."

I did. "You think me too young and rigid. You just said so."

"Let me put it to you directly."

"But Mr. Stewart—"

"Quiet!"

I steeled myself and dug my toes even deeper into the bear rug. I took a deep breath as my spine tightened.

"First, call me Duncan."

I wondered if he even listened to me.

"You are a most peculiar man, sir."

"As are you, Andrew Wyndham, and I say that in the most complimentary sense. In most houses a tutor, granted, as inexperienced and young as you—"

My eyes narrowed into slits and the frown across my face happened before I could stop.

"—who spoke and acted so rudely, would be discharged without question. However, my parents encouraged an atmosphere of free speech at Seacliff. In your case, I have thought over what you said, and concur that my actions, not yours, were improper. I would not want you to entertain leaving because of my brashness. As you know, there has been a period of unpleasantness in the house. It is my desire that your arrival here will put the past behind us, forever."

I found his apology, it was an apology—almost too much to absorb, but I answered, "You have great faith in the abilities of one so 'young and inexperienced', sir."

He chuckled and I softened in the chair. How one minute his eyes could change from coal to silk fascinated me.

"Why don't you tell me of this love of art that motivates you to endure employment from such a tyrant as I? Frankly, I find it hard to fathom that a person as stodgy as you could manage to be creative."

Although cloaked in an insult, I was pleased he could be interested in what I enjoyed doing, and with some hesitation I opened myself up to him about my past. Duncan Stewart gave me his complete attention, creasing a brow or nodding in silence to show my story was not falling on disinterested ears. I was impressed that when he wanted to, he could be a sympathetic listener. In the brief time we talked, I attempted to relax. I did not want him perceiving me as "stodgy" by any means.

In return, I learned he had no interest in hunting: his father and grandfather had claimed the animal heads. Looking over at the white bear rug, it no longer mocked me with its missing teeth. Duncan Stewart's eyes followed mine.

"I kicked them in. I was twenty-three and furious at my father. I walked out that door and did not contact him until my son was born almost one year later."

"You were insolent," I said, thinking, *then as now.*

He laughed. "As are all young men. For many years there was bad blood between us. I tell you this for I want life at Seacliff to be different than before. For my son's sake."

"I returned home with Tim, and tragedy struck. Over and over," he said, motioning to the wall with his chin. The light from the chandelier overhead cast an unusual glow upon an ornate revolver in one of the walnut cases. "That pistol killed my father. Then Albert turned it on himself."

My face revealed my thoughts, and he nodded.

"I see you've heard the other version of events." He swiveled in his chair, facing the window. "Damn Leo!"

The kiss and the scent of lemon floated into my mind.

Duncan Stewart picked up his cigar, inhaled, and pitched it into the marble tray. "I assure you I am not the ogre Leo Van Horne presents me as, nor as my conduct may have led you to conclude."

His eyes traveled up and down my body, different than a moment ago, but similar to the way he examined me yesterday in the library. This made me twitch, and I didn't like it. He continued, "It really doesn't matter who killed them, does it? They will remain dead, regardless."

Had he just confessed?

"I would like to help you, however I can."

He poured himself another drink, leaving me sad that such troubles pushed him to liquor early in the morning.

"Perhaps another time, Andrew."

The clock's chime informed me we had talked for over one hour. It seemed only minutes. I spoke up.

"Mr. Stewart—"

"Duncan," he corrected with firmness.

"—I thank you for your faith in me."

I had buried my feet so deep rug I couldn't see my shoes and it was a struggle to stand up. Duncan Stewart eyed me, and again I felt uneasy.

"I should like to see your artwork, Andrew. I have always been most envious of those with such gifts."

Steven Charles and his handsome piano downstairs came to my mind. "I'm afraid I've not the talent Steven Charles does. You must have enjoyed his skills immensely."

His face clouded over. The cool businesslike demeanor of the day before returned.

"That will be all, Andrew. I will not join you and Timothy for breakfast. However, I'm certain that you won't hesitate to correct me if I err in any other way."

By mentioning Steven Charles I undid all that had been accomplished. I had taken three steps forward and four back with my employer. Now he mocked me. Still a bully. And like most bullies, he hid a deep hurt. I walked out without a further exchange.

Walking past the gallery of Stewart ancestors, in the light of a new day they seemed to challenge me to solve the mysteries of the house. The door to Tim's room was open, but the child was not in sight. Again, my charge had eluded me. Stopping at the vivid portraits of Janina and Gordon Stewart, I stared up at my employer's father, and I sensed a communication from his soft black eyes, as if he asked for help. But turning to Janina Stewart's emerald eyes I saw only the cold sea, and heard the angry waves crashing outside.

Downstairs, I glanced through open doorways into the library and the sensation of Leo's mouth on mine returned. I wasn't certain what my impressions were regarding his kiss. I'd always thought there would be more magic in such a kiss, but perhaps this was because Leo was a stranger. Kissed by a stranger; the neighbor and childhood friend of my employer. I thought of the schoolbook I found. Had there been affection between Leo and Duncan, long ago? Nonsense, I answered. Duncan Stewart was not like Leo or me. That might be what kept them distant and distrustful of each other. But he was devastated over Steven Charles' hasty departure; that I knew. Could there have been an intimacy between the pianist and his benefactor? No, my mind was out of control. Duncan Stewart embodied masculinity. He had a son.

"Are you alright, child?"

Mrs. Johnson's face was lined with concern. She smelled of pine soap and was wringing her hands with her apron. I thought about the grief this woman carried. Seacliff was an unhappy house. Duncan said my presence would put the past behind us.

"Yes, everything is well. Thank you," I said sitting down at the table.

No sooner had I placed my napkin in my lap then Tim skipped into the room whistling, stopping short when he saw me.

"I thought you'd been sent away."

"Come and eat your breakfast." I waited. "Would that have pleased you?"

"I don't know."

"I appreciate your honesty, but it does not appear that I'll be leaving in the immediate future. And there's no need to gobble your food."

The child acted preoccupied, cheerful almost, and not by the sight of me, nor my announcement. "I understand you saw your father this morning."

"Yes! Oh yes! We went for a ride early this morning along the beach. It was great. Just him and me." Tim took another bite of his hotcakes. "If he'd do this always there'd be no need for you."

How the child's eyes lit up when he spoke of his father, and his face glowed when he said the words "just the two of us." I wished Duncan Stewart could see his son right now. Maybe I could have an impact after all. I watched Tim, who settled back in his chair and continued eating, and realized again how similar he and his father were.

"Finish your breakfast, and we'll go to the schoolroom together. I believe you'll be telling me about Greek Revival architecture today."

Tim's eyes widened and he drank his milk with a solemnity and dedication I had not seen the day before.

One month passed and had it not been for the warmer weather and an increase in the length of daylight hours, I would have thought it only minutes from my meeting with Duncan Stewart, when I expected to be discharged.

I felt confident that Tim and I made progress, both as student and tutor: and as friends. I learned if I told him it was something his father would do, or it related to the Stewart business interests, I could garner his complete attention and thus motivate him to concentrate on his studies.

Duncan Stewart departed for New York, Boston, and Philadelphia after our eventful meeting in his study. I debated if his apology to me was motivated more to offset an inconvenience— if I were dismissed Tim would have no one— than a true change of heart. I prayed he was sincere.

Tim was lonesome for his father, and this manifested itself in all sorts of impish actions. I admitted missing my employer's presence as well. I wanted to forge a friendship with him, for Tim's sake, and believed I could. I also wished to trumpet his son's progression with his education. Duncan Stewart's communication to the house seldom inquired after Tim, and I was unable to convince Fellowes that a report on the heir to Seacliff should be given to his father.

"If there is a problem, I will advise Mister Duncan without haste. Otherwise, he should not be disturbed. Mrs. Stewart said that Seacliff should run like a well-oiled timepiece, and the master need not be bothered with inconsequential details."

It was pointless to argue with the valet, especially when he invoked the name of Duncan's mother, which he did quite often. Plus, it was clear he was disappointed I hadn't been tossed out.

I had better luck with Mrs. Johnson, and I spent several afternoons with her. I learned that any hint of cold, minor ache, or feeling of failure on my part, prompted the housekeeper to prescribe her "home remedy," which amounted to syrup laced with a generous dose of brandy. Although I could not bring myself to ask further about her daughter's suicide, she spoke often of Albert Brown. Encouraged at last, I asked her thoughts on why he killed Gordon Stewart.

"Mister Gordon was involved in some pretty shady business deals; and both of 'em was a being called to court. I think that rather than speak against his old friend, Mister Albert thought this was the way out of it."

"But those rumors about Duncan Stewart—"

"Mister Duncan is mostly bark. He wouldn't have killed those men, even if he did get the business." She looked at Ash, who had come in and nestled by her, but while staring up at me with his large gray eyes. "Besides, if Mister Duncan were caught and sent to jail, we'd all be out in the street. And Lord knows how we'd take care of this boy."

Her statement did not reinforce complete innocence on Duncan's part, and I thought it best to stop asking questions for awhile. However, Mrs. Johnson continued, "Mister Albert loved this house; knew every stone and crack. Only Miss Elena knows as much about Seacliff as he did. Now look at this." She pressed a panel within the cupboard and a door popped open. "Secret place to stash valuables," she winked. "I keeps my remedy in there now."

It was during Duncan Stewart's absence that Elena Van Horne called almost daily, or invited me to her home for tea. I found her to be a pleasant light of contrast among so much somberness at Seacliff. She was eager to hear of Tim's progression in his lessons. In return she gave me advice on handling him in his more difficult moments. Thank goodness one other person took an interest in my pupil.

"You're so much more disciplined than Miss Jones was. One would think you'd been tutoring for years. Tim is quite a handful, and she was in over her head from the beginning."

"Leo mentioned some missing earrings."

Elena shook her head. "Fellowes had it in for her. I pitied the poor woman and located a position for her along the Hudson River, as a companion to an elderly friend, so I don't entirely regret her departure."

On that first visit to their home, Leo was conspicuous by his absence. I found myself looking for him to appear, and Elena noticed this.

"Once in a rare while, my brother actually has to earn his living. I'm afraid our family has never shared the business acumen of the Stewarts," she laughed, offering no details on her brother's whereabouts. The Van Horne house, Glendower Hall, was not as grand or well maintained as Seacliff, but there was a quiet casualness about it the other house lacked.

I developed a fair knowledge of my way around Seacliff and the immediate acreage within a short amount of time. After my second week, I began taking late afternoons and Sundays to resume drawing. The excitement of having my old sketch pad and pencils available close at hand and not hidden in a box under my bed and being able to utilize them without reproach was a new experience for me. This freedom renewed me, but I still hesitated to share my art. Only Duncan knew of my passion; which I thought strange, for I expected he would be the last to confide in.

Often when I walked the grounds, little Ash would appear, silent, but often hovering near me. Elena commented on this one afternoon while we walked by the greenhouse.

"It is funny, for he was the same way with Steven. Ash would sit beside him at the piano for hours, absorbing it all in. Steven never complained, either. I worry about that child; no parents, no education."

In time Leo Van Horne did return, and began coming around to Seacliff. He demonstrated only his best behavior, at least in a physical sense, which confused me. He never brought up the kiss, and I was too nervous to do so. Perhaps his actions that night were like the daily storms—brief, intense, and forgotten the next day. While walking one afternoon in the Roman garden, with its colonnades of firs and statuary, I confessed to Leo my desire to go to France and be an artist.

"Excellent. Let's sail immediately! You'd fit into the art circles of Paris deliciously and may I add, with open arms."

"I think there's just a little matter of money, Leo. I'd have to work, and my French is rather limited."

"We'll live on the goodness of others, and your talent."

"Your talent, Leo, for charming people far exceeds any skills I have with oils and brushes. Plus, I suspect my artwork would do little to keep us fed and clothed."

"Who needs clothes? I know a little island off Haiti where the natives roam freely without the constraints of clothing or prejudices. Let's go there instead." He punctuated this with a leering grin and a wink. His eyes traveled my body, and my face flushed at the implication of his words. He had a knack for saying things that shocked me, but never went further. After listening to Leo's ribald jokes, I anticipated Duncan Stewart would not find me so "stodgy" when he came back.

When Fellowes delivered the news of his return, Tim became more difficult than usual, which I attributed to excitement. I was impatient for Duncan Stewart's arrival also. I decided my initial perception of him was based on my own uneasiness. At times he was brusque, but if I could befriend him, it would work out. Practicing French for Tim's lessons and my own future, I stumbled through the text of a book in the library of a farm girl who tames a monster that is revealed to be a prince. I could apply that to my experience at Seacliff, casting Duncan Stewart as the beast of the tale, although I had no hope for his salvation.

My life settled into a pleasant routine; the deaths that were so part of the history of the house were far from my mind, and on this warm Saturday afternoon, with most of the other servants off, I ventured onto the terrace to draw. Rather than sitting in one of the heavy wrought-iron chairs, I opted to sit on the grass under a large spreading elm tree, filled with leaves. With my sketchbook in hand, I began a study of the stately trees down the hill. Even with the ever-present fog, they stood out, majestic in their guard of the house. I could hear the ocean waves crashing on the distant rocks. The sea was angry today, as angry as they were the last time I saw Duncan Stewart.

I looked up to the second floor, to his bedroom. He had arrived late the previous night, and I had not yet seen him. The heavy green drapes were closed when he was away, but today they allowed every beam of summer sunlight into the room. *He even controls the sun,* I thought, staring out toward the ocean.

"Sitting on the ground in that thin suit will give you a chill. Take a chair."

I looked up to the window. Duncan Stewart leaned out, grinning much like a cat that had cornered a mouse.

"Welcome back, sir. I'm quite comfortable here, but I thank you for your concern."

In a minute, he had strolled through the glass doors to me. He wore an open white silk shirt, his black riding pants and boots. His hair was the unruly mane I had seen the first day, but otherwise he looked sober. I admired the confident manner with which he walked upon the earth. Yet again, I felt nervous in so male a presence.

"Is this a sketchbook, Andrew? You mentioned about wanting to paint, or write or design monuments, didn't you? I can't remember which."

"Did I give you permission to look?" I snapped, as he jerked the sketchbook from my hands. Irritated he had forgotten our previous conversation, I bit my lip to keep silent. I must remember my place in the house as employee.

He read my mind. "It is Duncan, not 'sir'. And you are in my employ."

"Employment, yes, however, slavery was abolished by President Lincoln over three decades ago. Come to my classroom and you can brush up on your history."

"If you'd let me finish, my dear young man, I was going to add that I was being rude in snatching the book from you. But I don't think you'd offer it if I politely asked, would you?" The gruff tone had vanished. He was teasing, like the last time we talked. Feeling quite embarrassed at being called "dear," my face turned bright red.

"Why are you blushing?"

"I'd prefer you not look at it. I'm not good; it's more of a hobby . . . really." I was so tense at sharing this aspect of my life with one who was a success in everything he tackled.

"A hobby? I believe your sole reason for educating my son, whom I understand is markedly more focused now, was to take my money and dedicate yourself to your craft. Besides, I prefer to look. I'll be the judge of your artistic abilities. Who knows, I might be harboring another Rembrandt."

I shifted my mouth into a grimace. "I hardly think so, but I'd like to achieve what Monsieur Monet does with his watercolors."

He thumbed through the pages, then with care handed me the book. "These are quite lovely." He looked me square in the eyes. "Sketch me, Andrew."

My heart skipped two beats. "I'm afraid I wouldn't do you justice. Once I get to France I intend to really develop my talent."

"You are too modest. This study of my son is excellent," He pointed to a drawing I had done of Tim inside the sketchbook. "As your employer and master of this house, I command you."

"Command me? Am I in King Arthur's court?"

He smiled with perfect white teeth, and again my cheeks reddened. "If that's what you'd like."

"I do not know whether you are pretending or when you are serious," I said, rising to my feet and strolling toward the stone railing.

In my haste to make a clever escape, I failed to see where the terrace ended and the lawn began. I stumbled and fell against the wall. I'd never felt more clumsy and awkward then at that moment.

He was beside me in an instant, keeping me from toppling down the hillside.

"Please be careful. I'm not ready to engage another tutor." He laughed, "I think throwing yourself off my terrace is a bit extreme recourse for not wanting to draw me." His strong hands stayed on my waist, and I liked them being there. "Your drawings are superb, Andrew. You are indeed gifted."

Perhaps his hand on my waist was the reason for my newfound confidence. The sensations coursing through my body were indescribable. Like Leo's kiss but more intense. I heard myself agree.

"Let's move over here," he said. Guiding me to a small wrought-iron bench at the east end of the terrace, we sat. The sea, sensing the master of Seacliff was near, quieted down. I could only hear the occasional crash of waves. Duncan watched with intensity as I prepared.

He said, "When I was in Paris—"

"You've been to Paris? How fortunate."

"I met Tim's mother there. The street artist used his thumb to center the page. You are not so inclined, Andrew?"

"I am already familiar with your face. I need for you only to be quiet, please." How in charge I sounded! Me, Andrew; the shy and meek, telling the mighty Duncan Stewart to be silent.

My hands never worked with such efficiency. It was if an unseen power controlled them. Duncan Stewart sat, patient, and did not interrupt, either with questions or comments, while I completed my work.

As I felt his penetrating stare, I wondered if he looked at Steven Charles the same way. I could see them in the drawing room, Steven at the piano, Duncan on the sofa smoking his cigar. Those were happy days in the house. I finished a rough sketch in minutes, and with a flourish, gave it to him. Nodding his approval, he smiled.

"Excellent." Looking at my charcoal pencil, he concluded, "And you did it with the simplest of tools. I am impressed. May I keep this, Andrew? I predict it may be quite valuable in time."

"If you wish, however, I would like to add some color and shading. I can do that without your being present, Mr. Stewart."

"Can't you call me Duncan? It is such a simple name to pronounce."

"I will try, sir."

"And drop the 'sir'." He paused. "I understand from Fellowes my son is regaining the educational ground he lost while without a tutor."

"Tim is a bright child."

"No more tricks?"

"None." This was a lie. Tim surprised me the day before with a long green snake in my desk drawer. Having sworn Mrs. Johnson to secrecy, I hoped word of this would not get back to his father via Fellowes who captured and disposed of the serpent. As if my thoughts summoned him, the valet appeared at the terrace door.

"Mister Duncan. The correspondence you expected from New York has arrived by a special courier."

"Excuse me, Andrew. Some lingering business."

"Yes . . . , thank you . . ."

He wrinkled his face. "Duncan."

"Duncan." It sounded too familiar to call him by his proper name. I looked at the sketch; I had done a good job.

Three days later, the experience on the terrace must have emboldened me, for a feeling of assuredness surged in my body as I marched down the hall to Duncan Stewart's study. Having sketched him I felt more relaxed, and in turn, I could sense he tried to curtail his temper, at least where Tim was concerned.

The door was open, but I knocked anyway. He sat at his desk, engrossed in a mountain of documents. His cigar dangled from the right corner of his mouth, ashes ready to fall onto his papers. The smell of him filled the room as before, and I inhaled because I found it comforting. He did not acknowledge my knock.

"Duncan," I began.

He flicked the ashes from his cigar onto the bear rug, inhaled and blew a cloud of smoke into the air as he leaned back into his leather chair and stretched his arms above his head, acknowledging my presence. My completed drawing of him was in a handsome frame on the wall, next to a colorful rendering of his horse that Tim created. This made me smile, but I could sense he was in a cantankerous mood. As I sat down, he shoved his papers to the side and broke into a grin, which concerned me even more.

"Alright. The cold, calculating businessman is gone, replaced by a friendlier fellow. Is that the Duncan Stewart you prefer?"

"A blend of both would be welcomed at any time."

He scowled and I half expected to be thrown out of the room. Instead, he leaned in. "A gentleman more like Leo Van Horne, perhaps."

My face turned from pink to crimson at the mention of Leo's name. Duncan continued, "I understand you spend a great amount of your personal time with him."

Fellowes must have passed this bit of news on. The valet had surprised us in the garden, as Leo demonstrated a new dance he learned on his last trip to Lisbon. "Leo and Elena have been most kind since I came to Seacliff."

"And I have not, is that the inference?"

"You are putting words in my mouth. In fact, you haven't been around."

He blew a bellow of smoke into my space, but I refused to break under this show of power. Seeing me maintaining my position, he raised his voice.

"I advise you to be wary of Leo. I have known him since childhood and he is trouble personified. Always has been." To add weight to these words, he stamped out his cigar in the glass ashtray on his desk.

"It's not my personal time I have come to discuss with you. I came to ask your permission to begin tutoring Ash as well as Tim."

Duncan reached into his humidor and removed another cigar. He propped his boots up on the desk, with no regard for the papers on top. "An interesting proposal. Why?"

"Tim has made excellent progress in a relatively short time and is completely current on his schoolwork. The boys are close enough in age and I think it would be only logical that Ash benefit from an education as well. This would not take any time or attention away from Tim, and I think that both would learn more if they are studying together." This portion of my speech I had practiced several times in front of my bedroom mirror.

He seemed as unreadable as the Great Sphinx that Tim and I read about the other day. The minutes dragged before he rested his chin in his hand. I saw how his thick brush of a beard covered his fingers. But his black eyes were softer as he spoke, calm and cool.

"I think that's wonderful, Andrew."

My elation was incredible. Duncan Stewart came around the desk and I flew out of the leather chair. Throwing my arms around him, I said,

"Thank you Duncan, thank you so much."

Saying his first name this time came as natural as if I had always used it. But I realized in my jubilation I probably overstepped the line between employer and servant by embracing him.

I started to break away when his strong arms enclosed me next to his body. I looked up from his blue ruffled shirt and black paisley smoking jacket into his handsome face. The musk cologne he wore was strong and it overpowered my senses. For a second I saw a different man than the one I thought I knew.

"You are welcome to make any changes you wish at Seacliff."

Then his eyes clouded over, and he broke away. I followed his eyes to the pistol that killed his father and Albert Brown. Why did he keep such a thing?

He mumbled, "Forgive me, you seemed so happy, I don't want to spoil it."

"I am happy. Thank you again." I felt awkward. The mysteries of Seacliff cast a pall over everyone's lives, even its master. Now, he rubbed his neck and made a face.

"I really shouldn't slouch over that chair. My neck feels like I've been pulling a coach."

Here was a chance to help. "Let me rub your neck. It will make you feel better."

"I will be fine, Andrew. Uh . . . thank you, just the same."

"My uncle always appreciated it. I used to go to Chinatown, and one of the ladies taught me some wonderful remedies. I'm really quite good."

"Alright," he said, sounding defeated, but upon sitting back in his chair, he pointed at his neck in a dramatic fashion. I stood behind him and began massaging the olive skin underneath his hair. His neck was thick, powerful, and difficult to manipulate.

"Your muscles are so knotted; I wonder how you move your head at all," I said, wanting to add it was no surprise he was cranky by turn. Working my hands down to his shoulders, I was impressed how solid and wide they were—so unlike my own slim body. "I wish I was as large as you."

"I'm turning to fat. The house has a complete gymnasium downstairs; I haven't used it in months. This feels quite nice, by the way." Absorbed in his papers again, I felt him start to relax. "Perhaps I could educate you on physical fitness. Father was an expert. Fit as a man half his age."

The thought of being beside Duncan in a gymnasium terrified me. Then again, if he was willing to teach me, perhaps I should take advantage of his offer. No other man had taken interest in my physical development. This was like having the brother I'd always wanted. He groaned as I hit a tight knot between his blades.

"Why are you so tense?"

"The pressures of running a successful business. There was a time when I argued violently with my father regarding my responsibilities in his company; meager assignments compared to what I thought I knew. He wanted to turn over control to one of his cronies until I proved myself. Albert and Mother agreed with him. But I wouldn't take no for an answer."

My mind wondered if that was the motive for killing the two men. Was he again admitting guilt?

He continued, "Be glad you have a talent for art and teaching. I don't know how Father did it. Even with my mother and Albert's help. He'd laugh if he could see me now, I know. The old bastard."

"Your father . . ." I started.

He straightened his back. "I need to get back to these papers, Andrew. I've broken my own rule about discussing the past." He shrugged my hands away and bent back over his desk.

I did not press, but his granting of my request to tutor Ash caused me to float out of the room, and I don't think I told him goodbye. I went for a walk around the grounds, and wandered up the winding path to the top of Whispering Hill, I found myself at the wrought-iron gate to the cemetery. Perhaps I'd find Ash and tell him the good news.

Since my initial visit with Tim, I had only been back once, when my student led me on another fanciful chase through the grounds. But seeing the pistol in the case in Duncan's study set my mind to thinking. I combed the headstones for several dozen minutes, locating it at last. The marker was only a few yards from the entrance to the mausoleum, and Ash was nowhere to be seen.

I stared at the marble tablet, weathered with age from the harsh winters, as if it had lain there for decades instead of only eight years. The stillness surrounding me made my eardrums want to burst.

"Would that he could speak," a voice from behind me said.

I yelped and whirled around to face Leo Van Horne. With a sardonic grin, he clicked his heels and bowed.

Today he wore a green coat that complemented his eyes, and a purple silk cravat. Everything about Leo was so bright compared to Duncan Stewart's darkness: and I fell in somewhere between the two of them.

"You've frightened me half out of my wits."

"Why are you so fascinated by Albert Brown's death?"

"I don't know," I said, but confessed to myself that if I could ease Duncan's pain over the death of his father and Albert Brown, I would. Life at Seacliff might become happy. Maybe Duncan would dress in bright colors like Leo. He would be more cheerful and less brooding. His neck wouldn't be as immoveable as the granite markers surrounding us. We would exercise side by side.

"It has more than a bit to do with the master of Seacliff, I suppose. Steven Charles shared a similar curiosity. We had numerous conversations about the subject. I believe he learned the truth and that is why he left, and was later dispensed with." Leo's face had a grimness that I had not witnessed before.

"The truth that Duncan murdered his father and Albert?"

"Precisely. The two men were cutting Duncan out entirely from his inheritance, despite the fact that Duncan had a son. He killed them in cold blood. I'm also certain Steven learned this, and escaped. That is, until we had the séance. Now I believe Duncan . . ."

"Stop it Leo. I will not . . ."

Leo put his hands on my shoulders and held me firm. Would this be a repeat of our kiss in the library?

"Duncan is trouble. We were close as children, but as he grew up he became darker, more calculated and cunning. Were it not for Elena, I doubt I would even socialize with him."

I could not believe that Duncan murdered his father and Albert Brown. I would not. And yet, it made perfect sense.

Chapter Six

Ash took to schoolwork as the summer flowers welcomed the sunlight that poked through the foggy days. An eager and willing student; and although I failed in my attempts to get him to speak in more than halting tones, his eyes beamed with gratitude and respect. This was more than I could say for Tim, who regarded me with varying degrees of disinterest.

I determined the reason behind Tim's behavior. He wanted attention from his father, and if being good didn't work, being naughty did. I kept many of his pranks from Duncan Stewart and debated whether the secrets that haunted Seacliff now extended to me. When Tim's actions could not be overlooked, a screaming match between father and son ensued until one or the other would stalk off, leaving me to mend the damaged fences. Trying to settle their differences, however, often resulted in an argument between Duncan Stewart and me.

"Your indifference to your only child is most certainly the cause of his mischief," I said, after determining he was interested in having me sit in his study. Many days this was not the rule. As was often the case, he did not respond to my statement.

I rapped on his desk, much as I did to get Tim and Ash's attention. "Did you hear what I said?"

He yawned and pointed his cigar at me. "It is your job to look after my child. I have a business to manage. I am not above harsh discipline to make the child obey, if you cannot control him. Perhaps you have bitten off more than you can chew with two students."

"Certainly not, why only yesterday—"

Before I could defend myself, he waved me off, ashes from his cigar trailing across the desk. "I have much work to do. Close the door behind you, as I have no further desire to be disturbed. Oh, ask Mrs. Johnson to send up some food at seven o'clock. That's a good boy."

"I am not a boy!"

He had succeeded; I had lost my temper and was now yelling at him. As usual, he laughed loud, knowing he had won and hunched back over his

The Master of Seacliff
Published by The Haworth Press, Inc., 2007. All rights reserved.
doi:10.1300/5778_06

desk to work. I was furious, and resolved again not to try and involve him. But I always forgot that vow after a couple of days. Duncan seemed to sense when I avoided him, and went out of his way to bump into me, usually with some obscure excuse as to why he needed to see me. I was coming down the back staircase when he appeared before me one afternoon.

"I see today is a brown day, Andrew. May I predict that tomorrow shall be a gray one? I must admit; your clothing is most suitable for a schoolmaster—were he eighty."

"Is there a concern about my appearance? My clothes are neat and clean. What more do you require?"

"Yes, there is a concern. Don't you have anything else to wear?"

"Had I known my employer would expect me to vary my clothing when tutoring, I would have brought my opera cutaway from my uncle's store. Or for variety, perhaps borrowed a costume from a carnival clown."

"Bright colors such as that would be refreshing. And while you're at it, you could stop oiling your hair. This severe look makes you as interesting as a mathematical textbook."

On purpose I styled my hair into what I thought appropriate for my position. Ridiculous statements about my appearance just didn't agree with me.

"What do you care? I hardly ever see you."

He nodded his head with an unnerving smile. "I'm surprised Leo Van Horne hasn't provided you with a new wardrobe. He is always on the crest of the newest fashions."

"Leo Van Horne is not my employer."

"Noted and filed." He bowed, which I knew was his own display of sarcasm. I was so furious I spent an hour washing and trying to restyle my hair, but gave up.

Although he did not fulfill his promise to instruct me in physical fitness, he rededicated his own self to exercise. Quite by accident I passed by the gymnasium window. Glancing in, I saw him struggling to hoist a long bar over his head. He did not see me but I caught a glimpse at my employer, wearing snug exercise trunks that exposed his thick legs. Shirtless, Duncan Stewart owned a powerful and most hirsute chest that caused me to marvel at his natural manliness yet feeling ashamed for spying. Later, I overheard Mrs. Johnson and Fellowes in the kitchen.

"'Tis a pleasing sight to know he's down in that gymnasium. I don't think he'd been in there since Mister Steven left. He was gettin' awfully paunchy and even more disagreeable."

"I believe he was surprised how soft he had gotten, despite my pointing out his waistline had expanded. However, the fact that he is again exercising is not for household knowledge, Mrs. Johnson. His orders."

"Getting fit for Miss Upshaw, perhaps?"

"That is none of your business."

"Tell him that if he wants to be sneaky then not to groan and swear at the top of his lungs when he lifts those irons."

That same rainy afternoon, Fellowes, the one remaining member of the household I hadn't come to terms with, knocked at my door. "I am to obtain your measurements and bring you some fabric samples. Mister Duncan requests that you order five new suits, at his expense." His expression again telegraphed his annoyance with me.

I was sorry I had invoked Leo's name to Duncan. I did not want it to appear I had goaded him into buying me things. Fellowes' cold stare continued, and I answered, "That's most generous of him."

The valet returned a thin-lipped smile that caught my attention. "Mister Duncan is dining at the Van Horne home this evening, with other friends. The Upshaws. Do you know of them?"

"No, why would I?"

"Mister Duncan finds Miss Victoria Upshaw quite fascinating. There have been rumors of marriage. It would create a powerful business dynasty and Seacliff would have a true mistress again."

He said nothing else as he closed the door. I had heard Victoria Upshaw's name before, and if she and Duncan did marry, that would not change our friendship. When certain Fellowes was gone, I left my room. While crossing the Great Hall, I heard Duncan's angry voice carrying down from above me.

"Damn it all! How could he just vanish?"

I wasn't sure to whom he spoke, but I knew he meant Steven Charles. Not wanting to confront him when agitated, I ducked down a small hall, only to see a shadow pass before me at the side door to the garden. Trying the handle on the door closest to me, I found it locked, and, panic stricken, I ducked into the room across the hall.

Inside, I had an immediate feeling of being watched, which alarmed me. Walking over to the drapes, first peeking to see that no one was outside, I pulled them open. Light flooded the room, and I discovered I was indeed being observed, surrounded by shelf after shelf of dolls. Hundreds of pairs of eyes, in a variety of sizes, expressions, and costumes, stared at me in mute silence. They appeared to be sentinels, guarding an ancient treasure, and the rain pounding outside sounded like war drums. No matter which way I turned, their eyes followed me.

The room had a musty smell, and the grim daylight revealed a cloud of dust that floated in the air from the long-closed curtains. Wanting to sneeze, a search of my pockets revealed I didn't have a handkerchief. I opened the drawer to a small writing desk by the door and began rummaging through it, hoping I'd find something inside to blow my nose. A glance at the desk revealed pale green stationery and a monogrammed letter opener, waiting for its owner, although she was long dead. This had been Janina Stewart's office, and she must have collected dolls. Still searching for a handkerchief, toward the back I found an opened envelope. Inside was a pair of steamship tickets on the *Diana,* made out in the names of Gordon Stewart and Albert Brown. I recognized the sailing date: two days after Gordon Stewart's murder. The destination was the island of Barbados.

Hearing a noise in the hall, I placed the envelope back in the drawer and glanced around at the collection of dolls, who watched me with as much interest as I did them. One was dressed as a cannibal, with wild hair, a bone necklace, baring fanglike teeth of ivory, holding a smaller head by the hair in its clenched fist. Not all the figures were grotesque, and I became intrigued by a small doll atop a gilded box. Dressed to resemble Queen Marie Antoinette, when I touched the pink satin hem of her gown with my index finger, music began playing and the doll began to move in a most delicate manner, opening a tiny fan and waving it. Fearful someone might hear the music and investigate, I crept to the door and opened it. Finding the hall deserted, I snuck out and ran up to the schoolroom, my steps cloaked by the sound of the rain hammering the terrace.

Two weeks later I experienced another tedious afternoon, returning to find all the chalk and pencils missing from the schoolroom. Neither child would confess and I realized that introducing Ash to the schoolroom exposed him to Tim's knack for inventing pranks. My attempt at punishment by having them clap erasers only resulted in them returning laughing, covered head to toe in white dust. Admitting defeat, I ended class for the day and returned downstairs.

Opening the door to my bedroom, I stepped back at the sight of a gigantic package in the center of my bed. Wrapped in elegant gold paper, it was accented with a bright red bow the size of my head. There was a card atop it, addressed to me in a bold script. Picking up the card, I could smell a hint of the musk and tobacco from the hand that had written it.

I grabbed the letter opener from my dresser and sliced the top of the ecru envelope. On the back was a wax seal, the large *"S"* prominent as on everything at Seacliff. My fingers trembled as I read the contents aloud.

Dear Andrew,
I trust you will find these most useful in your pursuits.
Sincerely,
Duncan

I shredded the paper into fragments. In the bottom right-hand corner of the box lid the B. Altman name was revealed. This had been sent from Manhattan. Practical man that he was, the box would contain more books for teaching. I had found a list Miss Jones planned on ordering and requested their purchase. After this afternoon, some additional chalk would be most welcome as well.

As I was about to lift the lid, a knock came at the door. Not waiting for my invitation, the door swung open and Duncan Stewart walked in.

"Ah ha! You've received my gift. I want the pleasure of seeing you open it myself."

He was dressed in sand-colored trousers and a light blue cotton shirt, open at the collar, with dark brown boots. He had discarded the worn out clothing he seemed to live in when I first arrived, and took more pride in his appearance. Indeed, he no longer drank alcohol before the late afternoon. Now his musk cologne wafted into my room with him. For me, this room had been the only harbor that didn't resonate of him. That was gone now.

"I was about to open the box when you knocked." I arched an eyebrow. "I'm so glad that you chose to walk in rather than wait for me to admit you."

"You've a rather dry wit, Andrew. And how fortunate you are to have an employer who knows when you are joking with him. Otherwise, I would be forced to reprimand you. Severely." His black eyes sparkled. I liked to see them that way.

"If you are finished with your wisecracks, may I open my present? My curiosity is getting the best of me."

"And curiosity killed the cat, so please continue," he said, sitting down in the small corner chair in my room, and filling it with his massiveness as he surveyed my modest quarters. "This room is deplorable. No wonder you dressed as you did."

"I thank you again for the new clothing. As for my room, I find it suitable."

"Nonsense. It is in desperate need of painting, and the curtains are faded. I don't think any maintenance has been done since Gwennie . . . You should have told me, Andrew. This is your home too, not a monk's cell."

I'd stopped listening, for when I pulled off the top of the B. Altman box I saw the most wonderful items inside: a long tin of paints, a dozen or so brushes bound with gold twine, a box of pastel chalks, a small mountain of quality paper, two books on art I had seen in Manhattan but had never dreamed of owning, and, most delightful of all, the components to assemble an easel. I was numb.

His deep voice came from the silence. "I don't think Timothy was this speechless when I gave him his new horse. You look as happy as a young kitten in a stable of dairy cows."

"I . . . thank you." My emotions climbed my throat, and I remembered the day in his study when I threw my arms around him. I did not want a repeat of such impulsiveness.

"You mentioned Timothy has shown some promise in art. I don't think it would cause harm to allow you to give him some light instruction in your craft."

"It certainly wouldn't harm him. A child who is forced to work, without recreation time would make for a very lackluster adult. You are blind-sighted by your own business interests."

"You infer that I am lackluster, I see. Perhaps you can teach me how to draw as well, then."

"If you were serious, I'd be happy to."

"Certainly your own talent is worthy of such an investment. That is my real purpose in presenting these to you. We should look for a room in the house you can use as a studio." He scratched his chin. "I know the perfect place, too. Perhaps Ash also has some hidden talent. Steven taught him a few piano pieces, and he did rather well."

He sounded calm, confident, and matter-of-fact. I wondered if there was any ulterior motive for giving me the paints. I didn't want to act foolish, so I extended my hand.

"Again, I thank you. We shall make good use of these."

He got up from the chair, shaking his head. "Last time I gave you what you wanted you flung yourself at me. Now that the heat of summer has set in, I suppose you are conserving your emotions."

I wasn't certain of if he was teasing me, or if he wanted me to react as before. That was the trouble with Duncan Stewart. I could never count on what lay beneath the bluster. He could be so contradictory. But he had mentioned that last time . . .

My room was small, and all I had to do was turn to be next to him. With extreme gentleness I hugged him, as if this giant of a man would break if I held him too tight.

"Thank you, Duncan."

Regular exercise had made his body firmer than before. He pressed against me, and I thought how glorious it would be to stay like this for awhile. The soft glow from the disappearing sun made it all seem like a dream.

"That is a much better thank you than would be customary under the circumstances," he said, almost whispering into my ear. His moustache and beard tickled against my neck and I heard myself giggle. He stepped back from me, looking quizzical.

"What in the devil was that?"

"For the first time since my parents died, someone has cared enough to give me a present that I truly wanted, did not ask for, and who requested nothing in return, except a gesture of thanks."

"I'm sorry about your loss," he said, and the gentleness in his eyes reminded me of the portrait of his father on the landing.

I began laughing like an idiot. "This whole situation seems so absurd!"

He held me next to him. "Andrew Wyndham, I would like to make all your wishes come true."

I leaned back from him, wiping my eyes. He produced a handkerchief and I took it. "I'm sorry, Duncan . . . it's just . . . I'm so . . ."

He put his hands on my shoulders. Thick black hair jutted out from his shirt cuffs, traveling to the base of his knuckles. He gave a deep laugh, and held me tighter. "But as for expecting nothing in return, I . . ."

I remained silent, waiting and breathless. His eyes grew more intense, and closing them, he leaned over, parted his lips—

"Mister Duncan, your business associate has arrived and awaits you in the drawing room. I should also like to speak with you, alone."

Duncan stopped, opened his eyes, and turned, his broad body unblocking my view of Fellowes, who scowled at us with utter disgust. Duncan winked at me.

"Fellowes, old boy, your timing is always impeccable. Excuse me, Andrew. I suggest you find some remaining sunlight and try out your new supplies. Meet me in the library for drinks at six-thirty."

With that, he was off, striding out of my small space into the larger hall-way. Fellowes looked at me, the box on my bed, and then back. I knew he saw our embrace.

"Yes?"

"Never has the master of Seacliff dared to go into the servant's quarters unless it was an absolute emergency. It simply isn't done. First you bring that mongrel child into Master Tim's schoolroom —"

"Don't call Ash that. I had Duncan's permission—"

"And you dare to call him Duncan. I surmise you shall move into his bed at your earliest opportunity."

My face turned bright red, and I was speechless at the valet's accusation. Sensing my embarrassment, he grabbed my shoulders, and the coldness in his hands cut through my jacket.

"I've seen your type before, Andrew Wyndham. Young and fresh faced, supposedly helpless and exuding a wistful innocence that is quite appealing to men such as Mister Duncan. He is a strong and virile man, naturally pro-tective, and you've made him think that he needs to take care of you." He lowered his voice. "But we are not fooled; you use these wiles to capitalize on Mister Duncan's weakness. You've worked quickly these past two months, we must hand it to you."

I looked around, wondering who the "we" were he spoke of.

"Mrs. Stewart trained me well. Don't play your childish games with me. You think me old and stupid. No doubt you've assessed Leo Van Horne's fi-nances are not satisfactory. Perhaps having conquered him on your first day out, you feel that the prize catch can't be too far out of your league."

I was stymied by these accusations. He made every interaction I had with the two men sound so dirty, so calculated, yet the way he held me and the leering look on his face was even worse. I took a deep breath. "You are asso-ciating me with ideas I have never entertained. Leo is my friend, and Duncan is—"

"Your friend? Spare me your unholy excuses. I've seen you with Mister Leo; I know what is going on there." His eyes narrowed into slits. "You may tempt them by pouting your lips and tossing your head to get your way, but Mister Duncan will listen to the voice of reason."

Releasing me, the valet turned on his heel and walked toward the kitchen. My shoulders ached from the pressure he had applied, but more-over, I felt I had been kicked in the stomach by his words.

I thought of Duncan's arms around me and then of Leo's kiss the night of the séance, then of Duncan again. Wondering what kissing Duncan Stewart would be like, I realized I wasn't thinking of a kiss as one would give a brother or receive from a father. I was thinking of a kiss like Leo's: no, even more than that, passionate, deeper, longer; more intense.

I stopped myself. My fantasies had gotten wilder since I'd arrived. A whole different world had indeed opened up for me; a world I never dreamed existed. I reviewed the facts. Duncan Stewart was my employer, and while we had reached an understanding and a friendship, it was nothing more, would be nothing more than that, ever. There was Miss Upshaw to consider. Mrs. Johnson told me his dinners in Manhattan with her were more and more frequent. I had to focus my responsibility on Tim and Ash, and using the remaining time to practice my art. If I concerned myself with feelings for Duncan, I might wind up like Steven Charles, sneaking out in the middle of the night.

Steven Charles: Duncan must still have feelings for him. I wasn't sure what the depth of those sentiments was, but from Leo I'd sensed there was more between Duncan and Steven than that of an employer and an artist. His abrupt departure had been painful to Duncan.

I was someone he wanted to make happy while under his employment. He had stated that I should use my art supplies to teach his son. That was all there was to it.

It took me no time to head upstairs and onto the terrace, and I indulged myself in drawing for what was left of the afternoon, trying to put Fellowes' hateful inferences out of my mind. I experimented with all the different materials in the box, discovering at the bottom a handsome leather case to carry my brushes and paints in. It was monogrammed; not with the Stewart crest, but my own initials stamped in gold, announcing to the world these were mine. For the first time in my life, I was proud to be an artist. I smiled as I thought that every afternoon could be like this, drawing until sundown, and as Seacliff was so vast I could select a new place each day.

Returning to my room, I rested my leather case atop the dresser as if it were an infant, and stood the easel in the corner with pride. I washed my face and dressed with haste, as I wanted to be in the library before Duncan.

He had changed his shirt into a handsome white silk and now wore black trousers, but he looked preoccupied.

"Your business meeting went well?"

"As well as could be. The gentleman was a private investigator I obtained to locate Steven Charles."

I was right. He retained feelings for Steven.

He crossed to a small cart, selected a large glass and poured himself a drink from the square crystal decanter. "His trail now leads to South America."

"It must be quite troubling for you, to have him leave so abruptly and without notice," I offered as I joined him at the cart. I cautioned myself to tread almost catlike on this subject, I didn't want a stray comment to set him off and ruin our evening.

"What would you like to drink, Andrew?"

I pointed to his glass. "The same please." I tried to sound sophisticated, having heard this interchange of dialogue in a play once.

"Scotch?"

I nodded and tried tossing my head in a flip manner.

"I think a light sherry will be best for you, young man. This would have you ill, and I do not think you're quite as versed in liquor as you might have me believe. And if you are, perhaps you should be fired." He reached for a slender bottle that contained liquor the color of watered-down tea. He took the smallest and most delicate glass and poured it as if he were a chemist.

"I've drank liquor before."

"With Leo Van Horne, no doubt. All the more reason to use caution."

As he nosed our glasses together and lifted his chin, I asked, "Do you hope to locate Steven Charles?"

"If only to forward the numerous debts he left behind. But after so many months, it's pointless. In fact, I discharged the investigator tonight. I shall have to push extra hard to eliminate those bills."

"I'm sorry."

His face darkened: I had overstepped that invisible boundary. He took a drink. "Why? You didn't know Steven."

"Because I can see how this hurts you. And I . . ."

"Andrew, your desire to help is not unnoticed. However, Steven Charles is none of your concern. He is a closed chapter in my life."

I followed him over to the fireplace. "I would like to help you Duncan, I gather you and he were close and—"

"You gather nothing. Why is this not clear to you? You are too young to understand."

I wanted to hit him. This was so typical of Duncan Stewart. Do not discuss this or that. I was always too young. There were too many "closed chapters" at Seacliff.

Tim appeared in the doorway, eyeing his father with caution.

"Tim, please come here," I said, beckoning to him. "I'm sure your father would like to hear how your reading is improving," I kicked Duncan's boot and he looked up from his Scotch.

"Yes, Timothy. Come and read to us." He walked over and pulled a book down from the upper shelf, the title of which I couldn't pronounce. Although an astute businessman, Duncan Stewart had no idea what an eight-year-old could read. I intervened, handing a book of poetry to Tim containing the shorter verses I knew he would not be so intimidated by in front of his father.

Tim's reading was excellent, and even I was surprised at how he mastered some of the more difficult words.

"Timothy, I am quite impressed. I see Andrew is teaching you well."

The child hesitated as he looked up at his father. "Thank you."

He read a few more selections, and I noticed Duncan's attention was held the entire time. Tim beamed at the attention he received. Duncan sent him to wash up before supper and we were alone again.

"My son appears quite on target, Andrew. I thank you."

"Tim is an exceptionally bright child. He only wants to please you, Duncan."

He smiled, but his eyes were far away. "Julianka would have been proud." Seeing my expression, he added, "his mother."

Her name had never been mentioned, by anyone in the household. "She is in France?"

"Yes, Paris. Père-Lachaise Cemetery. She died giving birth to my son." I didn't know how to respond.

Duncan's face grew darker than when I mentioned Steven Charles' name. "It was my fault. She should never have become with child."

Tim rushed back in; his energy welcomed after this revelation. So much unhappiness hung over Duncan's head. I so wanted to ease his pain.

Having finished another day's lessons with Tim and Ash, and relishing the time that was now mine alone to spend on my art, I walked up the hill west of the great house. I set up my new easel and paints in the Roman Garden. I had fallen in love with this area the moment I saw it, orderly rows of firs trimmed like giant lampshades, and classical statuary lining the stone walls. I perched myself below a flower pot as tall as myself near a gurgling fountain of one of the muses pouring a vase of water into a seashell. It was a glorious afternoon without a hint of fog or gloom. A wren danced on top of the branches of a bush. Ivy tumbled in a lazy fashion down the walls. Sketching the fountain in two minutes, I experimented with my new charcoals.

I held and reread Duncan's card that came with my gift. Life at Seacliff was turning out better than I expected, with the exception of Fellowes. The master of the house encouraged my art, and he was my friend.

A pair of eyes observed me and I looked up. Elena Van Horne stood at the end of the reflecting pool. She looked resplendent in a pale blue dress. Her smile was as warm as the sunshine.

"Please don't let me interrupt."

She glided along the ground and only the slight rustle of her skirts interrupted the wren's song in the bush beside me. Elena looked at my work and placed her hand at the cameo at her neck.

"Andrew, this is wonderful! I can't wait to see it completed."

How marvelous it was to be in a place where my talents were welcomed. The freedom to express oneself, a definite advantage of life at Seacliff.

"Thank you, Elena, but I'm afraid I have much work ahead of me before I complete this." Although she exuded warmth, I felt shy discussing my art with her.

"Has Duncan seen, or more likely, is Duncan even aware of your talent? He would be most impressed— if you could get his attention."

"It was he who gave me the easel and paints." I had put his card in my pocket, and I touched it for reassurance.

She sat down beside me, curious but not pressing and I opened up to her. I told her of my plan to study art in Paris. She listened, and I could see her mind formulating a plan. She snapped her fingers and spoke.

"I have a friend, Edgar LaVina, in New York. He is a prominent artist that could use an apprentice. I will speak to Duncan; I know he would support you."

"That would be wonderful Elena, but I did promise Michael I would remain at Seacliff through the summer. That's another month." And I now considered remaining through the fall, life was going so well.

She put her hands on my shoulders and looked at me with her emerald eyes. "That's all well and good, but if art is your passion, you should pursue it. I applaud your willingness to tutor, but we should be realistic." She frowned, "That was Steven's problem."

We had not mentioned his name since the séance. I was intrigued to hear about him, particularly since Duncan would not open up.

"Steven was a talented pianist, and Duncan was willing to support him. Instead, Steven languished here, doing nothing. A fitting way to repay Duncan's generosity."

"And he left Seacliff."

"I saw him to the train station. His leaving was for the best, trust me." She said this with a finality and coldness that seemed unusual. Then she brightened.

"If I persuade Duncan to endorse your career, you must not disappoint him by staying on, regardless of your promise. I shall speak to him at the earliest opportunity." She checked the small timepiece pinned to her bodice. "But now I must be off. I have visitors from New York who should be arriving as we speak."

"Elena, are you blushing?"

She laughed, "One of my suitors is arriving, I guess you could say. Arthur Upshaw." Then she whispered. "I'm afraid I'm only teasing him. There's another who always has had my heart."

My ears perked up and I stopped sketching. "The Upshaws dined at your house recently."

"Yes, Arthur, his sister, Victoria, and their father. Charming people, all."

I could trust Elena to tell me the truth. "I understand Miss Upshaw and Duncan are interested in each other."

"Fellowes, am I right?"

"And Mrs. Johnson."

"Their butler is Fellowes' first cousin. He would delight in predicting such an arrangement." She looked away. "Their family is quite wealthy and powerful, and I suppose a Stewart-Upshaw alliance would be an excellent business decision." She laughed, "But Duncan Stewart has never done what was perceived as the right thing." She gave me a small squeeze. "Forgive me, I must go; I will write to Edgar at once. You have my word."

With this pronouncement, Elena Van Horne floated away, a rustle of silk and the scent of jasmine in her wake. I was certain once her mind was made up, there would be no changing it.

I thought of her kindness in speaking to Duncan, but I was unclear if I wanted to leave Seacliff. And this realization shocked me, made me happy, and confused, all at the same time.

Only minutes after Elena left, Leo popped out of the bushes behind the fountain, and he slid onto the bench next to me. His fresh scent of lemon and the sea greeted my nose and his green eyes seemed so close, I thought we would bump noses.

"Good afternoon! How stunning you look!" He rubbed my coat sleeve. "A present from the master?"

The way he said "master" made me feel uncomfortable, much like Fellowes' insinuations that day in my room.

"I selected the fabrics and styles, but yes, these are a gift."

"Don't be fooled, dear Andrew. He's trying to win your loyalty. I've seen it happen dozens of times."

"I think you are exaggerating his intentions, Leo."

"I have known him much longer than you," he whispered. "You must be careful with Duncan. He may appear to have your interests at heart, but this—" he fingered the sleeve of my charcoal coat again, "—is all strictly for his own gain. You have good taste. I surmise since he's buying, you wisely chose the costliest goods available."

This remark stung, and I kept seeing Fellowes' leer in my mind. I let my face show my emotions. Leo shook his finger.

"Now, now, none of that. See how he casts gloom, even when he's not around? I came to tell you this: I was awake most of the night, composing a poem dedicated to you."

"A poem about me?" I couldn't imagine anyone doing such a thing, although nothing the lean and graceful Leo Van Horne did should be a surprise. Then I thought of the sketch I did of Duncan. Did he not inspire me the same way?

Aware that Leo awaited a response, I answered, "I should like to hear it, Leo."

"Not yet, my fair Andrew. It's not complete. I feel I must have more . . . inspiration."

In a flash he placed his arms around me, pulling me into him. I could see the kiss forming on his thin, rosy lips. I managed to break free and stand up.

"Leo, you are incorrigible." I tried to sound serious, but I knew I was more amused than shocked.

In a second he was up, his long arms around my body. Leo was so tall, lean, and strong. His emerald eyes glowed with a passion, directed at me. I tried to avoid his eyes, but it was as if I had been hypnotized.

"Don't be frightened of me, Andrew. Life is different here at Seacliff, different than most places. I told you we live by our own rules. It is a place to follow your instincts. I'm following mine, now."

It wasn't Leo Van Horne I was frightened of. It was my own inclinations and my cravings, which had been simmering since I arrived at this magnificent house. A house that breathed desires I could not admit were taking over my soul. The passion inside me was now at a boiling point, a thick, rich soup of emotions brimming over the kettle, waiting to be whetted by hungry appetites. As Leo held me, my thoughts were only of Duncan.

"I won't hurt you Andrew," he said, drawing me next to him. "Not like . . ."

The tall flower vase above toppled toward us. I pulled Leo away as it crashed to the stone pathway. In the now empty space, Duncan Stewart peered over, his hands on his hips. "Leo," he said in his lowest voice.

"Really, Duncan, I thought such theatrics were beneath you."

"I'll thank you to keep your hands off my son's tutor." The blood drained from my face as I wriggled from Leo's arms. I tried to straighten my rumpled clothes and hair, but I knew it was no use.

"Oh, Dunky. You've always been so possessive."

I wanted to crawl under the jade bushes and disappear.

Leo continued, "Might I remind you that Andrew doesn't have 'property of Seacliff' branded on his backside?"

"As Andrew's employer and benefactor, I must keep a watchful eye over him. Particularly from rogues like you," Duncan said, walking confidently and determined as if preparing for battle.

"Benefactor?" I said.

"Andrew has a real talent for art. It is a gift that should be cultivated and developed. I'm just the man who can do that. Your financial resources are fairly limited, as we all know." Duncan thrust his thumbs in his pants pockets and widened his stance as he came up beside me.

Both men became so silent it was deafening. Duncan stood on my right, and Leo remained on the left. I remembered when I was ten and my cousin and I fought over a small toy lamb. We tugged and pulled, until its head popped off. At this moment, I felt not unlike the lamb.

Leo snapped, "You were Steven Charles' benefactor also, and had you not been so controlling he might still be in this house . . . and in your bed."

Now I knew the truth of the relationship between Steven Charles and Duncan Stewart.

Duncan saw my reaction then turned back to Leo, his face red as fire.

Leo continued, "And what about your father? When will you learn that if you can't buy people's affection, you must kill them?"

Duncan lunged at Leo, growling like a grizzly bear, but I stood in the way. Leo backed up to throw a punch and I threw my small arms between the two men, feeling like a toothpick used to support toppling oaks. It was all I could do: had I not been there, the scene would have deteriorated into fisticuffs.

"Would you gentlemen please stop?"

Leo retreated, clicked the heels of his black boots together and bowed.

"As you wish, Andrew. I shall remove myself posthaste so as not to embarrass the master of Seacliff, but think about everything I've said . . . and haven't said."

With that, he left, his wool coat flaring out behind him. I watched him disappear behind the columned rows of hedges. Turning back, I saw Duncan with a broad grin on his face. I frowned.

"What is that grin for? You look like the cat that ate the canary, Duncan Stewart."

"Andrew, I know Leo has a certain charm, but you must be careful of him. Pay no attention to his caustic and dramatic remarks. I should like to help you in anyway I can."

"I wish you two could be friends."

"Elena and Leo are like a sister and brother to me. We have always been competitive, and deep down, we both use the same tactics to get what we want. Mine are applied to business; Leo's are personal—in this case to take advantage of your innocence."

I rolled my eyes. "Oh, yes. I'm a child."

"Yes, which is what makes you so endearing. And I mean every word about supporting your art studies."

I wondered if Elena had already spoken to him, or if his comments were unsolicited. Or, had his seeing Leo's arms around me prompted this sudden display of generosity?

"Duncan, employment here is more than enough to fund my art studies."

Now it was his turn to frown. "I see. Employer and employee again. I suspect next you'll return to calling me 'Mr. Stewart.' I notice, however, that it's always 'Leo, Leo, Leo.' No formality there. Actually, *quite* familiar, I'd say."

"But it was you who told Leo you were my employer, only moments ago," I said, not hiding my smile.

He made a move toward me, and hoping he would seize me as Leo did, I closed my eyes and leaned in toward him. I should have liked being wrapped again in his big arms, pressed against his strong chest, gazing into his black eyes. After a few seconds with no reaction, and feeling foolish, I opened my eyes to see him before me as red as a cherry. The implacable Duncan Stewart: at last out of sorts.

He barked, "Shouldn't you be preparing the children's lessons for tomorrow?"

"Tomorrow is Sunday."

Then eyeing the easel and sketch pad, he said, "Perhaps you should just be left to your art . . . alone." He turned on his heel and stalked off down the same path Leo had taken.

The color returned to my face and grew warmer. Although the entire interchange had been complicated and almost comical, I was certain of one thing: Duncan Stewart liked me, more than as my employer. And I, in similar fashion, liked him, more than I cared to admit.

Chapter Seven

On my way outside, I passed the door to the doll room, seeing it open with a harried Mrs. Johnson inside. Packing crates surrounded her and the dolls that had frightened and intrigued me were now wrapped in paper. In the light of early afternoon the menacing figures, no longer standing like a small army, looked defeated.

"Andrew, could ye pass me that crate?" she called, patting her forehead with her apron. "Glad to see these things heading out. Nothin' but dust magnets, they were. And those eyes all lookin' at me. Ugh."

I gave her the large box and handed her some additional paper. "These were Mrs. Stewart's?"

"She'd collected them for years from all over. There were more, if ye can believe that—Miss Elena took some, and Mister Duncan gave a few to the other maids." The housekeeper sighed, "Thank goodness he's sold the rest to that Mr. Upshaw in New York." She winked. "Guess he's trying to woo the old man, I hear he collects these for his daughter."

"Really?"

Mrs. Johnson cackled. "T'would only be to get control of the Upshaw business! I understand the old man's been holdin' out, sellin' off bits and pieces of things at a time, but Mister Duncan will prevail, even if it means having to marry that old maid daughter." She winked again. "I know a few folks who'd not be so happy 'bout that!"

Before I could react, Fellowes appeared in the doorway. The look he gave me was pure hatred.

"I see you are surveying your new art studio."

"Art studio? I—"

He cut me off. "I have assured Mister Duncan this room will be emptied by the end of the day. 'Inconsequentials' he called them. His mother valued these dolls more than anything." The valet surveyed them, now scattered around the room, and for once I felt sorry for him.

"And sold off, like that, at a fraction of their value. George Upshaw will just turn around and sell them at a higher profit."

The Master of Seacliff
Published by The Haworth Press, Inc., 2007. All rights reserved.
doi:10.1300/5778_07

Mrs. Johnson shook a tall doll fashioned of straw at the valet. "Mister Duncan's never made a bad deal in his life. I'm sure Mrs. Stewart wouldn't mind, if it means more money for the family. Remember when times was lean; she'd not hesitate to sell off some jewelry to help Mister Gordon."

"Because her reputation was at stake. If Mister Gordon had been a better manager instead of —"

The housekeeper hissed at Fellowes. "That's a fine way to speak of the dead! When he was murdered right across the hall."

I had been half listening, bowled over by the news that this room would become my studio. Now I looked past Fellowes at the door across the hall. It was the one that I had tried to enter before and found locked.

Fellowes caught my glance. "We are not to discuss that, per Mister Duncan." He turned and walked off and I heard the side door slam shut. A moment later the valet passed by the window.

Mrs. Johnson tossed the straw doll into the box and closed it. "Bet he's gone up to the graveyard to tattle. There's nothin' wrong with visiting the dead, but I don't think she's a'hearin' his complaints."

I tried to hold my laughter.

"He'd rather have this room preserved than used again. Same with that one across the hall. Been locked up since their deaths, and he's the only one with a key. Doesn't bother me; less for the girls to clean."

The housekeeper bent back over the crate and continued to fill it with the dolls. "All the work I've to do, and he refuses to touch 'em! Well, Mister Duncan always has let him do as he pleases, because he's been around longer than the pyramids. More trouble than it's worth to challenge that one, I s'pose."

"Can I help?" I offered, still trying to comprehend the news that this room was now mine. With Duncan's gesture, I felt pronounced an official artist.

"No child, this'll all be out by the end of the day. Then Mister Duncan wants a fresh coat of paint thrown up, which me husband will do. Should all be ready by day after next." She shook her fist at the window. "Not my job, you understand, but that one t'would have nothin' to do with it. So here I am, with a load of work backed up in the kitchen."

Remembering the steamship tickets I had seen in the desk, I got up from the crate I was sitting upon. Perhaps Mrs. Johnson would answer some of the other questions I had. I looked at the closed door across the hall. "Elena said Albert's mind snapped knowing he was being sent to a sanitarium."

The housekeeper motioned for me to close the door. She then crossed herself and lowered her voice. "Mister Albert seemed alright to me—they'd all been under a lot of worry over some business doings that wasn't quite up to snuff." She dropped her voice to a hoarse whisper and wiggled her fingers. "It was only *after* they died Miss Janina said Albert had been acting a'strange. What she didn't say was Mister Gordon and Mister Albert had been called to testify by the court. The old man had his hands in a lot of crooked deals, but I never said nothin' for he gave more than his share to the church. While I don't think ye can buy your way into heaven—"

"Could it be Albert was being sent to Barbados to escape any scrutiny by the courts?"

She wrinkled her face. "Oh, no twasn't there. Mrs. Stewart told us that Mister Albert was going to a rest home called Oak Lawn. It's just up the river from Manhattan. Real nice place too, she said. I think she owned part of it."

"Are you certain it was in New York?"

"Me daughter Gwen almost worked there."

I always avoided mentioning Gwendolyn, for fear of upsetting Mrs. Johnson. "What do you mean?"

"Gwen wanted to get out of Seacliff; she'd lived her whole life here. I think her sailor awakened the rover in me daughter. Good money, it would have been. Mister Duncan wrote up a fine recommendation, and kept the possibility of her a'leavin just between the two of them. Low and behold, she got a letter offering her a job."

"And changed her mind?"

"She threw herself off the cliff that afternoon. We'd all been celebratin' her good fortune. I guess she couldn't leave after all."

It didn't make sense Gwendolyn would commit suicide if she had a way to escape Seacliff.

"There were steamship tickets in this drawer for Gordon and Albert. To Barbados. They were to have sailed two days after—they were murdered."

Mrs. Johnson shook her head, and leaned on the crate she had sealed. "Can't be, child. Miss Janina and Mister Gordon made the arrangements for Oak Lawn. But she said later when they told Albert about it, he just went loony." She sighed, "He'd been here so long, helpin' Mister Gordon build his riches, guess he felt he was just bein' tossed out like an old newspaper."

I opened the right drawer. To my dismay it was empty; the entire contents of the desk had been removed. The housekeeper watched me, and opened the door, pushing one of the larger crates with her foot into the hall.

"The only thing Fellowes did was clear that desk out this morning." She stuck her nose up in the air. "Said it was Mrs. Stewart's 'personal' papers. He's probably saving them like precious relics. Do you think you might want to keep that desk in here? Sure is hard to move, that thing."

I walked into the hall and tried the handle on the walnut door, which did not move. Mrs. Johnson followed me.

"Mister Albert kept his room as neat as a pin. But oh, what a mess it was that night! Furniture toppled over, clothes all cross ways. All packed up he was. Mister Gordon had given Mister Albert one of his fine steamer trunks and a bunch of his clothes. From the amount of trunks you'd tell on sight he warn't comin' back!"

I thought again of those tickets. I wanted to ask if it were possible that Gordon Stewart packed a trunk for himself, and that in the disaster that followed, the intention had been misconstrued. But Mrs. Johnson wouldn't let me get a word in. She continued, waving her hands in the air.

"And the blood! Everywhere! Took poor Gwen hours to sop it up. And that rug Mister Gordon and Mister Albert bought in Persia—we had to throw it out. Their bodies was right across the middle of it." She splayed her arms outward. "And Mister Gordon, clutchin' a Bible in his dead hands. Miss Janina guessed he tried to get Mister Albert to remember the Commandments as a last resort." She shrugged, "Shot him dead, anyway."

"Could it be they were going away together? Mister Gordon and Mister Albert?"

Mrs. Johnson scratched her head and secured the stray strands of gray back into her bun, and laughed. "Land sakes, yes. Those two men traveled all over the world, like two little rascal boys they were, always getting into mischief! But not that time. They had to testify in court the following Monday. Would have gotten into more trouble if they skipped out."

Fellowes' voice came from behind us. "Did I not tell you Mister Gordon's death is not a topic of discussion?"

Mrs. Johnson muttered something under her breath and resumed packing.

I confronted the valet. "I'd like to see inside that room."

"No one goes in. If your father had been murdered by an insane killer would you want to see a constant reminder of your grief?"

"But isn't sealing it off just as bad?" I countered, looking into his steel eyes. He said nothing, so I pressed on. "Fellowes, there were papers in this desk."

Was it my imagination or did the valet flinch at this question?

"Those were Mrs. Stewart's personal correspondences. I gave them to Mister Duncan."

He straightened his coat. "Master Tim has requested that you see him in his father's study. At once!" The valet turned, checked the door handle to ensure it remained locked, and marched away, triumphant.

"Ears like a lynx, that one," Mrs. Johnson said.

"Mrs. Johnson, who found the bodies of Gordon and Albert?"

"I . . . I don't remember."

Her tone did not convince me. "Was it Mister Duncan?" I asked, hoping it wasn't.

She saw my expression. "Things was a'crazy that night. People were all over the place. I know old fussbudget was with Miss Janina; she collapsed when the sheriff arrived."

"Where were you that night?"

"I don't recall . . ."

"On such a night as that?"

"Down at me own house. They'd all gone to a party so there was no need for me to be up here. I made dinner for Gwendolyn and James. That's where I was."

"James?"

"Her sailor. They had just started a'courtin'. Were on their way to the tavern in town when—"

Tim's voice, calling my name, echoed from upstairs. I wanted to tell Duncan my theory about his father's death. The men could have been leaving together to escape testifying. And if so, then who shot them?

Running up the stairs and down to the study, I found Tim rolling around on the polar bear rug with a set of metal soldiers his father had given him. They were his newest favorite toys, and Duncan now allowed his son in his study on certain afternoons. Duncan watched him, his customary cigar languishing aside this time, all ash. Before I could open my mouth, the child jumped up from the floor and grabbed my hand.

"You're going horseback riding with me. Father is busy."

I balked each time this subject came up. Now it seemed Tim had enlisted his father for help. His overcoming a fear of Duncan was a good thing, I told myself, even if my penalty meant riding a horse, a task I had done once: the day Leo rescued me from the zoo and brought me back on his.

Duncan gave me the once-over and having made an assessment, shook his head. Then the study clock's chime and Tim's voice broke the silence together.

"Please, Father, please!"

"I don't see why not, son. Have you any riding clothes, Andrew?"

Tim leaped for joy and wrinkled his nose at me. "I told you my father would make you! See you downstairs!" Watching him dart out of the room, I turned to Duncan.

"About your mother's dolls . . ."

"Would you like one?"

"No! I—"

"Now you will have a fitting place to paint." He lowered his voice. "Honestly, I had more selfish reasons than that. This transaction may net me a much larger gain in the future with George Upshaw."

"Duncan, I've discovered—"

"Me too. After months of playing hide-and-seek, Upshaw is ready to sell his interest in the new railway being built underneath Manhattan. It's called a subway, Andrew, and it's the transportation of the future."

Business, he always thought business.

"This is concerning some correspondence I found in your mother's desk . . . by accident."

"Tell me later. Right now the goal is to overcome your fear of riding."

"I don't have a fear of riding, it's—"

"I'd like to go out with my son, but I'm close to closing this deal with Upshaw; months I've been wearing him down. Mother's dolls may do the trick. And there's nothing to riding, don't be timid."

His crack about my supposed fear of riding annoyed me. "You're mistaken, Duncan Stewart, if you think I'm afraid of riding a horse."

He grinned wider, then laughed. "This I'd like to see."

"You don't think I can ride, do you?"

"The fearless city boy. Not to worry, I know just the mount for you. As for clothing, Fellowes can outfit you, I'm sure. My old riding clothes are too big. They'd swallow you up." He looked me over again and I shifted my stance, nervous yet exhilarated with the way his eyes traveled my body.

I would have liked to have worn his clothing, oversized or not. To be enveloped in his scent, overpowering my own; it was an intriguing thought and quite appealing to me. As if I could actually become him for a short time.

"But in your mother's desk—"

He lit a fresh cigar. "We can talk about whatever you'd like at supper. Now, go off and have a good ride."

Fellowes returned, received his instructions, and looked me over as if it were our first meeting.

"My riding experience is rather limited. Perhaps the right clothing will make me feel more at ease," I confided outside the study door.

The valet cracked a smile, revealing a crooked front tooth. It was the first sign of pleasure I'd seen since I'd arrived.

"I know of exactly the garments that will suffice, please come with me."

We walked down the long hallway, past the portraits of ancestors, to the double doors at the other end.

"Mrs. Stewart's room has the answer. Always has, through the good and the bad. Many times I would come here and ask for her guidance. We were friends."

He looked at her massive portrait and smiling, turned the slender brass handle, and I wondered if he inferred that I would wear her clothing. I was of slight build, but that idea was ridiculous.

Fellowes continued with his quizzical grin, which unsettled me. "Wait here, Mister Andrew, while I open the draperies."

The room was dark and foreboding. I strained my eyes as Fellowes walked catlike through the dimness and drew the drapes. Midafternoon illuminated the room. Overhead, droplets of crystal glimmered from a chandelier while the sun's rays danced off them.

Looking around, I longed for my sketch pad to capture the room's beauty. Crocus-yellow draperies covered a magnificent expanse of window, set with innumerable individual panes as if in a cathedral, along the eastern wall. Opposite the windows, a well-done oil painting of a seascape stretched across. Another wall was mirrored from one end to the other, and I imagined that the palace of Versailles must look quite the same way. It was immaculate; not a hint of dust existed.

"It's lovely," I said.

"Mrs. Stewart personally designed this space, from the paneling to the appointments. There was no end to her talents."

The focal point of the room was its bed, which was easily three times the size of mine downstairs. It was covered with an embroidered yellow silk spread that had the tiniest fringe along the bottom like delicate, suspended spun gold. Four enormous pillows of ruby and sapphire, in round and square shapes rested at the head. Beneath my feet, a lush emerald rug almost covered the shining oak floor and my toes sank into it, like a thick lawn.

Although breathtaking, the room remained cold in its beauty and temperature. I looked into the hallway at the portrait of Janina Stewart, whose painted eyes followed us in. The portrait complemented the haughtiness of her room to perfection.

"There is a silver key on the dresser; would you bring it to me?"

A four-foot high dresser rested against the wall and I noticed dozens of jars and bottles of different shapes and colors arranged atop a long lace runner that rested on the mahogany surface. The bottles appeared to contain a variety of colognes and ointments. The brand of spiced cologne that Michael Betancourt favored caught my attention. I purchased some for his last birthday and remembered how nervous I was going into the elegant men's store where it was available. Upon closer look, I recognized several of the bottles as being masculine toiletries.

"I do not see a key, Fellowes."

"Perhaps it is within that chest."

In the center of the dresser rested a handsome container of burled wood and I flipped up the hinged lid. It held an array of silver chains, jeweled cufflinks, boot pins and rings. A broach, fashioned like a piano, was encrusted with glittering stones. The sunlight caught the piece and it radiated fire in the lifeless room. Mesmerized, I picked it up and moved it back and forth in my hand, watching the play of light against the stones. It was expensive, but gaudy. Looking back in the chest, I found the key; underneath a large signet ring inset with sapphires and the telltale initials 'S.C.'— Steven Charles.

"An incredible collection, don't you think?"

Fellowes had watched me the entire time. Dropping the piano broach back into the box, I looked straight into the mirror above the dresser, and noticed a sinister gleam in the servant's eyes. I had been set up to find these things.

"Fascinating he would leave so many expensive baubles behind, isn't it, Mr. Wyndham?"

"I assume so," I answered, shrugging my shoulders. Although intrigued, I acted aloof. I extended the key toward him.

"Here it is."

"Assume nothing, Andrew Wyndham. Mister Charles loved his jewelry. He had collected them from his travels around the world. Many were gifts from admirers, male and female. An incredible bounty of riches, tossed at him in exchange for a mere glance, an aside."

The valet picked up a silver pocket watch.

"Mister Duncan gave this to him two Christmases ago. From Tiffany's store in Manhattan. It is valued at hundreds of dollars. Yet, he left it behind. Don't you think that absurd?"

"I know very little about Steven Charles. Only the Van Hornes have spoken of him before now."

"They were close, indeed. Many times when Mister Duncan would be out of town, the three of them would be up all hours with guests, here in this room. People not of our social circle, I might add."

"Mr. Charles was Mr. Stewart's guest. I'm certain if there were any visitors invited, Mr. Stewart approved of them."

"Guest? Indeed, it was much more than that, child."

I would not discuss that with the valet.

"You don't think his leaving was planned?"

The valet didn't hear me. He stared at the portrait of Janina Stewart in the hallway. "He was never really suited for this house. Mr. Charles was a creature of society, and Seacliff can be most desolate. But he would not have left these treasures. Very content, he was, living off the generosity of Mister Duncan . . . and others." He arched his left eyebrow, looked around the room and exhaled.

"If Mrs. Stewart had lived, this arrangement would have killed her. Putting that sort into her room, as if he were her equal. She had no equal, ever. Never—"

The tobacco and musk scent reached me before Duncan's voice did.

"Never what? Exactly what have you deduced from this, Fellowes? I would be most interested to hear your theories directly after so many months of whispering behind my back!"

Fellowes paled and I took a deep swallow. Duncan looked as angry as the night of the séance when he burst into the library.

"Mister Duncan. I—"

"Your instructions were to find Andrew suitable clothing to wear. Timothy is dressed, and if you two weren't wrapped in your own speculations you would have heard him screaming at you from downstairs, as I did from my study. I expect Andrew to dress with promptness. And, I expect there to be no further discussions as to the prior occupant of this room between anyone else in my house."

He wouldn't even say Steven Charles' name, and I saw no emotion in those black eyes.

In silence, the valet walked over to the mirrored wall, inserted the silver key, and the panel slid to the right revealing a wardrobe. Row upon row of handsome suits, cutaways, shirts and pants hung neatly and color coordinated inside. Hatboxes stacked three deep lined the shelf above the brass rods that held the clothing. Dozens of shoes sat upon the floor below them. My eyes fell upon an orange silk smoking jacket with the bold 'S.C.' embroidered on the left pocket. These clothes waited for their owner's return. However, he had been gone well over ten months. Leo Van Horne and Seacliff's valet were suspicious of his departure, and its master did not want it discussed.

Fellowes produced a jacket and riding pants of a camel color, studied them, then me. "These will accommodate you."

I walked over to the closet, but as I looked out the window I saw Duncan Stewart heading across the driveway toward Whispering Hill, cigar smoke trailing behind him. His brisk stride emphasized his agitation. He had been too preoccupied with business to ride with his son, or listen to me, but now he had gone out.

The sandalwood scent, closed up for many months, flooded the room. I remembered the séance, and felt ill. Behind a screen, I noticed another door, tucked in the corner near the dresser. Fellowes' eyes followed mine and they narrowed.

"That connects to Mister Duncan's room, via a private bathroom. You may dress behind the screen," he said, handing me a yellow chamois shirt, and a beautiful pair of dark chestnut boots that looked brand new.

The riding pants were of thick twill and felt heavy on my skin even before I put them on. As I changed I thought of the times Steven Charles had dressed in front of these mirrors with Duncan in an adjacent room, and mulling his fate made me uneasy. Steven Charles had broader shoulders than I, and narrower hips, but I was able to get the clothing on with relative ease. While I would have liked Duncan's cologne, Steven Charles' sandalwood made my nose and throat close. Praying I wouldn't start coughing, I hoped the fragrance would evaporate once I got outside. Pleased with how the riding costume looked, I called out.

"These fit nicely. Thank you."

I emerged from my dressing area to an empty room. Fellowes was gone, but he had left me with a myriad of thoughts: amazed that Steven Charles would have left so many of his belongings here; accepting the relationship between Duncan Stewart and Steven as more than a wealthy man entertaining a successful pianist. This was an intimate relationship, and I was surprised I wasn't more shocked. I remembered the newspaper accounts of Mr. Wilde and his trial, but the lurid, whispered gossip on the streets that wasn't printed was easier to recall. I wanted to know what had driven Steven Charles to leave. Such a falling out must cut Duncan even deeper than the death of his father.

I walked over and grabbed the handle to the connecting door. Duncan was out on the grounds. Fellowes had probably gone to the kitchen. I could sneak a glance at Duncan's room and perhaps learn more about his life with Steven Charles.

"Andrew! Andrew! ANDREW!" Tim's voice echoed throughout the house from downstairs. I would have to investigate another time.

My pupil danced in wait at the bottom of the stairs. As I rounded the last step, Leo Van Horne emerged from the drawing room with an afternoon cognac in hand. It was no surprise to see him; in fact I expected Leo to show up anywhere, at anytime.

My borrowed clothes made an impact on him. He stared at me with an unusual coldness in his eyes.

"Where did you get those?"

He lifted my arm and inhaled the cuff of the chamois shirt.

"I don't think he ever wore this."

I pulled my hand away, as Leo had moved his nose from the fabric to my skin.

"I'm going out for a ride and needed the proper clothes. It was Duncan's idea."

"They fit you well." He strolled off but continued talking. "Have a good ride. But remember to come back, unlike the prior owner of that outfit."

Tim grabbed me by the forearm and dragged me out the side door. I could see Leo watching us from the window, as we disappeared down the flagstone steps to the path that went to the stables.

Once there, Tim dropped my hand and took off.

"John will have a horse for you. Father told him to."

I had been at Seacliff for over two months, and yet John was an unfamiliar name. I thought I'd met everyone who lived and worked on the property.

Rounding the corner to the stable, a man was visible beyond the arched entrance. I recognized the pronounced limp, his hair the color of dried grass, and the thick spectacles. He was not a stranger: he was the horrid man I met in town upon my arrival.

"Name's John Middleground," he said with a laconic stare. "You didn't stick around long enough to ask before."

I closed my eyes at the intense smell of alcohol. "Based on your dislike of the Stewarts, I'm amazed you work here."

He ignored me. "Mister Stewart told me himself to give you the gentlest horse we got, so I got Flowerbell all ready for you."

Tim squealed, "I stopped riding Flowerbell when I was four!"

I looked at the collection of horses in their stalls, Duncan's sleek black stallion, the coach horses, and Tim's young gelding, Cornelius. Across from them was Flowerbell, a lumbering, dapple-gray animal with a tired expression, who acted bored. Another horse, more trim and gleaming like a chestnut, was in the stall next to her.

"What about that one?"

"Angel? She's tame enough. Suit yourself."

I could tell John Middleground was irritated I had to be helped onto Angel, and he almost pushed me over the animal, instead of astride her. But I was out to prove everyone wrong. Flowerbell resembled a creature that would enjoy pulling an ice wagon rather than be ridden upon. For once, I would not be treated like a child. I wished I'd thought to put some sugar cubes in my pocket for additional insurance.

"Andrew's never ridden a horse, John. Can you believe it?" Tim said with mock disbelief as he climbed with ease atop Cornelius.

The stableman snorted, "Don't know why someone your age would attempt to ride any horse when they haven't done so before. All sorts of accidents can happen."

"I suppose that's how one learns, by trying." I wasn't about to let him or anyone else make me feel any more insecure than I did already.

Tim and I set off farther down the hill from the stables to the safety of the flat beach. We rode in silence along the coast up toward the Van Horne estate, and I wished Elena would appear to console me with her quiet calmness. Passing their home, Glendower Hall, I noticed how unkempt the lower grounds were. I allowed Tim to ride ahead, but he returned back to me from time to time. I was certain he would prefer galloping along as he did with his father, but I would not. It was enough getting used to the motion at this slow pace. I looked down at the reins and my hands, which were bone white. Remembering books I had read on riding, I tried talking to Angel, who was a good sport about it. I hoped she was pleased just to get out of her stall for awhile. I told her I'd bring her some carrots tomorrow if she'd cooperate with me today.

We stopped at a small cove, which gave us a break from the breezy shoreline. Up the cliff, Whispering Hill loomed above. Getting off Angel, who turned out to be a calm beast, was as difficult as mounting her, and without John's hands to assist, I sort of slid off, but was thrilled to stand for a moment. I checked my pocket watch. We'd been out only an hour. It was chilly and I stuck my hands in the riding coat pocket, wishing Fellowes had provided me with gloves.

My left hand hit an object in the pocket and I withdrew it with caution. I held a small brown leather book about the size of my hand. 'S.C.' was stamped on the cover in gold leaf. I opened it. An inscription was inside:

> *My beloved Steven-*
> *Always make time for me*

I did not recognize the dedication as being in Duncan's definitive bold handwriting. On instinct I flipped to the last entry, dated September 2, 1898.

> *Must order new suits from Brooks Brothers and discuss the painting with*
> *ELV. 2 p.m. Order new watch from Tiffany's. Consult D about party*
> *invitations and confirm date for end of month.*

I moved back a few pages. To my dismay it was not a diary or journal, but more of an appointment book. Similar notes of daily life at Seacliff were the primary entries, with occasional musical notes drawn on some of the margins. Scanning the pages, I saw nothing that suggested his departure was planned.

Sticking out of the corner of the book was a page that had been torn out, and tucked back in. Written in haste, but by Steven Charles.

> *Ask J about key and G.*

This was interesting, but I wished Steven Charles had written out proper names. Who was "ELV" and what was the painting? "D", of course had to be Duncan. "J" must be Mr. or Mrs. Johnson. Ask J about G. Gordon Stewart?

Leo said Steven suspected Duncan murdered his father. Perhaps the Johnsons had information that would clear Duncan, or incriminate him. What if Steven confirmed Duncan's guilt and fled Seacliff? I placed my hand back into the pocket, and removed an ornate key on a beaded chain. The key Steven referred to in the note, no doubt.

"Come on. Let's go up the hill this way."

Tim dug his heels into Cornelius and started up the steep wide path to the top. By utilizing a boulder, I climbed aboard Angel. After insincere congratulations from Tim on this feat I followed him up the path.

"Lean forward, then you won't feel like you're falling off," he advised.

I smiled at the child, who looked confident and secure in his well-worn riding togs. My lack of experience, on the other hand, would be obvious to the most untrained of eyes. Wrinkling my mouth, I admitted, "You're quite a horseman, Tim."

"I've done this for years, silly."

Tim rounded the top minutes before me and I breathed a sigh of relief as I joined him. The cemetery entrance was ahead of us, and I could see Ash sitting outside the mausoleum as he had on my first day out.

Tim shrugged, "He's always there at the same time."

Since he started schooling, I hoped the sad child with the white hair had stopped playing alone among the headstones, but I was wrong.

"Why do you think he does?" I said, stroking Angel's mane.

"Who cares? And see, he's gone now. He knows his grandpa will give him a whopping if he stays out too late."

This was indeed true: Ash no longer sat by the entrance. Tim saw my look of concern and brightened.

"Let's go into the cemetery and find him."

"No. It's time to get back to the house. I'm cold. Come away from the cliff."

"I've ridden here a thousand times, what do you know?"

We had such a nice ride; I'd enjoyed it. Now, predictably, Tim would be difficult.

"I'm ready for some hot tea." In moments we could be back at the stable. I hoped Duncan would be back from his walk and calmer. I would march into his study and insist he listen: the steamship tickets, Steven Charles' appointment diary, the strange key. They were connected.

"Can we race back? It's flat," Tim said as he prodded Cornelius into action.

I opened my mouth to consent when I saw movement in the shadow of the cypress trees. But it was not Ash. The gray-cloaked figure I'd seen that first day watched us from the brush. I could not discern whose face lay behind the heavy, layered hood, and everything else blurred after it raised its arm. I saw the rock coming at Angel, heard it whizzing through the air. The horse reared, emitting a sound from out of this world. As I sailed into the air and then back down I realized I was no longer astride Angel but falling toward the edge of the cliff. And Tim's scream scared me more than my own predicament.

Chapter Eight

The rustle of wool awakened me, and I cracked open my right eye. A plump hand holding a steaming cup of jasmine tea cued me Mrs. Johnson hovered near. I was flat on my back and unsure where I was or how I had gotten there. Wanting to disappear under the blankets that covered me, I tried shrinking away, but the housekeeper was not to be dismissed. My head throbbed and muscles I didn't know I possessed ached up and down my entire body. I remembered riding along the sea: the cliff: the shadowy figure.

"Tim. Where is Tim?"

"Down at the stables helping John put away the horses. Nothin' to worry with that one. Drink this, now." She winked, "An *extra* dose of my special remedy."

With this news, I gave in to Mrs. Johnson's fuss. The liquor was welcomed.

"Poor dear," she clucked under her breath while folding the blankets around me. "Now I'll be bringing some of me chicken soup up directly. Lay back and rest." The expression on her face was as soothing as the hot liquid but I couldn't forget how much pain my body felt.

Nodding, I snuggled in deeper but kept my eyes open, trying to figure out where I was. Pastel angels holding musical instruments floated over my head on a magnificent ceiling. It reminded me of something I'd seen in the Metropolitan Museum, a "fresco," they called it. I turned my head into the soft down of the pillow. The bed linens were fresh but there was the faintest trace of another scent, coming deep from the center. Sandalwood. Steven Charles. I was in Steven Charles' room. I could not stay here.

I must have fallen asleep, for Mrs. Johnson had left when I next awoke to the sound of the piano downstairs rising up to my ears. Again, I looked up at the ceiling, the crystal chandelier casting shadows onto the cherubs. Blinking my eyes, I saw Duncan Stewart standing over me. He held a silver tray heavy with dishes. The smell of chicken and fresh bread caressed my nostrils. Soup. Mrs. Johnson promised soup, hadn't she?

The Master of Seacliff
Published by The Haworth Press, Inc., 2007. All rights reserved.
doi:10.1300/5778_08

"Andrew." His voice was deep, rolling and soft like the distant thunder. He looked worried and his creased brow accented this.

"Tim . . ." I couldn't remember.

"Tim is alright."

I managed a weak smile. This brightened his dark countenance. He set the tray across me and pulled up a chair.

"I was worried about you."

I began to raise myself, thinking I was imagining these words, but Duncan pressed me back with extreme gentleness, and then plumped the giant pillows to prop me up. How soft and plush this bed was, not only to my aching body, but also to my fingers. Running my hands along the sheets made of a heavy silk, they were quite a contrast from the simple cotton ones I slept on downstairs. The smell of sandalwood remained faint enough to remind me where I was and I wanted to get out of this room and return to my own. Duncan kept his hands on me, and I felt secure having his powerful presence in this room that on instinct I hated.

"Have some soup." He reached for a spoon.

"What time is it?"

Duncan turned, and behind him stood a celery-green clock, hand painted with flowers and vines, next to the dresser. "I forgot that damn clock stopped running." He pulled out his pocket watch. "A little after nine. Doctor Nickles from the village examined you. He says that no doubt you'll be terribly sore, but luckily there are no broken bones."

I had been unconscious for over five hours.

Managing what I hoped was a smile, I answered, "I can't imagine being any more sore than I am now."

He took my hand in his left and caressed my cheek with his right. I was touched by his show of affection for me, the first since presenting me with the art supplies.

"I do not understand it. Angel is a gentle animal, although Flowerbell would have been best." He wrinkled his mouth. "Stubborn boy. Had to prove yourself."

My mind remained muddled and I needed a clear head. I opened my mouth and Duncan spooned the warm broth inside.

"Don't worry. There will be no 'I told you so.' No reprimands, at least not until you eat all of this soup and this bread, as I am going to feed it to you. Besides, Mrs. Johnson would be most offended if you did not finish it." He ladled the soup, slow and deliberate, alternating it with pieces of bread cut into tiny triangles, I had no time to speak. I reached up and stopped his large hand.

"Duncan, I want to tell . . ."

He broke into a wide smile, and the brilliant whiteness of his teeth framed by his wide black moustache warmed me more than the soup did. Whispering, he leaned over. "What do you want to tell me?"

My cheeks flushed. His mind was in another place. It must be this room. I sat straight up in bed, biting my lip as swords of pain penetrated me.

"It wasn't an accident."

"Certainly it was. You think Angel reared on purpose?"

"Please listen to me. A rock was thrown at her from the woods."

He looked at me with surprise, as if I was Tim, telling a tall tale, and did not wait for my answer.

"Andrew, no one would—"

"He did."

"Nonsense."

"I saw someone in the woods. The same person I saw the first day I was in the schoolroom. He meant to deliberately frighten the horse. Or horses. Tim could have been injured as well."

Duncan's face hardened. He took my hand and placed it back on the blanket. "Andrew, think about this logically. Who? And why?"

I could cast suspicion on just about everyone in this house. Duncan knew I'd asked questions about his father's death. He had caught Leo and me embracing. Another, more frightening thought came to me. What if Steven Charles had never left? His diary gave no indication he was planning to go. No one knew I had it. Had Steven remained at Seacliff, misreading my wearing of his clothing as Duncan's interest in me, perhaps? I looked down at what I wore now, a handsome linen nightshirt that wasn't mine.

I glanced around the room and thought about its vibrant former occupant. Was Steven watching us now? I was in his mahogany and velvet bedroom, being fed soup by his male lover. Theirs had been a passionate relationship. How easily my presence here could be misinterpreted.

Duncan's deep voice brought me back.

"You are not telling me everything, are you?" He put his thumb under my chin and lifted my head so that I had to face him. His strength resonated through my slender body. I searched his black eyes for an answer; for trust, but only saw a reflection of myself.

"I know what I saw."

"Tim is asleep but I shall ask him in the morning what he saw . . . if anything."

"You don't believe me."

"I don't see a reason for anyone wanting to harm you."

I put my hands on his forearm. "I do. I believe your father and Albert were murdered. I—"

"Not again. You think the murderer is me. I suppose I threw the rock."

Fear shot through my back, realizing that Duncan could have thrown it. He had been on the grounds. I had seen him walk toward the hill.

He straightened his back, and in an instant I was aware of what a vulnerable position I had placed myself in. Duncan could crush my neck with his hands if he wanted to.

"Allow me to finish. I discovered two steamship tickets with your father and Albert's names in the desk in your mother's office. They were planning a trip together."

"They were forever taking business trips together. I am certain that if you searched the house, you'd find dozens of tickets belonging to them."

This information disappointed me. I was certain it was a clue.

He ran his fingers through my hair, which I had stopped trying to manage. It had grown longer and thicker through the summer, and I was sure looked wild. "Your tousled hair makes you look so innocent, Andrew. No one would want to harm such innocence. You present no threat." His hand lingered under my hair; and with the gentlest of movements he stroked the lobe of my right ear, and traced the line of my chin with his finger.

The blood rushed through my body responding to his touch. In another moment I might embarrass myself. Thank goodness my lower body was hidden under several quilts. For added insurance, I bent and raised my knees, and almost howled with pain while doing so.

He frowned. "Will you remain still? Doctor Nickles wants you in bed until tomorrow afternoon."

The nightshirt was riding up my thighs. Steven's nightshirt. Another thought came to me and I expressed it aloud. "Could Steven Charles have returned without your knowing?"

Duncan's eyes clouded at the mention of Steven's name. He turned toward the large paned window. "Ridiculous."

"I heard the piano."

"Your imagination. No one plays that piano except Elena." The rumble of thunder signaled the approach of an evening storm. Duncan walked to the wall of windows and peered through the drapes.

"I should have gone riding with you. I thought I had important business matters regarding George Upshaw. That was foolish, based on what has happened."

I had to press further.

"What was the date that Steven left Seacliff?"

He wasted no time in responding. "The third of September." Then, in a rather absent-minded tone, he added, "Why?"

"I found Steven's appointment diary."

Still looking out the window, he answered with an annoyed air, "I didn't know he kept one." His voice then grew sarcastic. "I'm sure it provides most extraordinary reading."

"The last entry was the day before he left. Duncan, he had plans involving a party."

"Yes."

"The diary mentions no plans to leave."

"And what does that have to do with your belief a rock was thrown at you today?"

"Perhaps someone knew I found the diary." *Perhaps Steven,* I said to myself.

Duncan walked back over to the side of my bed and rested his hand on my covered knee and the blood rushed through my body again. "Steven is gone, Andrew. I assure you he will not return. His departure was sudden. I don't wish to explain why, but he is gone."

His tone and face showed a conflicting blend of temper and remorse. I was terrified that in my haste to trust him, I revealed too much. Leo was right about Duncan being responsible for Steven's departure. Thus, he could have been the robed figure on the cliff this afternoon.

"I want you to rest now, Andrew. I will take care of things. The most important issue is that you get back on your feet soon. As for what you have just told me, including the rock throwing, that shall remain between us exclusively for the present time."

He pulled me toward him, and I became lost in his masculine smell. He whispered in my ear, his moustache brushing against it, and my body relinquished into his.

"I care for you very much, Andrew. By God nothing will happen to you in this house. I swear."

His beard caressed my cheek as he positioned me back on the yellow silk bed pillows. He pulled back, and his eyes were moist. Another aspect of Duncan Stewart had shown itself to me, one that I liked.

I did not hear or see him leave the room. I fell asleep in an instant.

I awoke just as the rooster crowed. The dreams I had were too fantastic: in one I was running through a fog along the edge of the cliff, in another Duncan Stewart appeared as a half-man, half-goat creature poised above my bed. The most disturbing dream concerned a faceless Steven Charles pointing a revolver at me, while Fellowes and Leo cackled.

No matter how kind Duncan Stewart may act, how comforting I felt in his embrace, I must not forget that this was a man who was a suspect in a murder, a questionable disappearance and now, an attack on me. He was a tangible link between these events. I needed to listen to my head and not take his concern to my heart. I should have kept the discovery of the diary and the tickets to myself until I knew more. The ache in my back and legs as well as the throbbing of my left temple reminded me of yesterday's incident.

The door squeaked open and I looked up.

"Ash! Tim! Come in. I'm alright. I was more worried about you."

With some caution, the children entered the room and without speaking, came over to me. Tim searched me for some visible sign of damage, and seeing none, he plopped upon the bed, shaking his head.

"You should have ridden Flowerbell."

"Tim, did you notice what made Angel rear?"

"I told Father you probably pulled the reins wrong. Or something stupid." The boy sighed, "Are we having lessons today?"

"You didn't see anyone in the woods?"

"No, no, and no! I was heading toward the house just as you told me. Are we having lessons?"

He was ahead of me on the trail. The rock couldn't have been thrown at Tim. I was the target.

"We can have lessons here if you'd like. The doctor and your father think it's best for me to remain in bed."

Tim hopped up as if it he had been burned, which sent a bolt of pain through my body. "Oh, then I won't disturb you anymore. You rest. We can study anytime. Bye."

The child dashed out, but in a second he jumped back into the room. "I'm happy you're not hurt."

"Thank you, Tim," I smiled. Ash lingered in the room. He wandered over to the wall of clothing, peered inside, and now came back across the room to the dresser. He pulled a footstool to it, climbed atop and searched Steven's jewelry box. Finding what he looked for, he dragged the footstool alongside the bed and offered me a silver pin shaped as a lion's head with a ring in its mouth.

"What is it, Ash?" If only I could get the child to speak.

He closed my hand around the pin, turned his ear toward the door, jumped off the bed, and ran out. I heard Leo greet him, and then sweep into the bedroom like a proud peacock in a blaze of color: emerald, gold, and earth. He surveyed the room and pursed his lips.

"Amazing. Just amazing. Nothing ever changes except the occupant. Quite an operation Duncan has. Out with old, in with the new."

"I'm not in the mood for your sarcasm, Leo. I was brought here because it was the easiest place to do so."

"I suppose Duncan forgot to tell you that it was I who discovered you at the edge of the cliff? Lucky for you I happened to be riding by."

Could Leo have thrown the rock, in order to rescue me?

"And the moment I brought you to this house, Duncan took over. He recommended you be brought up a flight of stairs when your own quarters are directly off the side entrance. If you think this coincidence, dear Andrew, your head must have been affected."

He gestured to his left. "No doubt you've deciphered that there is an adjoining corridor to Duncan's room behind that Hunan Dynasty screen." He perched on the side of my bed and clasped my hand. How different his cool touch was from Duncan's warmth. He removed the silver lion pin from my grasp and studied it.

"Christmas, a year ago. I really don't think Steven and you share the same taste in jewelry though." He tossed the pin back into the jewelry chest and produced a small wrapped package from under his coat.

"I dropped by to give you this; a gift to keep your mind occupied while you are confined. I hope you'll be up and around soon. I'm dreadfully bored."

"Leo, you don't believe Steven left by his own will, do you?"

"My sister saw him at the station. My assumption is he and Duncan came to an inevitable parting of the ways, and it was more lucrative for Steven to exit the stage when he did."

"Lucrative?"

"No doubt Steven had proof Duncan murdered his father and Albert, and demanded a price for silence. If Duncan were disinherited the Stewart monies would have fallen under Janina's control and on her death would revert to a charitable trust." He clicked his tongue. "Headed by me."

"By you?"

"You didn't know? The trust was formed eons ago by our grandparents."

Leo continued, "Not only would Duncan be in jail, but he'd be penniless and Seacliff would belong to my family. I'm sure Duncan's condition of payment was that Steven would remove himself as far from here as possible. Why do you think he's working so hard on this mysterious business deal with George Upshaw? His funds are surely depleted."

"But if Duncan went away, Tim would . . ." I started.

Leo shrugged. "A bastard child. Perhaps you could recommend an orphan asylum for him."

This was a different Leo than I knew. And I didn't like him.

"Why do you hate Duncan so much, Leo?"

Leo gave a loud laugh and turned to view himself in the mirror. "It's not hatred, Andrew. Pure jealousy." He lowered his voice. "You see, for all our pretense, my sister and I are not in the best of financial situations. I fear in another generation, the Van Hornes will be back on a boat to the Netherlands, rowing the entire way. Duncan would jump at the opportunity to purchase Glendower Hall and send me packing."

I wasn't sure if Leo was honest or if this was another of his inventive tales. "Why?"

He fingered the cuff of my nightshirt, rose from the bed and walked to the door. "I feel the need for a drink. Would you like one?"

I shook my head.

To my surprise, Leo did not leave, but knelt down by the green clock and ran his left hand along the side of the base. In a second, a door popped open at the bottom.

"Steven discovered this. Seems Janina didn't want to trundle downstairs to get her liquor." Leo removed a bottle of brandy and two glasses. "Join me? Makes the pain go away."

"Duncan went overseas looking for Steven. If he didn't want him back—"

Leo filled his glass, replaced the decanter and closed the secret door.

"As far as that grand display of combing the corners of the earth for his lost love, I've come to doubt those motives. My guess is that he actually tracked Steven down."

"And?"

"Andrew, Duncan Stewart has contacts all over the world, from heads of state and religious leaders to some of the most dangerous thieves and blackguards since Ali Baba. I suspect he paid Steven to leave, but as a trump, I wouldn't be surprised if Steven was dispensed with by an assassin shortly after. That would explain why his clothes remain here after so many months. And don't forget our visitor during the séance."

Except for the séance, his theory made sense.

"What does that matter, my heir apparent? I see you've acquired not only Steven's wardrobe, but his bedroom as well." He looked to the door behind the screen and his lips curled at the corners. "And room to spread out. How do you find—"

I was in no mood to be linked to Duncan, especially by Leo Van Horne's cruel innuendos.

"I'll be returning to my own room as soon as possible."

"I most certainly hope so. I'd like to see more of you—" He started lifting the sheet that covered me. When I put my hands down to keep it secure he took my hands in his and kissed them.

"— when you are up and around and free of Duncan."

"I have no romantic feelings for Duncan, or anyone, Leo."

Leo's face lost its color and for the first time, his expression scared me. "Don't reject me Andrew. You may regret needing a true friend in this house. Steven located some documents. They stated Gordon's intent to disinherit Duncan. I have them now. If you find anything else, you must come to me at once. I—"

"And what if I believe Duncan innocent?"

"He is fond of you, Andrew. I don't deny that. Perhaps if you get him to confess . . . in a moment of weakness . . . using your charms."

"Duncan is not guilty of killing Steven," I said. I wished I could be as confident about the deaths of Gordon and Albert.

"Then prove it to me." Leo gave a light laugh. "But now, I must fly; until later. Think about what I have told you, and perhaps you'll be ready for some liquor at tea time. Or, if you get thirsty, remember our hiding place."

He swirled out, all green velvet and gold silk, leaving on the nightstand a small box tied with a bright yellow ribbon.

I clasped my hands together and shook my head. The thought of these two men trying to win my favor put Steven Charles' fate right out of my mind. Plain Andrew Wyndham, heretofore resigned to a lonely life as a tutor and artist, now attracted two powerful men, in a grand mansion above the ocean. One a possible murderer; and the other determined to prove it. Seacliff brought me an escape from my old life, but I debated the price of that escape. If Duncan were found guilty, my plans of going to France would be just a dream. As for Leo's thoughts on Steven Charles, I suspected that was a blatant attempt to discredit Duncan, and cast himself in a better light. I couldn't believe Duncan would have the man he loved killed. The man he loved—would I ever experience that?

I opened Leo's package with curiosity. The box contained not artist's tools, but a leather-bound book. I thought of Steven and his appointment diary. Was it still in the jacket? With a fair amount of grimacing, I crawled out of the plush bed and hobbled over to the dressing stand where the riding clothes were hung. I put my hand inside the narrow coat pocket and felt the leather journal inside. I removed it and climbed back into the bed to examine it further. I had only really studied the first and last entries. Perhaps there was another clue hidden within the ecru pages: a clue that would clear Duncan's name. I set Steven's upon the coverlet and opened my new one, reading Leo's inscription:

> *Andrew, write only thoughts of me*

I had seen this before. I flipped open the cover of Steven's journal, and lay the two side by side. The handwriting of the inscriptions was identical. Leo had given Steven his journal, and now had given one to me.

Sitting up in bed, I flipped to Steven's first notation, surrounded by musical notes, and reread it:

> *Presented to me by the most vibrant and exciting individual I have known.*

He wasn't referring to Duncan, but Leo Van Horne. I started reading, but began skimming the pages, aside from the torn page referencing the key, there were no other extraordinary details that struck me, as Duncan had stated. Perhaps if Leo and Steven were as close as the journal entries intimated, Leo was correct in his suspicion of Duncan.

My thoughts of Duncan were telegraphed, for the bedroom door opened and he appeared, balancing another silver tray laden with food, and a small stack of books from the library. The smell of fresh fish and potatoes calmed the swimming thoughts in my head. This time, I must be cautious and not let his charm disarm me. I closed the journals and slipped them under the blanket.

"Good afternoon. I am pleased to see you awake."

"Thank you. I'm feeling much better. Quite eager to return to tutoring tomorrow . . . and to my room downstairs."

His smile became more forced. "Why go back to that little space when you have all this at your disposal?" He dropped the books on the nightstand beside me. "Here are several books to keep your mind occupied. I deliberately eliminated the works of the Bronte sisters and Oscar Wilde from this selection. Your imagination is active enough. I suggest *Sense and Sensibility*."

I attempted to get up, to show him I was fine. But I was too hasty and made what must have been a horrible face. In a second he was beside the bed, tucking me back in. I liked the attention, but remained stoic.

He winked, "If you are not going to follow my instructions, then you must stay in bed indefinitely. And I'm just across the vestibule, so I can keep my eye on you."

I turned to look at the door behind the screen, and his eyes followed me. I thought of Leo's comment and wished the door were locked from this side.

"And yes, that door connects the two rooms. Leo Van Horne has been up here, hasn't he?"

"Yes."

"I suppose you agree with him that I murdered Steven?"

"I did not discuss anything with Leo." I hoped he hadn't been listening outside the room. "He spoke of some ancient agreement about Seacliff and his own property."

He brushed my hair with the back of hand "Yes, if there are no Stewart heirs, Seacliff becomes part of the Van Horne estate. Obviously, Tim and I aren't going anywhere."

It clarified why Leo was determined to get Duncan out of the picture. I opened my mouth and Duncan shook his head.

"Andrew, don't try to solve other people's problems."

"But I want to help you."

"You've done wonders already. Let's have lunch, shall we?"

He had a plate for himself.

We sat and ate in silence. No discussion of the hooded figure I had seen, the rock-throwing incident, or my discovery of Steven's diary. I watched how Duncan's large hand dwarfed the teacup, yet how graceful he moved. I could envision how he could eliminate those who crossed him, and not think twice about it.

Only when I had cleared my plate of all its food did Duncan allow me to get out of bed, although I was slow to move. It felt good to stand up and

stretch and the plush green rug felt wonderful under my bare toes as I pad-
ded over to look out the window. I liked the feeling of the yellow drapes
against my cheek. Looking past the gardens, toward Whispering Hill, I
knew the answer to the mystery of Seacliff lay there.

"Fellowes will bring your belongings up here, Andrew."

"This is Steven's room."

"It shall be your room. Make what changes you wish. Draperies, carpet,
burn the furniture if you'd like. I'll have Fellowes dispose of his, uh, Steven's
property. It is a long-overdue project anyway."

Saying Steven's name aloud, I noticed, made Duncan uneasy.

"I prefer my own room, downstairs, with the other servants."

"Have you been treated as a 'servant' since you came to this house? Andrew Wyndham, you are much more than an employee, more than the tutor to my son. The changes you have brought to Seacliff have been
incredible. Timothy is as well behaved as I've ever seen him. Ash is coming
out of his shell. I would like this to be your room, I hope for as long as you
like."

"I shall be perfectly happy to remain downstairs. I am not sure I will remain here past our three-month agreement."

"It's Leo Van Horne, is it not? That snake."

"Why didn't you tell me it was he who found me on the cliff?"

Mr. Johnson interrupted us. "Mister Duncan, the carriage is waiting to
take you to the station."

I sunk down into the overstuffed chair by the bed. "You're leaving?"

"One moment, Johnson." He waited for the servant leave. "I'm going to
Manhattan to meet with Upshaw, now that he has my offering of Mother's
dolls. I am confident I can close the deal without having to resort to extreme
measures."

"Like marrying Miss Upshaw?"

"Don't act like a spoiled child. Marriage to her wouldn't change my feelings for you. An arrangement—"

"Such as the one Oscar Wilde had? Look at the trouble it caused him. I
do not think I would be interested in any 'arrangement' of that kind. It is ridiculous."

He frowned. "You make this very difficult, Andrew. Unfortunately I
don't have the time to discuss the nuances of my proposal with you."

"You assume I would move into this bedroom without concern."

He lifted his eyebrows. "Go on."

"Once settled, you most likely believe I would open that connecting door and allow you to satisfy whatever needs you may have."

"I see you've figured my intentions are entirely selfish. Trust me, you would be well compensated. But the difference—"

"That situation may have worked for Steven Charles, but not for me. I believe in true love, Duncan Stewart, and my heart is not for sale."

"It worked well for my parents, and Albert."

Another stupefying revelation had made itself known. However, I was more furious that Duncan Stewart again took a business approach to every aspect of life.

"Is that why the room where your father and Albert died is locked?"

"What?"

"The room is sealed and apparently has been for some time, per your direction. Is it a museum to their 'arrangement'?"

Duncan called for Fellowes at the top of his lungs to no response. This infuriated him more. "Damn it all, I don't have time for your priggish suspicions, but I shall resolve this matter at once. You stay here."

"I'm coming with you, I . . . " the words trailed off.

"You need to believe that I didn't murder my father, is that it? What is in that room, eh? The dark secrets to the unhappiness in this house, perhaps? Perhaps Steven is down there as well?" The eyes were darker than night. I had pressed too hard.

Mrs. Johnson appeared in the doorway as I was struggling to get out of the enormous chair. "I heard ye yellin' all the way in the kitchen. Fellowes left the house, Mister Duncan. He didn't say where he was going."

"Do you have a key to Albert's bedroom?"

"Why no sir, only Fellowes has a key . . . and yourself, I thought."

Duncan stormed out, leaving us. She turned back to me. "Best to batten down the hatches, Andrew. I've seen that look before. That temper's quick as a sudden storm, and just as terrible."

The key in the pocket of Steven's coat must access the locked room. The pieces of the puzzle were falling into place with stunning alacrity. I hobbled over and pulled it out of the pocket.

Mrs. Johnson's eyes grew wide. "Wherever did you get that?"

"It's the key to the room downstairs isn't it? I knew . . ."

"'Tis Gwendolyn's."

I grabbed a robe, trying not to notice Steven Charles' monogram as I slipped it around me. With pain shooting through me, I managed to get to the bottom of the stairs. Mr. Johnson looked at his pocket watch and shook his head.

"We've got to get him to the station, Mister Andrew. What in heaven's name has him all worked up?"

I came down the hall behind Duncan who slammed into the door with his full weight and growled with the animal rage that was in him. Another mistake, and I had caused it.

"Duncan, I didn't mean . . ."

"By God I won't have them haunting me further! Damn them and damn these oak doors."

I was seeing the full extent the legacy of his father's death. It tormented Duncan. On top of this was the suspicion of guilt brought on by myself. He had never spoken of it before now, and when it had been referenced, it was usually accompanied by a quick shut down of all feelings. Those emotions had been released with the fury of a volcanic eruption.

The lock gave way, and with a splinter of wood and snap of metal, the door opened. I peered around Duncan's back.

It was an ordinary room, as simple as its twin across the hall. In my mind perhaps I did expect to see everything frozen in time, covered in cobwebs like a chapter in Mr. Dickens' novels. There was a hint of mustiness, but white muslin sheets covered all the furniture. Aside from that and the heavy drapes blocking out the sun and the sea on two sides, there was no real indication of death, or that the room had been closed for eight years. Duncan's eyes were transfixed on the floor.

"Their bodies were right there. I can still see the revolver in Albert's hand."

"You found them?"

He shook his head. "I was on my way back, and I blacked out along the path. I couldn't stop it."

I tried to comfort him.

"It's all in the past, Duncan, let's open the curtains and allow some fresh air into this room." I struggled with the drapes; after a moment they allowed sunlight to flood the bedroom. I opened the window and welcomed the fresh sea air as it filled the room. When I turned back, Duncan had seated himself on the bed, and had buried his face in his hands. I looked down; the mark of tragedy could not be erased in the midafternoon light. The naked floor had two enormous stains that darkened the wood in the center.

I put my hand on Duncan's shoulder and he looked up at me.

"The truth is I am responsible for their deaths. I'm completely guilty as charged. Everything I have ever truly loved has been taken from me. But I did not shoot them, Andrew. You must believe me."

I tried to understand if this was a confession.

"Mister Duncan, we have to leave for the station," Mr. Johnson called from the hallway.

Duncan stood up and the cold composure I had so often seen was back. He acted ready to face the world, but I had a glimpse at the deep wounds within his heart. Sweeping into the hall, he did not say goodbye. I heard his heavy footsteps as he walked out the side door. This bedroom overlooked the walkway and I hurried to the window to see him disappear around the corner to the coach. This room was at the center of Duncan Stewart's pain. Had I done more damage by forcing Duncan to confront his past? Perhaps Fellowes indeed protected the son of the couple he worshipped by keeping the room sealed.

Now the valet loitered before me, studying the dust on the wainscoting around the door. "I see you would not rest until you forced him to reopen this room." He looked down. "Congratulations. Mister Charles never succeeded."

"You believe Steven Charles' disappearance and the death of Gordon Stewart are related?"

The valet's eyes narrowed. "If you know what is best for you, Andrew Wyndham, you'll leave this house at once. I will take you to the station tomorrow or to the Van Horne's tonight if you'd prefer. It's for your own safety, and you must trust me. I warned Mister Charles, to no avail."

He left. Threats would not deter me. I had to find some way to convince Duncan he was not responsible. Before Leo proved otherwise. For my own sake as well as this man and his son.

Chapter Nine

Two days later, secure in my own room, I awoke from a nap with a clear frame of mind, if not still sore as the doctor warned. I had returned and found my room had been searched, and it was clear from the condition of my nightstand and bed that a journal was indeed what was hunted for, as nothing else was disturbed. After restoring the room to order, I washed my face, when Mrs. Johnson bustled in.

"'Tis good to see you up. Best thing is to keep movin'!" She dropped her voice to a whisper. "Dreadful news from New York, though." Checking the hall as she closed the door behind her, her voice became even lower. "Mister George Upshaw dropped dead last night!" She grabbed her throat and stuck out her tongue. Before I could reply, she put a floury finger to my mouth.

I moved her hand away. "Surely Duncan isn't suspected?" Although I hadn't decided his guilt regarding his father, I could not imagine him doing this.

The housekeeper threw her hands up, spreading a waft of cinnamon in her wake. "Lord knows trouble just follows Mister Duncan. He's been accused a' plenty, and the talk! How any of us can show our face in town, I don't know."

"Has he returned?"

"Not yet. Bein' questioned by the New York police, or so I heard. Miss Elena and Mister Leo have arrived; they're in the drawing room. Don't let on that you've heard this awfulness from me."

I put my arm around the older woman and pulled the key out of my pocket. "First, tell me about this. It was the key to Albert's room, correct?"

The woman turned red and put her hands on her hips. "And why would me daughter have a key to Mister Albert's room? A good girl my Gwennie was. No scandal from the Johnson family you'll find."

"I meant no disrespect," I answered, suppressing a laugh and trying not to think of the circumstances of Ash's parentage.

The Master of Seacliff
Published by The Haworth Press, Inc., 2007. All rights reserved.
doi:10.1300/5778_09

"Besides, Mister Albert wasn't so much interested in the ladies, except for Mrs. Stewart. And only because she was Mister Gordon's wife."

I kept my interest subdued by clutching the iron footboard a little tighter.

"Then what lock does it fit?"

The woman fingered the key in her careworn palm. "Gwennie had a carved chest her sailor gave her. He'd picked it up in some way-off land, and she just doted on it." She handed me the key. "But I ain't seen that chest in years. I imagine her sailor kept it with him. I always thought it contained some money they saved."

"Something valuable was in the chest."

"She always said James had a plan that would keep them set so none of us would have to work. But it still couldn't take the pain in her heart away. James drowned just before Asher was born."

"Do you know what their plan was?"

The housekeeper shrugged. "That chest is at the bottom of the sea. With them." The woman looked old and sad, and I felt I raised unhappy questions instead of getting answers.

"Maybe not, Mrs. Johnson. I found the key in Steven Charles' jacket. I think he knew this belonged to Gwendolyn, and was searching for the chest. Perhaps it wasn't lost at sea. It may contain the answer to her death."

"Most likely then Mister Steven found the chest, and took it with him when he left. That one always was rootin' around for extra money."

I thought of the king's ransom of clothing and jewelry that remained in the room upstairs.

"In any case, he wouldn't have left the key. And there was a note: *Must ask J about the key*. Could that be you or Mr. Johnson?"

The housekeeper wrinkled the right side of her mouth.

"I don't recall Mister Steven ever asking about Gwendolyn, but I'll ask me husband." She put her hand to her mouth. "Do you think it might tell us why she . . ."

Reaching out and putting my arm around her, I said, "I don't know for certain, but I'd like to find out."

I waited for the echo of her footsteps to fade away, and poking my head out the door, I heard the grandfather clock chime. Fellowes would be upstairs for at least the next half hour. Mrs. Johnson was secure in her kitchen supervising supper. I had this wing of the house to myself.

Creeping against the wall, I made my way to Fellowes' room. With extreme caution I opened the door. I had an excuse already prepared if the valet should return: I had left a volume of Shakespearian comedies in the library; it was now missing and I hoped one of the maids had returned it to his room by mistake. Having seen Fellowes in the garden reading the companion book of sonnets, this was a plausible ruse.

His room had the same simple furnishings as mine, but heavy drapes with a dramatic delphinium pattern loomed over his bed, making the room appear smaller than it was. It was immaculate and I would have to be most careful not to disturb anything while I conducted my search, unlike the unknown visitor to my own quarters.

I had to find the steamship tickets. Proof to Duncan that his father and Albert were planning to leave Seacliff when they were murdered. My eyes traveled to a gramophone in the corner, then a tall bureau against the wall. Upon closing the door behind me, I noticed the door had no lock, only a gaping hole where one had been.

Atop the bureau were two photographs of Janina and Gordon Stewart. Janina stood before her portrait, and the photograph captured the same detached coolness that was in her painting. Beneath her photograph lay a pair of sapphire earrings. The other photograph was of Gordon Stewart. However, he was not in Seacliff, but appeared to be at the summit of a mountain. He wore a broad brimmed hat, and his muscular chest was covered not by a shirt, but a mass of black hair. His booted foot rested on the remains of an elk, and he carried a rifle in his hand. Next to this photograph were several rabbit's feet assembled on a long cord.

Without a sound I opened the top drawer, finding nothing. I tried the next and the next, and again was disappointed. Then I froze upon hearing the rhythmic approach of the valet's shoes coming down the hall. I scrambled for a place to hide. The bed was too narrow a space to slide under. The tap of his shoes grew louder: I was running out of time. I darted into the oak wardrobe beside the bureau, catching my foot on the corner and making a distinct noise as I closed the door behind me. I prayed I would not be discovered.

I peeked through the louvered shutter of the wardrobe. The valet had stopped in his tracks upon entering and searched the room with his eyes. I was trembling in my shoes and my heart pounded in my ears. I should never have hidden. There would be no logical explanation if Fellowes opened the wardrobe. Through the louver, I saw his eyes narrow and I closed mine.

"What are you doing in my room?"

Waiting for the door to be flung open, I held my breath. But it did not.

"Asher! Give that back at once!"

Opening my eyes, I saw Ash holding a silver cane with a goat's head handle. He waved it back and forth.

Fellowes had his back to me and loomed over the small child. I swore that Ash's eyes met mine. Grinning, the elfin child flew out of the room, clutching the cane, which was almost as long as he was. Fellowes took off in pursuit. A few pounding heartbeats later, I waited until complete silence fell. I jumped from my hiding place and left.

Upon entering the drawing room, Elena floated over and greeted me with a delicate hug that smelled of roses. "I came to visit, but you were asleep both times. Thank goodness you weren't seriously injured. It's why I never ride; I detest horses."

I wondered at that moment what Duncan was saying to the police. I smelled Leo's signature lemon fragrance as he came up behind me.

"Hello," I said, turning and stepping back.

Elena looked at her brother, than back at me. "You haven't heard the news, have you?" Her face looked grave, an appearance I had never seen reflected in her Dresden-like beauty.

I knew what was coming, but more than Mrs. Johnson's request commanded me to play ignorant. Looking at Elena for what seemed forever, it was Leo who spoke. "George Upshaw is dead."

"Duncan was on his way to meet with him," I said.

"He did meet with him. And Upshaw dropped dead shortly thereafter. Foul play is most certainly suspected."

"Leo! You know no such thing!" Elena said as she crossed over and closed the drawing room doors. "You might as well hear it from me, Andrew. I'm sure once Fellowes' cousin sends word, if he hasn't already, the staff will be up in arms about it."

The servants already knew, but I continued with my charade. Leo was having trouble containing his glee. Naturally, he hoped for a turn of events such as this.

"Are you feeling light-headed, Andrew? Please, sit down." Elena guided me over to the brocade sofa and I sank into the plush cushions. She held my hand, her reassuring touch cool. "Nothing has been proven that it wasn't natural causes."

Leo struck a match from his boot and lit a cigar. "I'm certain Duncan will slip through suspicion as always. But perhaps, this will invite an investigation into the disappearance of Steven Charles." He gloated over this news, I could tell.

Elena narrowed her eyes. "The only good thing Steven ever did was leave this house. And you know it, my brother."

Leo started to respond, but instead looked at me and shrugged his broad shoulders. Tossing his head, he sat down at the piano and picked out a melody on the keys.

"There is no reason to believe Duncan did anything deliberate," I said.

Elena patted my hand, but looked concerned. "Certainly not."

Leo stopped playing. "Only the fact that Duncan had been pressuring the old man to sell his business interests to him. George refused, and now he's dead. Victoria will be the negotiator now, and she's soft clay in Duncan's hand."

Elena wrinkled her face. "But with this scandal there will be no wedding bells in the air. Victoria wouldn't dare accept any proposal, business or otherwise, from Duncan."

"He doesn't have to marry her darling; he just needs her to sign over her interests to him. You should like that news as well, Andrew."

I scowled at Leo.

"Speaking of marriage, notice what latest trinket I acquired from an erstwhile caller." She raised her left hand. An enormous diamond seemed to overpower her delicate finger.

"Elena! Are you engaged? Who? Arthur Upshaw?" I said.

She gave her rippling laugh and tossed her head.

"Richard Lawrence, at least he thinks so." She examined the ring. "It was such a stunning piece I couldn't possibly say no. Especially since he burst through our door while I dined with Arthur."

"My sister inspires high dramatics from men. You lucky girl."

"Poor Arthur, he'd tried so hard to woo me. Victoria will be practically green with envy. I think she fancied Duncan and Richard would duel over her. That dull goose." She arched her eyebrow as her brother often did. "I can't wait to see Duncan's face when I show this to him."

Leo frowned. "The police in Manhattan think there is enough suspicion regarding George's death to warrant an investigation, so you may be showing Duncan your ring through iron bars, sister dear."

"Duncan will persevere, Andrew," Elena said, ignoring her brother. "We know he is innocent."

"Andrew, I expected more of a reaction to this twist of events. I see there's no surprising you today." He studied me and lowered his voice. "Still angry about our earlier discussion?"

"Seacliff has given me enough surprises these past months to suffice several lifetimes."

"And through these surprises, you no doubt have broadened your mind. And to celebrate this new found self, I've brought you another present." He pointed to the small marble table at the end of the couch. A wrapped package rested on the edge.

"The journal was more than thoughtful, Leo." As I said this I could see in my mind Leo's inscription, the same as in Steven Charles's appointment diary.

"The journal was an impulse due to your accident. This gift is in more direct relation to your art studies."

I opened the package. It was a book of charcoal drawings by an artist of whose name and works I was not familiar. After perusing the first several pages, though, I saw through Leo's charade: the drawings were all of naked males. Had this been given in my first weeks at Seacliff, I would have blushed as bright as a tomato, or been too embarrassed to speak. Now I found that control and my response came as easy as if I had been presented with a book of Mother Goose illustrations.

"Leo, you are truly incorrigible. If I didn't know better, I'd swear you were trying to corrupt me."

"As long as Duncan doesn't trump me, I shall continue to do so."

I would give none of my heart's secrets to Leo. "Duncan is my employer. That is all there is to that. Don't forget it."

"I shan't. My hope is that you shan't as well. Please make a note of the drawing on page twenty-three. It's my personal favorite."

Turning to the page, my cheeks turned red at the overt display of sexuality. Elena peered over my shoulder and made a face as I slammed the book closed. Leo chortled with a wicked laugh as his sister moved to the piano and began playing a Chopin melody.

"Brother, you are despicable, really. Now Andrew, I bring good news especially for you. My artist friend would be delighted to hire you."

I knew Elena would achieve whatever she set out to do. "That's too wonderful. I can't thank you enough, but what . . ."

She smiled and lifted her chin. "Duncan embraces the idea—after I explained the benefit to your career."

Leo straightened his back and widened his eyes. "This is a turn of events. Perhaps the master is not as enchanted with you as I previously thought."

His remark bruised me. As I had refused Duncan's offer to move into the upstairs bedroom, I had brought this upon myself.

Elena looked at her brother and mirrored his earlier frown. "For goodness' sake, Leo. Not everyone is switching beds as in a Shakespearian comedy of errors. You really require a dosage of reality."

"Sister, you are as blind as you are beautiful. Particularly where Duncan Stewart has been concerned."

"I am under no illusions about anyone, particularly you, dear Leo."

Knowing this exchange could continue for hours, I interrupted the siblings' banter.

"Tell me more about your friend."

"You will meet him. You must travel to New York as soon as you are ready." She clasped my hands. Besides, you've been here three months. I'm certain you're probably homesick for your family."

The idea of going to New York and seeing my aunt and uncle was farthest from my mind. I hadn't received a letter or card from them since I arrived. But I could seek Michael Betancourt's advice. There were dozens of questions now.

She continued, "My friend is the well-known portraitist, Edgar LaVina. He has a delightful but thoroughly disorganized studio in Greenwich Village."

Leo fingered the gold chain around his wrist. "Why don't you have Edgar out here to see us? He hasn't visited in months, since Steven was here."

Elena checked herself in the mirror and sat beside me. "He says he is chained to his studio, and could use Andrew at once to help with his affairs." There was warmth in her smile. "You've done such a splendid job here, but I must confess Edgar is quite a handful. It would be a challenge."

"There is so much more to do here . . ." I started.

"Elena, no doubt you've told Edgar how Andrew's charms extend outside of the schoolroom." Leo looked at me. "In that case, perhaps I should escort you into Manhattan. A young lamb, lost in the jungle of the city."

The thought of Leo accompanying me made me uneasy. I had no interest in fending off his advances on a continual basis. And I kept going back to Elena's earlier remark, that Duncan gave his consent. His quick acquiescence made me sad, but Elena knew him best. And I had refused to enter into any type of "arrangement" with the master of Seacliff.

A shuffling sounded across the marble of the Great Hall, and then an erratic rap came at the door. We turned, all surprised to see John Middleground standing before us.

The stableman removed his cap. "I just . . . uh . . . came to ask after Mister Andrew. Awfully sorry about the horse and just uh . . . wanted to see if he was better."

I sensed John hoped I was alone. It was too strange that he would hobble to the house I knew he detested, just to inquire about my condition.

"Mister Andrew is quite fine, back to your horses, John," Fellowes commanded as he walked into the drawing room with a tray of tea, cookies, and fruit.

I offered him my hand. "Thank you. I'm almost back to normal and will expect to be riding again soon." I laughed and added, "I don't want Angel to think I've given up."

The stableman nodded, wiped his hand on his leg and took mine. His grip was firm and strong. His eyes searched mine as when we first met, and I sensed he wanted to talk, but wouldn't. Or couldn't. I took the lead.

"I'd like to come down and see Angel. Perhaps later?"

"That, uh, would be nice. See you then. A good afternoon to you all." He shuffled away and I turned back to the room finding Elena and Leo dumbfounded.

"Your powers of allure are incredible, Andrew. I think that's the first time John's been in the house since Gwendolyn's death," Elena said, with a twinkle in her eye.

"His last appearance here was quite a scene. Threatened to kill everyone, as I recall. Waving a bottle of cheap whiskey, naturally." Leo flailed his hands in the air, demonstrating.

Elena interrupted, "John's brother and Gwendolyn . . . well, John was overly protective of her after James's death."

"You mean John's brother was her sailor? Ash's father?"

"John felt the house somehow caused the sinking of his brother's ship, and Gwendolyn's subsequent suicide. Of course her death was a result of James being lost at sea, before marrying her. She loved him more than life itself, and I say that's a strong argument for ending one's life. Losing the one you love, forever." Elena's voice trailed off, and she gave a sigh. "She was a lovely girl."

Leo walked over and picked up an apple from its silver stand. "And that is why one should never fall into serious love." As he bit into it he winked at me.

I did not want to explore thoughts of love. "The prospect of meeting Mr. LaVina sounds exciting, but I hoped to help Duncan before I considered other employment."

"Help him, how?" Elena asked.

"To find out what exactly happened the night Gordon Stewart was killed. Duncan has taken the entire blame upon himself, and I don't think the circumstances were as they have been explained."

Leo crossed his arms. "You are correct, Andrew . . . and starting to sound precisely like Steven." He rolled his eyes and reached for another cookie. "What is it about Duncan that makes everyone want to be a living Sherlock Holmes?" He plopped down on the sofa and focused his green eyes onto the valet. "Fellowes old boy, you were there. Tell Andrew this is all his imagination, that Duncan had nothing to do with the two men's deaths. If you can."

"Mister Leo, with all respect, I do not believe that matters of Seacliff's past are any of Mister Andrew's business, or yours, for that matter."

"They are if their legacy affects the present and the future of the house," I replied in a calm voice.

The valet remained silent, and Leo crinkled his mouth.

"You are betraying no confidences, Fellowes. If you recall something that will bring an end to this speculation, now is the time to speak. If Duncan has done wrong, he should be judged and duly punished. Covering up for him isn't helping Gordon . . . or Janina. If he is innocent, then I rest my case."

Leo was eager to hear Duncan had murdered his father. I knew from the cold, uncaring look on his face; this was what he hoped to get from Fellowes.

"Leo! You are being absolutely ridiculous!" Elena cried.

Fellowes turned to Leo. "I've kept silent about it for years, but I shall tell you this: Albert Brown was obsessed with Mister Gordon, an unnatural obsession. He had it in his head that they eventually would start a new life, much in the way a man and a woman enjoy a Christian marriage."

"Albert murdered Gordon because he was in love with him," I said aloud. This contradicted what I believed.

"There was talk," Elena said, shrugging her shoulders.

"Gordon could seduce anything, men, women, or beasts. And he was quite proud of his talent to do so," Leo said, rolling his eyes. "Much like his son."

Fellowes looked at me, "I would not call Albert's interest in Gordon Stewart 'love'. And as for Mister Gordon, he tolerated those advances for as long as he could. At last he and Miss Janina had enough, and convinced Albert to seek treatment."

"Are you so sure of Gordon's refusals?" Leo laughed, and dropping his voice an octave, "I remember the old man being quite randy, and more than once I had to pry his hands off my backside. Maybe that's what made Janina tip the bottle so much."

"How dare you speak against her!" Fellowes roared. I became uneasy. I knew the valet's fanatical devotion to Duncan's mother would draw him out of his shell, but I thought Leo had gone too far. Elena's face reflected my reaction as well.

Leo continued, "It's a known fact Janina loved her Scotch—whether men or liquor."

"If she drank, Mister Leo, it was only because of the misery brought into this house by Albert Brown . . . and others like him. The behavior in this house since her death would most certainly have killed her if her own fragile heart hadn't."

Leo straightened his cravat. "Others? Watch out, old boy." He checked his reflection in a gilded mirror. "Didn't Steven catch you reading that naughty book, *Teleny:* A book so deliciously decadent Oscar Wilde wouldn't claim its authorship?"

"I know not of what you mean, sir."

Elena threw her hands up in the air, "Stop this, both of you. Janina found the bodies, remember? The gun was in Albert's hand. Stop trying to link Duncan to it!"

"I beg your pardon, Miss Elena, but when we arrived Mister Duncan was already in the bedroom."

Elena looked as if she had been struck. "Duncan . . . ?"

"Miss Janina returned to the house before Mister Gordon. She was tired and I was helping her upstairs. We heard shouts; then those awful shots. I flew down the stairs and into the hall. Mister Duncan was at the door to the bedroom."

"And me daughter, too."

Mrs. Johnson stood in the doorway. "I came to see how many there would be for supper. There's a powerful storm brewing outside, you might want to stay the night."

"I didn't know Gwennie was there. Why did you keep this from us all these years?" Leo said.

Mrs. Johnson looked at me and then away. She believed Duncan had killed them also. What had Gwendolyn seen?

Fellowes focused his attention upon the housekeeper. "The gun was in Mister Albert's hand. Mister Gordon was gone, and that night also began

Miss Janina's decline, and her own early death. Nothing can change that now, especially Gwendolyn's exaggerations."

Mrs. Johnson looked with disdain at Fellowes, and pursed her lips. "Gwennie was out on the terrace with James. She heard a terrible yell and told me they saw the whole thing through the window."

"Your daughter would do anything to draw attention to herself. I distinctly remember the draperies closed all afternoon," Fellowes said.

"You high-minded so-and-so. No exaggeration about such a horror as this. Gwennie told me she and James saw the murder with their own eyes."

Fellowes looked down his long nose at the housekeeper. "She was also under the impression that James Middleground would marry her. How many more brats would she have had before a ceremony took place?"

The housekeeper put her hands on her hips.

"Now you listen here, you snooty . . ."

"Enough, Fellowes! Mrs. Johnson! Please!" Elena stood up. Leo fell onto the couch roaring with laughter.

"Excuse me." The valet strode out of the room. At that moment a terrific clap of thunder followed by a bolt of lightening made the hair on my neck stand up. The whole house seemed to shudder.

Elena rose up from the couch and put her hand on Mrs. Johnson's arm. "Leo and I will stay for supper, and if this storm continues to be as threatening as it sounds, possibly for the night. I refuse to travel back through the woods in such weather. Will you arrange rooms for us?"

The housekeeper's face was still red. "Yes, Miss Elena, I will have Ellen attend to it, if I can find her. Supper is early tonight, since Mister Duncan's away. It'll be ready shortly."

Leo watched the housekeeper leave the room. "I'll bunk in with Andrew!"

"I think not," I snapped.

"Oh, I see. Saving yourself for bigger things. Bigger is not necessarily better, Andrew. And while the cat's away . . ."

Elena turned, the rustling of her gown like the summer leaves whirling outside. "Leo, you really should control yourself. It is not your place—"

"And neither is it yours. Must I remind you, Miss Van Horne? Reprimanding these servants as if they were your own, indeed," Leo snarled.

I did not listen to their arguing. Gwendolyn witnessed the murder of Gordon Stewart. Her missing chest might prove Duncan's guilt.

"If the murders occurred as Fellowes says, then why does Duncan feel such responsibility about it?" I asked. "And why would Gwendolyn contradict that?"

Both Van Hornes looked at each other. Leo then spoke.

"It's only Fellowes' word that Albert killed Gordon. His loyalty to Janina, even now, would prevent him from exposing her son as a murderer. She was generous, left him a nice amount of money when she died, probably with the proviso that he keep his mouth shut. Gwennie's not here—"

Elena answered, "Duncan takes the responsibility of the world on his shoulders. Believe me, I've tried to help him for years, and he brushes me aside."

I fumbled for an excuse to leave. "Leo, I'll take your gift back to my room, and will meet you both in the library." As I walked out I heard Elena speak low.

"Leo, you suspect the worst about Duncan. You always have."

"And you believe him perfect, darling."

I gave the book of drawings to a maid, asking her to place it in my room, and hoping she wouldn't be tempted to look through it. Next, I slipped through the side door, heading directly down the hill to the stables. Beside the bridle path John Middleground popped out from behind a wall of rhododendron bushes.

"Mister Andrew. I'd hoped you come to see me." He weaved back and forth, an obvious clue he had been drinking even more since leaving the house.

"What is it?"

"I heard Mrs. Johnson ask her husband about that key you found."

"What do you know about it?"

The stableman nodded. "Right before that fancy Steven Charles left, he came down to the stable and asked me the same thing."

Ask J about key. John. Another piece in place.

"What did he ask you?"

"If me brother killed old Mister Stewart, and where the chest was that this key fits."

"Your brother?"

"I told that no-good piano player that I ought to kill him right then and there for making such a statement. And I wish I had. James, uh, had his faults, but he didn't kill those men." He reached out and grabbed both my arms. "I have a good idea who did, though."

The wind began to swirl, and a deep freeze ran through my body. I backed up, but the rhododendrons blocked my exit. I was penned in. John Middleground leaned toward me; his whiskey smell making my eyes wince.

"Who killed them?"

"Mister Duncan Stewart."

I didn't know how to answer. I could only look at John's stained and broken smile of triumph.

"What no one knows except for me is that Mister Gordon Stewart planned on leaving town and was gonna let his son take the fall for some bad business deals."

The steamship tickets. "How do you know they were leaving?"

"Albert asked me to have the carriage ready that night at midnight. He and Mister Duncan had been pals, but Albert aligned himself with the father, to get his own cut of the Stewart fortune. So Duncan murders both of 'em, and gets it all."

John reached into his left pocket and produced a flask, taking a swig. He offered it to me, and I considered it before shaking my head.

"Mrs. Stewart told me the rest. She was a lonely woman, and, uh, needed a real man to talk to. He grabbed below his waist and adjusted himself through his baggy, soiled trousers. Turns out we had a lot in common," he said, wiping his mouth with his sleeve.

My stomach turned. "And Steven Charles knew this."

"He'd pretty much figured things out. He also reckoned that Gwennie didn't jump off that cliff by herself. A' course she didn't! She was a God-fearin' soul. But I never told him what they saw."

I wanted to sink to the ground. "James saw Duncan murder his father."

"Before James uh, left, he told me the chest contained a signed confession by the murderer, and a tidy sum of money. Who else would have that kind of money except for Duncan Stewart? He planned on collecting more, enough so he, Gwen, Asher, and me could set sail and make a good life for ourselves. I've heard how good you've been to Ashie. Teachin' him like he was equal to Master Tim. I figure if you find the chest, we can split the insides. You take the confession, do what you want with it, and I'll take the money and leave this Babylon."

"And if I don't?"

The stableman put his hand in his pocket. What if he produced a weapon to accent his point? Instead he removed a can of snuff, opened it, and put some behind his lip.

"You won't need the money if that confession proves Mister Duncan's . . . innocent, will you?" He leered at me and I never so much wanted to get away from a place as I did right now. But I also wouldn't believe Duncan was a murderer. And to prove his innocence, I would do anything.

"What if Steven Charles found the chest?"

"I told him me brother took the chest with him. I think if he'd found it, he'd a told me." He shifted his weight from his bad leg to his good one. "That one liked to barter."

"Do you have any idea where to look?"

"I thought you'd see things my way," he said, backing up. "Gwennie grew up in that house, could've hidden it anywhere. Wouldn't surprise me if she hid it right under Duncan Stewart's nose." He spit out a stream of pale brown tobacco and I thought I would faint.

It started to sprinkle. John pulled his coat collar up and I was able to disengage myself from the branches of the rhododendrons.

"Remember, I get the money in the chest. And don't double-cross me. You might have another accident."

He shuffled off down the trail and I went back to the house. At the top of the path was the window of the room where Gordon and Albert were killed. I could imagine Gwendolyn and James stealing a kiss in the moonlight on the wrought-iron bench when they heard an argument from inside. From this walkway they would have had a clear view. They blackmailed the murderer, and when James was lost at sea, there was no one to protect Gwendolyn. She had been murdered. If Duncan was the killer, she was another of his victims.

Sliding quiet as a mouse through the side door, I checked myself in the hall mirror to see if there was any evidence I'd been outside. There was none and I strolled into the library as the clock chimed the hour. Elena thumbed through a book on Egyptian antiquities and Leo was stretched across the couch.

Leo walked over to the decanters on the sideboard. "I think it's time for stronger libations." Filling three glasses and handing Elena and I ours, he raised his in salute as the clock began to chime. "Thank you Saint Andrew!"

"I hardly think I count as a saint."

Both Van Hornes laughed.

"Saint Andrew is the library clock's name," Elena said. "When we were children, Duncan, Leo, Gwendolyn, and I named all the clocks in the house. Duncan's grandfather was a clock maker: he made most of these."

Leo continued, "And Gordon was nutty about them. Long after they'd traded clock making for land and investments, he still tinkered with them."

"The clocks chime in a special sequence, you see. One starts, then the next, and so forth," Elena said, adding, "More or less."

"We made up little rhymes for each of them," Leo patted the old timepiece. "This one is Saint Andrew. Remember the rhyme, sister?"

"Tea time or brandy sings the bells of Saint Andy," she replied, laughing. "But when we were children, it was 'tea time or candy.' We've matured since then, I'm afraid."

By now the grandfather clock was tolling. Elena sighed.

"That's Big Ben. I can't say Duncan was original or very religious on naming him."

Leo raised his glass again. "The gap in melodies between the morning room and the library marks the absence of Saint Margaret and Saint Mary. Ding, ding, ding, Saint Margaret married a king."

I had noticed this interruption my first morning at Seacliff. "What happened to Saint Margaret's clock?"

Elena shrugged, "It never could keep time. It was the most adorable ormolu timepiece too, and one of the oldest clocks in the house. Gordon was fanatical about keeping them accurate. Had Gordon lived, he would have been after Duncan to get Saint Margaret repaired."

Leo looked at me. "Its twin, Saint Mary, is in Janina's room. Steven said it disturbed his sleep, so he stopped it. As if he really spent any time—"

Another clap of thunder and the lights flickered. Mrs. Johnson appeared. "Fellowes says he's ill and taken to bed, so I came to tell you supper's served."

Elena walked over to the older woman. "Thank you Mrs. Johnson. Everything will be perfect, I'm certain."

"'Tis only because of your help with our menus that I'm able to keep a handle on things. This house wouldn't run so well if you weren't looking after us when we needs it."

Supper was indeed perfect, with Elena and Leo at their most charming, while the weather rampaged outside. Tim also enjoyed a good mood, and both Van Hornes commented on his change in manners. But with him in the room, there was no discussion of George Upshaw or Gordon Stewart's death.

After dessert, we went into the drawing room and Elena entertained us with her musical abilities and we played charades. I brought out my sketch pad and created caricatures of everyone. It was still early but the storm's violence took its toll, and at ten we said our goodnights. Elena took Steven Charles' quarters, and Leo the room next to Tim's. I dressed for bed, and tried drifting into sleep, but to no avail. After lying there over two hours, I got up and went to the library.

The entire house was silent as I crept into the room. Looking at the floor-to-ceiling rows of volumes, I wondered which one, if any, might help me sleep. I roused the fire with the well-used iron and brass tongs and the light intensified in the room. I had just sat in the leather chair when I heard footsteps.

"Fellowes," I said out loud, certain the fright in my voice was apparent. The valet stood in the doorway. The light from the fireplace gave his stern face an even more sinister cast, as the wind outside howled.

"Is everything all right, Mister Andrew?" He said this with a finality that sent shivers up my spine. He walked over to the fire and warmed his hands. I doubted the heat could penetrate his iciness.

"I wasn't able to sleep and came to read by the fire."

"One needs a book to read, then." Walking over to the right of the fireplace; he scanned the shelves with his fingers and selected one. Placing it on the table beside me, he added, "This was one of Mrs. Stewart's favorites."

"Mrs. Johnson said you were ill."

"I could not sleep either, but hoped I would find you. I must talk to you about the night Mister Gordon died. I did not want the Van Hornes to hear." Fellowes sat down across from me in the wing-backed chair. I didn't know which was strangest: his professed desire to confide in me, or that he was still dressed as if it were early evening.

"The decision to send Albert to the sanitarium was twofold. There was a distinct possibility that Mister Gordon committed some unscrupulous dealings regarding business and that Albert would be questioned. By sending him away, well, no one would take the word of an insane person, would they?" He gave a queer sort of chuckle that made me long to run away.

The storm pounded the house and I feared it might waken Leo or Elena and cause them to join us. I needed this time to get as much information as I could. Focusing my attention on the valet, I nodded.

"However, unbeknownst to anyone, Albert had concocted a plan of his own. He convinced Mister Gordon to leave Seacliff and escape the entire business scandal. Their plan however, would leave Mister Duncan and Miss Janina to face the authorities. They found this out the night of the Van Horne's party and rushed back to confront the two men."

"Duncan and his mother . . . ?" I began.

"I had escorted Miss Janina to her room, and went to the kitchen to bring her some tea. But when I returned, she was not there as I told the Van Hornes, and at the time, the sheriff. From her bedroom I heard the shouts and the gunfire. I knew at once what happened. Miss Janina was there, as was Mister Duncan: standing over the bodies. She pleaded with me to spare her only child as she placed the gun in Albert's hand." The valet leaned back in his chair and sighed.

"After all these years you've told no one else," I stated. I wasn't quite sure I believed Fellowes, although it made sense that to protect his dead mistress he would also protect her son.

He gave me a thin-lipped smile. "If Mister Duncan is removed, Seacliff falls to the Van Hornes. I could never let that happen. Mister Charles knew this. He asked the same questions as you, but was not as discreet with his curiosity, and involved Mister Leo. That was the worst thing he could have done. There was a tremendous argument that reverberated throughout the house on the last night he was here. I overheard Mister Duncan ordering him to leave, and Mister Charles just laughed at him."

"But he did leave."

"I never saw him again. Now you know the truth, but if you discuss this with Mister Duncan I guarantee he shall dispense with you, too."

But unlike everyone else, I believed Duncan was innocent. There had to be more to the valet's tale. "You said sending Albert away had a twofold purpose."

He gave me the same thin smile. "It was also hoped the sanitarium could cure Albert of his obsession with Mister Gordon. Miss Janina and I often prayed about it."

The valet could not fathom that two men could share a love that was normal. Yet it had happened in this house not once, but twice.

"Cure? Albert was in love with Gordon Stewart, and from what I've heard, Gordon didn't discourage that attention—" As much as Steven Charles and Duncan shared a love, I concluded to myself.

"Do not say that! You do not know what the true circumstances were. Yes, Mister Duncan has the same weakness as his father. Since he cannot commit to marriage, it is best that he remain here at Seacliff, alone."

The fire snapped as the last log broke in half. An idea popped in my mind. "Fellowes, are you in love with Duncan Stewart?"

He almost catapulted out of his chair. Without a word, he stood straight up and turned on his heel. As he walked out of the library, I held my breath. The grandfather clock struck midnight and in silence I got up, picking up the book Fellowes handed me: Janina Stewart's favorite: *Oedipus.* Tossing it onto the sofa, I walked into the hall, when out of the darkness a hand grabbed my arm.

"Leo!"

"Having a little midnight quilting party with Fellowes?"

"I'm tired. I'm going to bed."

"Would you like some company? I'll be out by dawn."

"No."

I headed down the corridor to my room, saying nothing more. He called after me.

"Rejecting me twice in one week isn't healthy, Andrew."

I crawled into bed. I had to think of my next course of action. I would confront Duncan, as Steven had done.

John Middleground's raspy voice and Fellowes' cold monotone haunted me while I slept, and I awoke in the pitch black of my room hearing them hiss Duncan's guilt of murder. Feeling groggy, I struggled to open my eyes. I leaned over to look at the small clock on my nightstand, but I could not focus my eyes. And the men's words continued, this time louder. I tried to breathe, but the heavy air caught in my throat. The hiss grew stronger, unrelenting, and I strained toward the sound, seeing through heavy eyes the gas heater on the wall beside my bed. I had not turned it on. Straining to reach behind me, I struggled with the window latch, wanting the cold, wet, fresh air to flood the room. It wouldn't open and I grew weaker. Falling out of bed, I experienced anew the pain in my back and legs. I crawled to the door and dragged myself into the hall. It was then I became cognizant of what was happening. For the second time in two days, someone tried to kill me.

Chapter Ten

After shutting off the gas, it was impossible to sleep. There was no question this time an attempt had been made against my life. The incident with Angel was deliberate—my would-be assassin had failed, and tried again. I lay in bed, waiting, hoping he would return, but not so much as a sound was heard outside my door. As the sun rose I saw the reason I could not open the window: a rake from the stables had been propped against the glass. Another discovery: the book of drawings had been propped open on my nightstand to a most suggestive page.

Walking into the morning room, I expected to find Leo and Elena, and my mind focused on catching Leo's reaction upon seeing me. His parting comment the night before made him as suspect as Fellowes, who remained at the top of my list. It was plausible Leo had turned up the gas, and thrown the rock at Angel. After all, he had found me.

Neither Van Horne was there, nor was the room empty. Duncan Stewart sat in his chair. Looking up at me, he gave me a curt nod.

"Surprised, eh? I am as well. What a whale of a storm! Took all night to get back. Look at that sky now; clear as a bell."

I had crossed him off my list of suspects. Now I had to add his name back, perhaps as the prime candidate. No doubt he was still angry at my refusal to share his bed.

"You're looking rather pale. Don't tell me you missed me, or is it just a lack of sleep?" Now he was all laughter, and in a cocky, jovial mood. Or, was he masking shock at seeing me alive?

"Elena and Leo . . ." I began.

"They headed back home at sunrise. Apparently, there was some damage to the roof of Glendower Hall caused by the storm. Their man came over and rousted them up. That house isn't the rock of Gibraltar that Seacliff is, you know." He rested his hand against his chin. "Leo is notorious for walking in his sleep. I hope he didn't wander into your room by mistake during the night."

The Master of Seacliff
Published by The Haworth Press, Inc., 2007. All rights reserved.
doi:10.1300/5778_10

I opened my mouth to tell him of my night of terror but he held up his hand. "I'm sure the storm bothered you, but you're not still upset about the other day are you?"

Mr. Johnson stuck his head in the door. "Mister Duncan, I'm afraid I've got some bad news."

"I've just boasted to Andrew that Seacliff is as sturdy as they come. Don't make a liar out of me."

"John Middleground is dead, sir. Doctor's on his way."

I dropped the porcelain teacup; it shattered into pieces across the table.

"Looks like he fell from the ladder in the stable, Mister Duncan. Snapped his neck."

Duncan looked toward the ocean. "Damn. Thank you, Johnson. I'll be down in a moment."

The only sound in the morning room was the gentle tick of the clock. Duncan picked up another cup and spoke while he poured me tea.

"John was a wee odd, as father would say, but a damn good stableman. I don't get it; he must have climbed that ladder a thousand times . . . Andrew, are you all right?"

I had slunk into my chair. Duncan put his hand on my neck and in response, I jerked up.

He said, "This is more than old John's demise that has you on edge. What's wrong?"

"I don't think John's death was an accident. Someone tried to kill me last night. Again."

"What! Oh . . . I see." I could not look at him, but I knew his eyes smoldered; his face red. "You think I'm responsible. I suppose I disposed of John too." He tightened his grip on my shoulder and terror rushed through my body.

"The gas was turned up in my room after I went to sleep, and the window was blocked. I nearly suffocated."

"Why would I want to kill you?" his voice changing from less of a growl to a softer tone. "For God's sakes, I . . . oh, never mind!" He walked to the window, his back to me. I wanted to reach out to him, and at the same time wished he would hold me, to reassure me he could not have done this. Anchored to my chair, I battled an internal conflict between reason and emotion.

"Everyone is aware I want to know what happened to your father and Albert. I don't know who wants to stop me, but they do. Throwing a rock at Angel didn't work, so another attempt was made."

"And you think I shot my father and Albert to seize control of my business?"

"It's been speculated," I said. Duncan turned, his eyes registering neither anger nor surprise at my expression, but sadness. My honesty had struck a blow.

"How callous you think me. I am driven by a desire to succeed, Andrew, but not at that price. And I realize the death of George Upshaw doesn't support my defense. I gather that before you expose me, I must eliminate you. You've deduced things quite well."

"I don't want to believe any of it. Until Mr. Johnson came in, I'd hoped John was the culprit. He hates this house so. . . ." The minute I said that, a thought occurred to me: perhaps John had tried to kill me, and Duncan intervened. Returning from the train, he could have seen John prop the rake against my window. He followed him back to his quarters—this scenario paralyzed me with fear.

Duncan faced me, and I found the courage to look up at him. I saw only the concerned face I cared for.

"You think John Middleground knew more than he told? Quite frankly, he ranted so often, I'd stopped listening years ago."

"John told me his brother and Gwendolyn witnessed the deaths."

Duncan screwed his face, as if trying to concentrate. "Gwennie . . . what was it . . . before she . . . John said they saw it happen. Fascinating." He laughed. "You know for the longest time none of us knew Gwen and James were involved."

"And he believed Gwendolyn was murdered, too."

"Anything is possible with a bloodthirsty fiend like me on the loose, eh? I pushed her from Whispering Hill because she saw me kill my father and Albert."

I nodded my head, wanting him to again deny he was the killer. To confirm what Fellowes told me by the fireplace last night was indeed the truth or a vicious lie.

"I suppose I had James' ship scuttled as well," he said, staring at me. He put his hand on my head, stroking my hair, and I wanted to lose myself in the sensation, but I refused. He pulled out one of the brocade chairs and sat beside me.

"I shall tell you this, Andrew. I do believe all the unhappiness at Seacliff is related. There is a curse on this house, and God help me if you are intended next." He straightened his back. "Elena spoke to me about working for Edgar, and I've made a decision."

My mind traveled in a thousand directions, and I found myself rambling, talking to the broiled breakfast trout and steaming white rice on my plate. "Yes, it sounds like a tremendous chance, her friend, an artist . . ."

Duncan nodded his head and crossed his arms.

"LaVina is not my favorite person, but under these circumstances I think it best you do leave. I will make sure he offers you a job."

I glared at him. "Like that? Sent away so unceremoniously?"

He put his hands on my face, and the familiar rush of adrenaline began at my feet and traveled up to my waist. I wanted to throw myself at him, even with the possibility that he might kill me for knowing the truth. Cupping my chin in his large hands, he spoke.

"Andrew, your life is in jeopardy. I do believe that you are in danger. I promised nothing would happen as long as I'm around, but I'm beginning to think that it might—regardless of my good faith."

I grabbed his arm.

"I don't want to leave you." The minute I said this, I blushed.

His expression changed again. "You've reconsidered my invitation to move upstairs?"

"No."

"I see."

Fumbling, I added, "What I meant was, what will stop this person from harming you, or Tim?"

"I will not have your death weighing on my conscience."

"Why your conscience?"

Duncan called into the hall. "Fellowes!"

"Good morning, Mister Duncan, welcome back."

"Call down to the stable. Johnson is there. Find out from him if the tracks have been cleared yet. I'm returning to New York."

The valet nodded and left, giving no indication of shock at my being alive. Duncan smiled and brushed the hair away from my forehead.

"We're going to New York, all three of us. Pack a valise for my son. Andrew, I want you ready the moment we get the word to go."

"We?"

"You are right; neither of you is safe. While there, you can meet Edgar." He walked away. "You probably regret ever coming to this house. Damn me for thinking this would work."

"I'd rather be with you, Duncan," I said, but I didn't think he heard me, but then he stopped and replied in a calm voice.

"But what if your suspicions about me are correct?"

I closed my eyes and when I opened them, he had departed. From the window, I watched him walk down the lawn to the stable. Where John Middleground's body lay.

Leaving the remainder of my breakfast on its plate, I went upstairs to find Tim and tell him of our journey. At the top of the grand staircase, underneath the portraits of Janina and Gordon Stewart, I stopped. Janina's outstretched arm seemed to point to her room. The door moved as if her painted hand had pushed it, directing me inside.

The draperies were open and the room was flooded with the morning sunlight. I looked at the clock nicknamed Saint Mary. I knelt onto the plush carpet and running my left hand along the side of the timepiece, found the button that unlocked the secret panel. Crouching lower, I peered inside the hiding space. At the back, far behind small decanters of liquor and crystal glasses, was a wooden chest.

My pulse quickened. Steven Charles had found Gwendolyn's chest, and hidden it inside the cabinet. The contents would prove Duncan's innocence, or his guilt. My hands shook as I extracted it from its hiding place. Removing the simple box into the sunlight of the room, I pulled the decorative key that I now wore under my shirt. A small brass plate was mounted on the lid.

Property of Janina Foster Stewart

There was no lock, nor any trace of one having been removed. This was not the chest I sought. I flipped open the lid; inside rested a pistol. I removed the pearl-handled weapon and placed it in my coat pocket. It would protect me, as long as I could figure out how to fire it.

I poked around the empty room. Nothing was changed. Steven's clothing still hung in the closet; his personal items lined the dresser. Deciding I had best continue my search in haste, I walked to the nightstand and opened the bottom drawer. Nestled inside was a stack of envelopes, tied with an ivory bow. Picking them up, the sandalwood fragrance touched my nostrils. Steven's name was on the top envelope, and thumbing through them, I could see they were all addressed to him. I recognized the handwriting as well. Not wanting to investigate further but compelled to do so, I opened the letter and began reading what Duncan Stewart had written to his lover.

The language was bold, demanding, and passionate. Actions were described that I never imagined people would consent to do. Just like the time I was eight and had devoured an entire plate of chocolate candy in one sitting, I found myself reading every letter until I was overloaded on personal information between the two men. The blood rushed through my body again, making me tingle with desire, yet my heart sank with each note I read. This was proof of the deep affection Duncan had for Steven. I could never expect him to care for me the same way, and how foolish I must look to Duncan, after he had reveled in such . . . experiences. I was a total novice compared to the exotic Steven Charles.

I retied the stack of letters and returned them to the drawer. Of all the events I had witnessed at this house by the sea, even two attempts on my life, nothing would have convinced me that leaving was the best choice. But these letters were consummate proof that his love for Steven endured. Defeated, I left and went to pack Tim's belongings for our journey.

And thus, two hours later, I found myself on the platform, boarding the train that brought me to Seacliff three months earlier. Tim jumped around like a monkey upon learning of this unexpected trip. He was excited to go with his father, but I found him clutching my hand and clinging to my side. He informed me this was his *third* trip to New York City, and he made himself at home in the railcar, while I attempted to do some sketching, but gave up. Duncan busied himself with his usual stack of papers, and was not forthcoming with details as to what might have occurred, or what awaited him regarding George Upshaw's death. I spent my time learning the game of chess from Tim, who was quite skillful. Once or twice I noticed Duncan pretending not to be watching us, but he had a hint of a smile, causing his moustache to crinkle that gave his secret away.

How different this journey was from my solitary first ride. We dined on the train, and I met Lu, Duncan's Chinese manservant, who maintained the Stewart town house in Manhattan. He prepared an exquisite lunch, and I declared his culinary skills surpassed those of Mrs. Johnson. Afterward, Tim fell into a deep sleep across one of the large red sofas, and this gave me the opportunity to approach Duncan. He lit a cigar and stretched his legs across a plump ottoman that I perched on.

"Are you frightened at being questioned by the police?"

He laughed so loud, I was afraid Tim would awaken.

"Captain Ankrum and I are old friends. And, I have nothing to hide. You see, my little investigator, the truth is George agreed to sell me his share of the subway system over two weeks ago. Thus, I had no motive to kill him.

The dolls were in fact, a thank you gift. He wanted them for Victoria." His expression was a bemused one, and again I felt he had one-upped me.

"Oh, Duncan, really?"

"The transfer of Upshaw's rights is on file at the office of my very honorable attorney, Mr. Knight." He stroked his beard. "I suppose as a potential Jack the Ripper I seem less attractive to you now."

The train lurched around a corner and I tumbled. Duncan held me until the car stabilized. Once again, I found myself getting lost in his eyes of onyx.

"This is quite a comfortable position," he said. His grasp on me was not tight like Leo's, but more cradling. In another moment I could forget all our arguments and lose myself. Then I remembered the letters to Steven. I wriggled and he released me.

"I understand Albert was being sent to a sanitarium to keep him from testifying," I said sitting back down on the ottoman.

He registered no surprise that I knew this. "Father had his hands in many questionable dealings. An inquest was planned for the week after his death. Only after he died did I learn the extent of his guilt, when I took over the business. Albert would have been aware, and there was some talk that by having him declared mentally incompetent, an inquest could be avoided. However, I can't see Father going along with a scheme such as that. He would never have sacrificed Albert over the business."

"What about your mother?"

"That's another subject entirely. She took no real interest in how Father got his money; her chief concern was that it wasn't spent frivolously. Father neglected her, I'm afraid, as he did me. His passion was all-consuming."

"Consumed by the business, correct?"

"No, by Albert. That's what makes their deaths so painful."

"They loved each other," I stated, surprised at my own openness about it.

He nodded. "It was an arrangement that worked out for everyone involved, Mother, Father, and Albert." He looked out the window. "Perhaps that was an old-fashioned idea."

"Love is never old-fashioned."

He smiled. "You are hell-bent on the dream they were leaving together, aren't you?" He stroked my hair again. "Your belief in true love is refreshing. If only that would ease the pain I carry; the guilt," His eyes grew smoky and I knew not to press on to what true guilt he carried.

"I only want to help you, Duncan Stewart."

He grabbed my hands and pulled them to me. "I know you do. I wish I could erase the doubt from your mind that I would ever hurt you, Andrew."

A slowing of the wheels signaled our arrival into New York. Tim jumped off the couch where he napped and looked out the window, jumping with excitement. The train came to a stop and Tim pulled me to the doorway. As we exited, a tremendous flash of light blinded me for several seconds, and I froze where I we stood on the stairs. When the smoke cleared I saw a photographer in front of us on the platform. Duncan stood behind me, resting his hands on my shoulders, laughing, and after Tim rubbed his eyes he laughed too.

The photographer doffed his funny cap. "Picture will be ready tomorrow, Mr. Stewart."

Duncan leaned over into my ear. "A surprise of my own, Andrew. Welcome to New York."

An ebony Stewart carriage whisked us to the Waldorf-Astoria Hotel on Fifth Avenue at 34th Street. I had forgotten the myriad of sounds and sights and my attention twittered like a bird at each corner. Another surprise was there in the lobby: standing under the grand bronze clock. Michael Betancourt extended his hand to Duncan and hugged him. Dear Michael.

"Heart attack, Duncan. George Upshaw died as nature intended."

Duncan turned and threw open his arms. "You see, Andrew? I'm as innocent as they come."

I pried Tim off the base of the clock as Michael turned to me. "Andrew, I haven't greeted you properly. Forgive me."

I gave him a hug, and he responded in kind. I blushed, thinking of how naive I had been such a short time ago.

My relief at the news that George Upshaw died of natural causes allowed my interest to turn to the surroundings of the hotel. The artwork was exquisite, and the first thing that caught my eye. I turned to my companions, gushing, "I can't believe we will be staying here!"

Tim frowned. "We have our own house. Oh, Father, is Andrew staying here with the other servants?"

Three months earlier, it wouldn't have surprised me if Duncan had slapped the child there in the lobby. Instead, he grabbed Tim and held him up in the air.

"Your precocious mouth! I have told you, Tim, Andrew is not a servant. It is I who has actually taken a suite here."

I think both our spirits sank at that moment. Tim's, because he adored being near his father, and mine, for the same reason. Duncan wrinkled his face and leaned his forehead against his son's, and spoke in a low tone.

"Don't look so downcast, son! I will conduct my business here, and will be with you the rest of the time. My office is too indiscreet for these particular meetings. We've just stopped to check on the accommodations, and to say hello to Michael. Andrew, you, and I will all be at the town house together."

"I love you, Father," Tim said, throwing his arms around Duncan's neck.

"And I love you, very much."

Michael had wandered unnoticed to a magnificent Gainsborough painting of a landscape. I left father and son, and walked over to join my old friend. Michael put his hand on my shoulder, as he had many times, but this was different.

"Excellent work, Andrew. And you had no confidence in yourself."

"I've done nothing."

"Bosh! Look. Those are two changed individuals. Make that three. Andrew, you positively glow. Your hair, your clothing . . . why, you've grown up."

"It is to you that I owe all this, Michael, but . . . I must talk to you, alone."

Duncan's voice boomed across the room.

"Andrew! We must be off. Michael: breakfast here, tomorrow?"

Michael spoke under his breath. "Come by my office anytime in the afternoon."

"Andrew! Get over here!" Tim screeched, causing Duncan to clap a hand over the child's mouth.

Michael looked at Duncan, who looked at me. He smiled again and sent me to the master of Seacliff with a playful push. "Go to him, Andrew. They both need you. Breakfast at seven, Stewart." His eyes never looked so kind, but today they were a little moist. The elegant lobby of the Waldorf must be drafty, though I experienced no such effect.

I walked out of the lobby and climbed into the coach, thinking about what Michael said. If Duncan needed me, why was he determined to see me leave Seacliff? And how could I, in all honesty, stay with the specter of Steven Charles looming over our lives?

Up, up, up Fifth Avenue past the entrance of Central Park we rode, and stopped at an iron and stone fence, across from the Metropolitan Museum. Compared to Seacliff, the town house was tiny, and I fell in love with it on sight. Its three floors were grand, but as understated as Seacliff was over-the-top. Walking inside, the decor was a combination of Oriental and what I took to be an Arabian style. It even smelled of what I thought those two countries would be like: exotic, delicate, but masculine. Pure Duncan Stewart.

"It's so unique!" was all I knew to say.

Duncan tossed his hat onto the rack inside the door and helped me with my coat. "The decorations at Seacliff are the legacy of my mother, and as long as Fellowes can walk, it shall remain so, I'm afraid. I give Elena credit for her gentle attempts at pushing him toward the twentieth century; it pleases her, but I could really care less about that house." He grabbed the oak newel post of the stairway, and smiled. "This, however, is entirely my domain. If a piece doesn't suit me, I throw it away."

He explained there was only one maid, who came in during the day, and Lu would prepare our meals. Duncan took my valise up the staircase, and opened up a door to the left. He bowed in a grand manner and placed my bag onto the large cloudlike bed. "This is your room, Andrew. Please note no ghosts lurk here."

I took that to mean Steven Charles had not occupied this suite. That meant he and Duncan had shared . . . I didn't want to think about that.

There were boxes in my bedroom containing two complete new suits, as well as hats, shoes, and gloves. Town clothes, Duncan called them, and added that if I didn't like anything, to disregard it.

He presented me with his cards and gave me a list of stores to shop. "I'll be gone when you awake tomorrow. Lu will serve breakfast, then Tim and you are on your own to shop. Select whatever strikes your fancy, simply give them my card and they will put it on my account." He wrinkled his mouth. "And make sure you choose something special to wear to supper tomorrow night. It will be my treat."

I opened my mouth to oppose, and he put a finger to my lips. "No arguments. Tomorrow afternoon I'll spend with Tim, and during that time you will meet Edgar LaVina; the coachman has the address."

"Thank you, Duncan."

He stood with his hand on the white door handle. "My room is next to yours, should you need anything. At night, the servants go to their own homes. It's the most wonderful feeling—complete solitude." Taking a deep breath, he looked me over. "And be assured there will be no attempts on your life . . . or virtue . . . tonight." He gave me a wicked grin and closed the door as he left.

I knew I was bright red. How different he was outside of Seacliff! Maybe the house by the sea was indeed cursed. This home, while no means small, had an intimate and relaxing quality. Exhausted, I fell into bed and slept without moving until I awoke refreshed in the morning.

Duncan was gone, but left instructions to have Tim back by one o'clock. After a light breakfast, the coach whisked us down Broadway. We had been inside Lord and Taylor's mammoth department store for two hours when Tim froze where he stood and his eyes grew wide. He ducked under a display table of fine china, mortifying me. He had been so well behaved all morning.

"It's her! The witch!"

"You're talking nonsense."

"Miss Jones!" he whispered.

She had already seen him. She came over, an attractive girl, similar in coloring to Elena, but younger, about my age, I guessed. She called through the heavy lace tablecloth where the child was crouched.

"Timothy! Remember me?"

"Miss Jones," I replied, as the child remained under the table, silent. "I am Andrew Wyndham, Tim's tutor."

"How nice to meet you. I received a letter from Elena not too long ago stating that you had been employed there. I understand the situation worked itself out better for you." She seemed pleasant, but perhaps a bit too earnest.

"I'm very fortunate, I think."

"How is Mr. Stewart?" she asked, blushing.

"Quite well; preoccupied with his business. Tim, please come out and greet Miss Jones."

From under the table, barking sounds; followed by growls were emitted.

I sighed, "Well, now you see, there are some things still to be worked out."

She laughed, understanding. She seemed to be a warm person, but clearly no match for Tim's shenanigans. The young woman peered again under the table and I was afraid I would have to go underneath it to obtain my charge. I thought of Michael's compliment the night before and was glad he wasn't here now. When it was obvious Tim wasn't budging, she extended her hand to me.

"I shan't detain you. Please tell Elena I greatly enjoy the Vernon estate. It's almost identical to Seacliff."

"I can't imagine Seacliff having a twin of any kind," I said, wondering if the Vernon place was as unhappy a house.

"The house has not been as modernized as Seacliff, but the grounds are almost exactly the same, including the layout of the cemetery." She gave me a broad smile. "Architecture and American History are two of my passions. Elena and I talked for hours about the history of many American homes." She folded her hands and blushed, "And Mr. Stewart and I talked as well. You see, Albert Brown designed the Vernon home, Briarbramble."

I wished we'd had a little more time, and that Tim would cooperate, for Miss Jones seemed to be most interesting. "I'd find Seacliff most difficult if it hadn't been for Elena's kindness. It's Mrs. Vernon that you are a companion for, no?"

She glanced down at the table where Tim remained. "An aunt: Miss Genevieve Bink. Thank goodness yes, for it gives me time to pursue my interests in Revolutionary War history. Please tell Elena that I discovered a secret storage area for military weapons at Briarbramble. Seacliff must have one in exactly the same location."

At that moment, Tim darted out from under the table and shot across the floor of the store like a cannon. In his haste, he knocked over a display of table linens, which tumbled into a rack of silver that clattered to the floor causing silence to fall over the shoppers on the entire sales floor.

"Please excuse me," I called as I ran off, no longer caring who was listening around us.

"Good luck!" Miss Jones answered, but I didn't miss the look of complete relief on her face.

Tim didn't stop until we had reached the toy department two floors down.

"That was a ridiculous way to act, Timothy," I said, collaring him.

"I don't care, I can't stand her." He then stuck his chin out at me. "You should be glad I ran her off. She wanted to marry Father, you know."

"What?"

"No one thinks I know, but I do." He hopped upon a giant stuffed lion and kicked it with his boots.

I grabbed his hands, to keep them from pulling out the orange mane of the toy.

"What are you talking about, marrying your father?"

"Ask Elena. She and Miss Jones were friends, but then she turned out to be a thief! Nobody knows I know that, either!" The child was yelling, and I noticed again that people were staring at us. This was not the impression I hoped to make on New York society.

I clapped my hand over his mouth. "Shh!"

He jerked his head over to the enormous clock on the wall above the elevator. "It's time to go back home. My father expects me."

We returned to the townhouse with a multitude of packages: gifts for Michael, Mr. and Mrs. Johnson, Ash, Elena, and Leo. I bought nothing for my family; I still debated whether to see them or not. And I had an elegant evening suit. Duncan had telephoned a men's shop he recommended and told them I would be dropping in, and they had several selections prepared. I fretted over my choices for thirty minutes and only when Tim began to howl did I realize I had to get back to the townhouse.

The only person I hadn't really bought for was Duncan. I purchased a small bottle of his musk cologne, but I wanted a more personal item to show my gratitude. After meeting Edgar LaVina I would find a store with a distinctive gift for him.

Lu took Tim to Duncan, and I was given use of the coach for my appointment with the artist. To reach his studio we passed Michael's office, so I went to see my old friend first. To my dismay I found he had been called out on an emergency. I so wanted his advice on what to do. I was only a few blocks from my aunt and uncle's store, but I didn't want to be late, so I forewent going there, and instructed the driver to head onward to Greenwich Village. My breath grew tighter in my chest as I walked up the steps to Mr. LaVina's studio and pressed the bell.

Edgar LaVina was an intriguing man. I guessed his age at forty-two, the same as my father had he lived. He reflected my height and build, but he was taut and wiry whereas I had work to do. His eyes were small and dark, and he searched my face with an eagerness and energy that made him seem years younger. I did want to snicker at his unruly charcoal hair and goatee, both flecked with gray, and the spattered red cap and smock that made him look straight out of a French postcard. He surveyed me, and snapped his fingers in the air, sending the smell of charcoal and lime soap to my nose.

"Enter! Andrew Wyndham, I presume. Most pleased am I to meet you," he said in an odd accent.

His firm handshake sent a warm tingle of electricity through me and I lost all my nervousness. He welcomed me inside, which was scented with a pleasant combination of roses, polished wood, and to no surprise, paint. The first-floor quarters were modest, and decorated in an eclectic jumble of pieces that reminded me of an overcrowded yet intriguing antique shop near my uncle's store. When he showed me his office area, I saw that Elena was not withholding reserve when she stated he needed organization. The tiny area was a complete scramble of ledgers, bills, and invoices, all tossed in a rather haphazard fashion. This disarray was balanced by his vast but immaculate studio, which occupied the entire top floor of the building. It featured windows that extended from the floor to the slanted rooftop, every inch covered with completed artwork, works in progress, studies, or tools. It was what I had dreamed my own studio to be like. Looking out onto the cloudy sky above Seventh Avenue and below at all the activity, I could find a million things to draw. Edgar surveyed me, and snapped his fingers again.

"Very much would I like to engage your services, indeed, yes! Elena's word is endorsement enough: I love her, but I must admit I was surprised and flattered that Duncan would telephone me as well." His mouth punctuated this with a sort of smile, and he looked to some canvases resting against the wall. "We have not spoken in months."

Duncan's support saddened me anew, but I didn't let it show. I answered, "I am not surprised. He has been most supportive of my desire to become an artist. In fact, he is quite fond of all who have such talents."

"Ah, yes! How true this is! Come see!"

Edgar LaVina flew to the wall and began thumbing through the stack of canvases in haste. He snapped his fingers and whisked a small piece into the air. Holding it close, he walked back to me.

"I've been keeping this; I didn't really know what to do. Perhaps you can advise me." He turned it around, and I looked upon the subject.

My eyes traveled past the handsome square-cut jaw, the piercing blue eyes, and the tousled white-blond hair down to the breast pocket of the orange silk smoking jacket that still hung in his closet at Seacliff. The monogram was bold: 'S.C.' It was he. As I studied it, Edgar LaVina beamed.

"Quite handsome, isn't he? *Dorian Gray* come to life. And devilishly charming. He posed for me on several occasions. This portrait was to be a gift to Duncan. When I learned Steven left, I didn't know what to do with it. Steven hasn't written, and I couldn't contact Duncan . . . he . . . ."

A new connection to Steven Charles. I interjected, "Where do you suppose Steven is now?"

Edgar LaVina added just the slightest addition of color to his heart-shaped face, but snapped his fingers just the same. "I have no doubt Steven lounges in an exotic setting, enjoying the best of life's gifts, creating his beautiful music, or motivating another businessman to make a financial windfall. He is quite the inspiring individual, and often talked about tour-

ing South America. Perhaps he is in Argentina, he often spoke of it." He
sighed and stood the portrait against a well-worn desk by the east window.

A bell on the wall clanged three times. Edgar looked at a large clock
mounted on the wall and smacked his forehead.

"*Dios Mio!* I've completely forgotten! Please excuse me, I shall return!"
He swirled out of his studio and bounded down the stairs two steps at a
time. In a moment I heard him speaking in an excited tone of what sounded
like Italian.

I stared at the portrait of Steven Charles. I hadn't seen any photographs
or paintings of him, but it was as if I'd always known him. He was indeed
handsome, and his sexuality jumped off the canvas.

I knew now what my gift to Duncan would be. I had mended the relationship between Duncan and Tim, but I could not heal Duncan's broken
heart. I thought of Miss Upshaw, and Tim's comment about Miss Jones.
Both women's hearts he had toyed with. I thought my friendship with the
master of Seacliff might lead to romance. I was foolish. I would leave Seacliff, and dedicate myself to art, as I had planned. In time, I would forget
Duncan Stewart.

Edgar's effervescent style of speaking floated up the stairs like bubbles
and a female voice that matched his tempo and accent joined in. Deciding
they sounded engaged in conversation for several minutes, I walked to the
wall and began looking at his other work. While his landscapes were not of
my taste, Edgar LaVina was an excellent portraitist, and he appeared to spe-
cialize in works of men. Toward the back, I found a different study of Steven, then another. To my surprise, there were over a dozen in total. In three,
he was stretched across the chaise lounge I had just been sitting on, or
leaned against a Roman column that I had noticed now was tucked into a
corner. In these renderings, however, he was nude. The smoking jacket was
discarded at his feet. In one, he was in a full state of arousal.

Wanting to slam the paintings against the wall and forget that I had seen
them, I could not stop. I continued to be hypnotized by the subject, letting
the sound of the bustle on the street below lull me into daydreaming. Steven
Charles was the embodiment of male perfection. Once upon a time I
thought I could make Duncan forget Steven and go on with his life. Now after reading their letters and seeing his image, I laughed at the ridiculousness
of my dream.

Hearing Edgar's shoes tap up the stairs, I leaned the artwork back
against the wall in haste and moved to a study of a large calico cat by the

window. When the artist got to the top of the steps I could see he was out of breath.

"I'm so sorry Andrew, but I must conclude our meeting for today. I will be traveling to Paris in the fall and I would most like your assistance as soon as you can." He clicked his heels and bowed. "Most happy I would be to make you my apprentice."

Paris. At last I would get there, though not as I planned. "Thank you. If you don't mind, I'd like to take Duncan this portrait of Steven. Unless you wished to keep it . . ."

His eyes darted to the wall behind me, and again the mischievous smile crooked the corner of his mouth. I decided I liked Edgar, but tried not to follow his gaze.

"I believe I do have some other studies . . . elsewhere. Please, take this to Duncan, as I said that was Steven's intention."

He wrapped the portrait in heavy paper for me and escorted me to the stairs. As I started to descend, I noticed an eight-foot tall canvas covered with a textured green cloth leaning against the wall behind the railing.

"That size artwork belongs in Seacliff," I laughed as I balanced Steven's portrait on my knee and pointed.

Edgar skipped over to the wall and snapped his fingers. "You must be clairvoyant, my young friend. This will be another masterpiece!"

Fearing another naked image of Steven was hidden behind the covering, I bit my lip as Edgar whipped the cloth off. Instead, it was an incomplete work of Elena Van Horne in oil. She seemed more ethereal in this piece, though. Her face and hands had been completed, as was the background, the blue foxgloves in the small garden at Seacliff. But her clothing was only sketched, and had been corrected several times. The erasure marks were as numerous as the penciled ones.

"Beautiful, isn't she? We began this, oh, over eight years ago. When Elena marries, this shall be finished and will hang in her new home. *Dios Mio,* I've redone that wedding gown I don't know how many times. But my lady tells me that soon, quite soon, we shall complete it, at last."

I thought of Richard Lawrence's enormous diamond ring, and I chuckled.

The foreign woman's voice, in a tone I gathered as a little irate, ran up the stairwell to where we were. Edgar snapped his fingers and led me to the front door. The coach was there, and I returned to Michael's; this time he was in.

"I've only a moment before I see another patient. It's been one crisis after another," he said as he offered me a chair.

I would waste no time. "Albert Brown did not kill Gordon Stewart."

Michael lifted his eyebrows. "I examined the medical records that Dr. Stowe had. He was a good doctor for colds or muscle pain, but not murder. His records were not that thorough, and do not give a distinct conclusion that Albert shot Gordon, and then took his own life. In fact, it could be the other way around or . . ." His voice drifted off.

"Does Duncan know this?"

For the first time in my life Michael did not look me in the eye. Instead he shuffled his feet and rubbed his fingers against his palms. "I never told Duncan of my findings. This was research I did out of my own curiosity. You see, Andrew . . . it's rather tricky . . . if . . ."

"You believe Duncan killed them, don't you?"

Now he looked into my eyes. "It's what you believe that's important, Andrew. Duncan cares for you much more than he will ever admit."

I left Michael's office more conflicted than ever.

Chapter Eleven

In the coach, I put Michael's condemnation of Duncan out of my mind and tried to think about a life working for an artist. I would see Paris in the fall, but I felt no excitement or enthusiasm. Instead, I thought of Tim and Ash. Who would teach them? Would Ash be allowed to study under a new tutor or governess? What if Duncan should lapse back into his old habits of ignoring his son? Should I assume, like my most trusted advisor had, that Duncan was a murderer?

I returned to the town house and tucked Steven's portrait behind the wardrobe door in my bedroom. I was deep into a nap when I heard Duncan's voice downstairs. I washed my face and went out to greet him, but he had gone into his quarters and closed the door. On the small table outside my bedroom rested a single rose and a note.

We shall be leaving for supper at eight.

I only had an hour.

Taking extra care getting dressed, the results pleased me. I admired my reflection and brushed my hair until it crackled with electricity. Hearing the door to Duncan's room open and the sound of his shoes descending the stairs to the first floor, it was time to meet him. I double-checked the hiding place of the gun I took from Janina's bedroom—underneath my sketch pad—but now felt silly for bringing it along.

He stood at the bottom of the stairs, and his face brightened when I came down. His beard was as neat and trimmed as I had ever seen it, and his hair was at its tamest. It made the darkness of his skin and the whiteness of his smile contrast even more. And his suit accented his broad shoulders and trimmer waistline to perfection.

"You look stunning, Andrew," he said, extending his hand and punctuating this with a hug.

"As do you. Where is Tim?"

The Master of Seacliff
Published by The Haworth Press, Inc., 2007. All rights reserved.
doi:10.1300/5778_11

"Having a private social studies lesson: a night out with Lu and the Chow family in the better part of Chinatown. They will keep him overnight. He deserves a break from us as much as we do from him." He added, "Unfortunately, you may like a break from me as well, but that request cannot be accommodated this evening."

I gave him a gentle punch on his massive forearm. "You are a different man away from Seacliff. One I enjoy very much."

He pretended to be injured, then grabbed me around my neck and dragged me out the front door. The night was crisp and clear, and I felt taller than the town house. The coach was not in sight; in its place a shiny black motorcar waited. Duncan opened the door, and bowed.

"This is yours?" I said, catching my breath.

"My latest toy. It occurred to me, Andrew, that you and I have never had any fun by ourselves. And this is quite entertaining, as long as one can find available petrol. Come along, we haven't far to go—and this is the way of the future."

I climbed into the front seat, Duncan handed me a pair of goggles, put on his own, and we whisked down Fifth Avenue to Fourteenth Street. The feeling of the cool breeze on my face was exhilarating, and I enjoyed the stares of people as we whizzed by. Before I knew it, we had crossed into Greenwich Village.

Duncan stopped the car outside an old brick building. We went up and knocked, and a tall, elegant man, as dark as the night itself, opened the door and admitted us. I looked up at the sign, which read in bold script, The Looking Glass. It appeared to be a private club or saloon of some sort. A sumptuous one, I could tell upon entering. The striking difference was all the patrons were either male or female couples. Only a few mingled together. Everyone was well dressed: I believed I saw the entire contents of Mr. Altman's store offerings. An ornate chandelier cast soft light, and a fireplace crackled in one corner while opposite, under a carved mahogany archway, a small orchestra composed of five Japanese women—or were they men—played.

"What is this place?" I whispered. Duncan held my arm but I clung to his. I was not nervous, but taken aback at the complete comfort of it all.

"Down a rabbit hole, my little Andrew. This is one of my favorite haunts." He picked up an object from a table and handed it to me. "Souvenir matches. In case you want to return on your own," he winked. The room was bathed by the glow of gas lamps, and behind a long bar was a smoky glass depiction of French revolutionaries.

Several of the patrons knew Duncan and he began introducing me to them. The orchestra was rather loud, and I had difficulty hearing all their names. And here, in public, Duncan Stewart put his arm around me and held me close to him, while he took me around. It was as though the worries at Seacliff had never happened; he was another person; relaxed, calm, content. And I was at ease as well, this world seemed so natural. We were escorted to the back of the club, to a private dining area closed off by a red velvet drape. Duncan pulled out my chair for me, and seated himself to my right. An elegant woman with flowing red hair crowned with flowers and royal blue robes passed by and nodded. Duncan saluted her.

"That's Madame Marcella, the owner of this decadent yet delightful establishment."

A waiter appeared and filled two crystal glasses with champagne. As Duncan toasted me, I wondered how often he had brought Steven Charles here. And now I feared that Steven, his face clear now from the portrait in my bedroom, would appear from the shadows to spoil tonight's happiness and reclaim his lover. I thought again about Tim's comment regarding Miss Jones. I told Duncan I met her.

"Really? How is she? Finding Aunt Genevieve not to be the handful Tim was: or worse?" Nothing in his response indicated more than a passing interest. Feeling boosted by the alcohol I had been consuming, I pressed.

"Tim said . . . I'm sure it's quite ridiculous, about your marrying her?" I hadn't wanted that to end in a question, and it did. I gulped from my water glass. The champagne had gone directly to my head.

"Of the many falsehoods that dog me, that is the most far-fetched." Leo spread the word that she was on the make for me, and that I was actually interested in her charms. She was a bright girl, and we talked American history, nothing more," he laughed. "The shocking thing was that everyone from Mrs. Johnson to Elena believed him. Another of Leo's childish jokes: with disastrous consequences for an innocent victim. The poor woman never knew what hit her."

"But the stolen . . ." I started.

"A pair of antique earrings, and I wouldn't be surprised that the pieces she had 'pocketed' were planted by Fellowes, who feared her as an ill-suited replacement for my mother. Besides, only he and Elena knew where the jewelry was stored."

"Fellowes has such a pair of earrings in his room, underneath a photograph of your mother."

Duncan brushed this comment aside. "Look around you, my dear Andrew, and you will see where I am most relaxed. I hardly think Miss Jones would fit here. But you seem to adapt quite well, don't you?"

I didn't answer, for I thought of the handsome Steven.

Duncan looked through the gap in the curtain and nodded his head. A rather short, round gentleman in exquisite formal attire sauntered over to us, and shook Duncan's hand with what I could tell was a strong grasp. The gentleman turned to me and bowed. Duncan smiled as he stood.

"This is my good friend Marie Romano."

I kept my jaw from dropping open. Marie Romano shook my hand with a grip that rivaled Duncan's own.

"Pleased to meet you, Andrew. Stewart, I'll see you at the Waldorf tomorrow. This is my own time now, and I've got a young friend waiting." Marie gestured behind her, where I saw a woman, heavy with diamonds, sitting at a side table. Excuse me, gentlemen."

Duncan watched his friend leave. "She now heads up one of the Stewart Enterprises in Mexico. The Catholic Church's loss has been my best gain. A financial genius, that one." He nudged me. "Andrew, you should really close your mouth. And where were your manners? You should always stand when a lady enters the room," laughing loud and long at my expression.

Food began arriving, one course after another, all exquisite and supplemented by endless champagne, which we continued to drink. It was my first time eating oysters, and after devouring a salad of spinach, I enjoyed a steak so thick it must have been carved from a giant bull. Duncan had been more open than ever, so I tested the waters of his past, as the light from a beautiful candelabrum illuminated his face.

"Tell me about Tim's mother."

"Julianka was a French gypsy. The first night I arrived in Paris, I had too much to drink and stumbled into a small café along the Left Bank, where she told fortunes." He took my hand and squinted. "She predicted I would spend my life with someone younger, but who would be my teacher and salvation. Naturally, Julianka identified herself as the predicted teacher, although we were the same age. Quite heady stuff for a young man, fresh off a boat with only the clothes on his back, but a valise full of money."

"What had happened?"

"I had a terrible row with my parents. They called me into the study one afternoon and announced they had arranged a marriage for me. We had a screaming match like never before, and I took off for Europe."

"Proof such arrangements aren't for the best."

He nodded.

"She must have been beautiful to capture your heart," I offered, picturing the two dark-haired passionate people sitting across a table, looking at tea leaves while Romany music played on a violin.

"Beauty is not everything, Andrew. Yes, Julianka was beautiful—and incredibly charming. I think I've only met two people in my life that had such a combination: Julianka and Steven. As different and as similar as two people could be."

I was glad I obtained the portrait from Edgar. Duncan's voice brought me back from my thoughts.

"I had too much wine that night we met, and I was furious at my parents. Events just sort of happened. A month later she informed me she was with child—my child. My parents had demanded an heir, probably to leave the estate to and cut me out completely—"

"Is that where the rumor of your killing your father started?" Even saying it, I didn't want to believe what Michael did.

"Probably. The Stewarts had arranged marriages for decades, but I believed in following my instincts. I could not marry if I did not completely love. The arrangement between Father and Albert had worked for them and my mother, but I realize now I could never do that."

"Did you love Julianka?"

"I grew to love her, yes. She was a vital person; strong, fearless, but that was all an act. Had I known she was so physically frail I never would have let her gone through with carrying my child. I killed her, Andrew, and I accept that."

"It wasn't your fault."

"Yes, it was." He took a deep breath. "You see, Andrew, I am the curse of Seacliff. People I love, die."

The waiter had entered our private room. Duncan raised his empty glass. "Excellent timing. I'm ready for more champagne."

Other friends of Duncan's arrived and chatted with us, all of whom were most interested to learn who I was, but there was such a parade of people I couldn't recall all their names. Dessert was served, a magnificent concoction of cherries and brandy that was served aflame. I tried to ask more about his younger days, but Duncan wouldn't discuss it anymore.

"I told you, I dunna like to talk about the past."

I gave him an amused look. "Dunna? You're sounding very Scottish now."

"The Scotch in me comes out after I've been drinking champagne. You should have heard Father—born in America but a few whiskeys and you couldn't understand a word he said."

I tried to keep from laughing. Everything seemed so light and the problems that dogged my mind were banished inside this safe place.

Afterward, we danced together. How glorious it was to be in his arms, surrounded by other couples like us. We remained until the club closed. I was in a terrific euphoria by the time we motored back up to the town house.

Feeling more than tipsy, I started to go upstairs, when Duncan walked into the library and over to the liquor cart.

"One more for good measure, I think. Join me. What would you like?"

"Your choice," I said, walking in. How safe I felt being alone in this house with him.

He picked up a bottle, squinted at the label, then held the bottle out to me and puffed his chest out. "This is the grand whiskey of the Highlands. I'm not sure you can handle it."

I sunk down into the soft pink damask of the rosewood sofa and Duncan sat next to me after presenting me with a too-tall drink. He filled up almost all the space, but looked comfortable. He took a gulp and looked into his glass.

"Tell me, as we've avoided it all night. How was your meeting with Edgar?"

I took a sip of the whiskey, which burned my throat. "It wasn't much of an interview. He looked at me . . ."

Duncan rolled his eyes. "Snapped his fingers, no doubt, spouted some Spanish . . ."

"I thought it was Italian. He offered me an apprenticeship, and that was about it. He had forgotten he had another appointment."

"That's happened before. When does he want you?"

Looking at him, I frowned. For the past few hours, Duncan and I were alone in our own special world. Now, he was ready to toss me out. "You seem most eager to dismiss me, Mr. Stewart," I said, knowing that would get a rise out of him.

"I see we've come full circle. I take you to one of my favorite places for supper, introduce you to business and personal friends, and you end the evening calling me Mr. Stewart. That's a fine how-do-you-do."

"Since you are so eager to get rid of me, I felt a return to formality was appropriate," I said, hoping I sounded indifferent.

"I am sending you away from Seacliff for your own good, Andrew. You will thank me someday."

"Does that mean I might see you 'someday'? Because I have the feeling I never shall again."

"Have you forgotten someone wants you dead? It is best you leave." He got up with some difficulty and refilled our glasses.

"It is not for the best if two people care for each other. I love you, Duncan Stewart. Together . . ." My voice trailed off. There, I had said it.

"Does that mean you dunna want to leave?" His Scottish burr was becoming thicker, which I found more attractive than his usual clipped speech.

"What do you want, Duncan?"

"I . . . I . . ." He started to talk, but fumbled. I found this funny. I rarely saw him at a loss for words.

"I'd like to stay," I answered.

He looked up with sad eyes. "I know you do. In that case, I must tell you the truth, now. I cannot carry the guilt any longer."

The answers I had been waiting for were about to materialize. I placed my hand on his arm, and braced myself.

"I am responsible for my father's death." He looked at me, searching for my reaction. "No, I didn't kill him, but I just as soon could have."

"I'm listening." A single chime sounded the hour, and I thought of all the clocks at Seacliff.

Duncan finished off his drink, got up, and poured another.

"I loved Albert more than my father. He was always there when I needed him. My father could never be bothered. As I grew older, Father looked at me as more a rival than as a son."

I thought of the fable of the mouse and the lion, although a thorn in the lion's paw was nothing compared to the anguish Duncan Stewart showed on his face.

"Are you saying Albert murdered your father because of you?"

"Father was incredibly jealous of anything or anyone that came between him and Albert. It's why I was sent to Oxford. I wanted to remain in the States, but Father would have nothing of it. As soon as I graduated, I came home."

"Duncan, did it ever occur to you that your father was jealous because he knew you favored Albert over him?"

He looked at me as he would at Tim.

"You don't understand, Andrew. Although Albert was my father's age, as I grew older we . . . became intimate with each other. Father found out." Duncan buried his head in his hands and began to sob.

I was stunned at his confession, but at last I had seen the real person behind the egotistical façade. He continued, "Then they wanted me to marry, and I left again. When Julianka came into the picture, I thought I had beaten them. But then she died. At that point, I wanted nothing more than to come home to Seacliff. I had written Albert before I sailed from Europe telling him about Tim's birth and my eagerness to come back. Father was still jealous; he wanted Albert out of my life, and, based on what you have told me about the tickets, perhaps he did suggest the West Indies."

"To leave Seacliff together?"

"There were minor business interests there, but Albert would know he was being taken away from me. His mind must have snapped. He killed Father and then having realized what a horrible thing he had done, took his own life. Because of me, Andrew! I can never forgive myself. Julianka, Father, and Albert. That's why I can't have your blood on my hands too."

I believed him. But the other stories I had heard didn't connect with his version of events. "Mrs. Johnson said Gwendolyn and James saw the murderer from the window."

"Albert."

"But John Middleground believed that they blackmailed the murderer." I swallowed not knowing how he would react, but thankful that the alcohol had removed my reserve. "Fellowes told me it was you . . . and your mother." I could not tell him Michael's suspicion.

Duncan blinked his eyes, over and over, but said nothing. I worried if he had overstepped his bounds with his last drink.

"The truth is Andrew, I'd had a lot to drink that night; I don't remember much after I left the party." He rubbed his forehead. "I had a sense there was trouble."

"Why?"

"They all acted strange those last days; I thought it had to do with business. That night, I remember running up the path to the side door, hearing voices in the darkness, then I blacked out. The next thing I remember is waking up on the pathway and running into the house. They were dead. If I had only gotten there in time, maybe I could have prevented it."

"And your mother . . . ?"

"You said Gwen and James witnessed the murder? I wish I could remember what she told me that last afternoon I saw her. Nevertheless, I wouldn't put much stock into John Middleground's claims."

"I believe he was sincere. If only we . . ."

"It won't bring anyone back, Andrew. And I will always take the blame." He dropped his head but looked up at me with sad eyes. "Do you think less of me . . . because of my relationship with Albert?"

"I'm glad you told me," I exhaled. "I don't care what your relationship was with Albert." As I said this I thought how much my values and ideas of love had changed. But in my heart I wished he had been clear as to his innocence. Blacked out? That sounded preposterous. Duncan was a tower of a man, thick and strong. No one could topple him.

"I do remember my last conversation with Father, in the ballroom at the Van Horne's. We agreed my trip to Europe had given us both an opportunity to think about things. He turned to me, lifted a glass and said, 'the wisest thing is time, for it brings everything to light.' Then he asked me to synchronize all the clocks the next day. It was a seasonal ritual he and I did when I was younger and it drove him crazy when they didn't chime in the appropriate order. Then he gave me a hug—he rarely showed affection. I had thought that meant he forgave me."

I believed his story about his father and Albert. If it were true, Duncan could not have killed them, but it did not explain why Steven left. By not invoking his beloved's name I guessed there was some glimmer of hope that he might return. Steven the talented: the inspiring, the one who exuded raw sexuality. The portrait would comfort him. I could not heal Duncan's heart. I stood up.

"I have a present for you, Duncan. Let me get it."

"After what I have just told you, you don't think me a depraved invert?"

Our relationship had reached closure with his revelation. "Certainly not. I'm glad you've cleared your mind. Let me get your gift."

"Andrew, that makes me happy. And I have a present for you too. And a proposition." His countenance changed, and he looked nervous, not at all the Duncan I knew.

Without letting him continue, I ran upstairs and brought out the portrait from its hiding place. Duncan still sat on the couch, rubbing his eyes. He had removed his coat, cravat, and unbuttoned his shirt. He was scratching the thick curly hair at the top of his chest.

"I apologize for my outburst. It's been bothering me for such a long time . . . I needed to talk, and I hoped . . . I knew you would understand." He focused on the object in my hands. "That's an awfully large gift. Please tell me that you painted it."

"Since I am leaving I . . ."

He reached into his pocket. "Andrew, I'd like to talk to you about that . . . and give you—-"

I stopped him. I had to say what was on my mind. "I'd like us to remain friends, Duncan. I saw this today, it was intended for you." I flipped the portrait around, smiling.

The color drained from Duncan's face. His hand tightened on his whiskey glass but before it could shatter, he threw it against the wall, then picked up my glass and did the same. The anger that I had seen the night of our first dinner, the anger he had shown me when we argued about Leo, was back again, magnified a thousand times. He stared at the portrait of Steven Charles, looked up at me; his face in complete rage as he withdrew his hand from his pocket.

"I thought you understood."

"It's Steven . . ." I started, in a stupor at his reaction. I looked down at the portrait. Steven's blue eyes stared at Duncan, almost in an accusing manner. My legs trembled.

"I know damn well who it is," he growled.

"Duncan, I understand your relationship with Steven Charles. How much you love him—will always love him. There's nothing to hide."

"Damn you! You understand absolutely nothing! How well I remember the day that was painted. What makes you imagine, in your childish little mind, that I would want that here in this house with you?"

"With me? But . . . because . . ."

He started toward me and I moved back. What if I had misjudged him?

"With me out of the way, the road is paved for Leo, is that it?" His voice grew louder. "Or have you decided Edgar LaVina is more your style? Why be an artist when you can be buggered by one, eh laddie?"

I dropped the portrait and ran up the stairs, sobbing at his hateful and lewd suggestions. I slammed the door and threw myself atop the bed. Hoping at some point he might knock at my door and apologize, I cried until I fell asleep.

Waking up four hours later, I deciding it was up to me to find out what I had done wrong, but I found his bedroom empty. With a headache that was ready to split my head into a thousand pieces, I crept downstairs and tiptoed into the library. Lu was there, picking up pieces of crystal from the floor. The portrait was nowhere in sight.

"Have you seen Mr. Stewart?"

"He is gone to Waldorf with Master Tim." The servant smiled. You are to have breakfast, then carriage take you to Greenwich Village. Mr. LaVina's studio." He nodded, "You pose for artist. Like Mister Steven Charles, Mister Duncan says."

I shook my head. Just when I thought I had the mystery of Duncan solved, another one took its place.

Lu continued, "Your bags to be sent from Seacliff on next train. Mister Duncan's wishes."

I had been banished without so much as an official goodbye, or the opportunity to pack up my own belongings. My good intentions had been misconstrued. His grief over his lost love was so great; the portrait had sent him into a tirade. Theirs had been the greatest romance. My actions poured salt into a wound that would never heal.

Lu chuckled as he picked up the last piece of broken glass. "This remind me of before. Mister Steven Charles and Mister Duncan have many fights in this room. Break much china. Very loud; say mean things."

I ran my hand through my hair, wishing the servant would be quiet. I wrinkled my nose. "There's an awful smell, Lu . . ."

"Mister Steven Charles' portrait. Very nice likeness, what remained of it, Mister Andrew."

I turned away, shaking my head even though it felt like it would fall off each time I did.

Lu pointed to the fireplace. "I take what was left to ashcan, Mister Andrew. Mister Duncan only wants happy reminders in house—his rule."

I sat down on the couch, holding my head in my hand.

"All Mister Charles' other belongings thrown out long ago. Would you like me to get what remains of painting?"

I wished my head would stop throbbing, so I could absorb what the Chinese servant was telling me. "He burned the portrait?"

Lu nodded and chattered away, and with a pounding head I walked back up the stairs.

Looking into Duncan's empty room, I remembered our conversation last night. The room was cold, as freezing as Duncan had been when I ran out of the library. An object on the dresser caught my eye and when I focused on it my heart fell to my feet. The photograph of Tim and I getting off the train was in a handsome frame atop the dresser, facing Duncan's bed. It would be the first thing he saw upon awakening. Only then did the significance of Lu's words sink in. I ran downstairs.

"Lu, Mister Charles and Mister Duncan; weren't they happy together?"

The servant laughed so loud my head throbbed. "Like cat and dog. Peace return when Mister Charles leave."

I could not join Edgar LaVina today, for my job at Seacliff was not done, despite Duncan's attempt to throw me out. I would not leave until I had proven to him that he was not responsible for his father's death. I did not believe Albert Brown killed his own lover over an infatuation with his son. If that were the case, then a sinister force wouldn't have gone to the trouble of keeping me from finding out what happened.

I did not understand why Duncan reacted the way he did to the portrait of the man I thought he loved, but I would find out. The answers to these questions did not lie here in the peaceful harbor of Duncan's town house, but in the malevolent house of secrets above the sea. As much as I feared returning there alone, I would go back. Calling to Lu, I lifted my chest and raised my chin.

"Will you arrange for the coach? I am returning to Seacliff, today."

Chapter Twelve

Standing on the platform, the cold wind hammered me. I'd left my heavy coat back at the town house, as I was in haste to get back to Seacliff. Now, wearing a lightweight wool jacket that was more suitable for late spring, I regretted that decision. I had foregone the private car for general boarding on the train, which would ensure my anonymity. After last night's outburst, I was certain Duncan would prevent me from returning to Seacliff. Pulling out my watch, I noted the time: Lu would have told him by now. After his outburst at seeing Steven's portrait, he would be as determined to stop me from learning the truth as I was as earnest to find it.

I had not telephoned the house. Fellowes would pick up the receiver. Likewise, I did not contact Glendower Hall. Confiding in Elena might result in her telling Leo I was returning. I searched the street and found a friendly face.

"Well, hullo Andrew! Good to see you about!"

It was the New England accent of Dr. Nickles, calling from his wagon.

"Thank you so much for tending to me when I fell." Returning his smile, an idea sprung to life. Little did the sandy-haired man know he was about to come to my rescue again.

"Would it be possible for you to drive me to Seacliff?"

"Are you alone?"

"Yes, it was a rather unexpected trip. I must collect an item I left behind and return to New York tomorrow," I offered, hoping he would not question me further.

The doctor gave no indication that he thought my statement as anything other than honest. "I'd be delighted to give you a lift. Please come aboard."

I hopped in beside him on the comfortable green plaid cushion that covered the buckboard. The doctor instructed his horses to depart and continued his pleasant small talk.

"You were quite lucky you weren't seriously injured. One has to be particularly careful at Seacliff, it seems." He gave a chuckle. "I'm beginning to believe that house does indeed have a jinx of some sort upon it. That's what the locals say, you know."

Another idea came to mind. I turned to him.

"Yes, Dr. Nickles, take the case of Duncan's father. Murdered by that crazed assistant of his."

"Precisely! You know, you should have worn a heavier coat. A chill can become pneumonia without warning. The weather has changed early this year. Cover yourself up with the blanket."

I bobbed my head in agreement, but I wasn't interested in my own health. "You know, I've been quite fascinated by the death of Duncan's father. Michael Betancourt mentioned you still have the medical examination Dr. Stowe conducted on the bodies of Gordon Stewart and Albert Brown."

"Why such morbid curiosity? From what I understand it was a clear case of murder and suicide."

I hadn't expected to be questioned. "Oh . . . it could greatly help me with my study of anatomy. I shall be going to New York to study with the well-known portraitist, Edgar LaVina, soon."

My traveling companion shrugged his shoulders. "I gave those exact records to Leo Van Horne just the other day. A bizarre coincidence, don't you say?"

"What?!"

"I hope I've done nothing wrong. I know what good friends the Van Hornes and Duncan have always been. Leo told me he was doing research on types of murders for a book he was writing. I had no idea he was a novelist."

"Nor did I," I muttered, not bothering to hide my sarcasm. If what Michael said were true, Leo would use the information to incriminate Duncan.

"Perhaps you two could collaborate on this, say together? I'm sure Leo would be glad to share those old files with you. As I recall, he only needed them a few weeks; he was going to show them to a detective friend I believe, to make his story genuine."

I pulled the blanket around me a little tighter. If only I'd known about those files earlier! Giving them to Leo was like providing dynamite to a posthole digger.

"Doctor, did you reach any conclusion about the cause of John Middleground's death?"

He reined the horses to a slow trot. "It appears that John fell from his ladder during the storm. Most likely he was intoxicated and lost his footing on one of the rungs. Mr. Johnson told me his roof was always leaking, but he was too stubborn to try and repair it correctly."

"At least there's no mystery there."

"Oh, you're quite wrong on that. Had to call in the sheriff. It was while we examined his quarters—if you could call that filthy area livable. I doubt there'd been any cleaning there in years. That's what happens from being a bachelor." He nudged me. "Remember that, and find a good wife."

I had a feeling of disaster, and my upper chest tightened. "What did you find?"

"No one outside of Mr. Johnson and the sheriff knows this; I even doubt Mr. Stewart has been made aware of it, unless Mr. Johnson has informed him." He looked at me. "It's a difficult situation to believe."

I stared at the doctor in silence, listening to the clip-clop of the horses' hooves, and pulling my coat tighter around my body. As we continued toward the coast, the fog began to swirl around us, and the large trees along the road waved their branches as if conducting some pagan ritual. An owl hooted a warning from the gnarled oaks above.

Dr. Nickles whispered, "The remains of a body had been buried in the back of the stable, near where Mr. Stewart keeps his stallion."

My stomach churned: Steven's body. John had killed him: John who told me he had threatened his life. Or had Duncan, who flew into a rage whenever Steven was mentioned?

"Macabre, isn't it? I gather you're wondering who the devil it was."

I did not want to hear his name, but I nodded my head as if in a trance.

"From what I understand, John had a brother presumed lost at sea five years ago. Well, we found a skeleton clad in a sailor's uniform, and a duffel bag with the name James Middleground in the grave beside it. Looks like John killed his own brother. Why he would have done such a thing, heaven only knows."

"Money," I said aloud. "John told me his brother had a chest filled with money."

The doctor twirled his moustache. "A logical deduction. Maybe you should be writing with Leo!"

I did not know how much more death at Seacliff I could absorb. The house on the hill was a place of evil. There was still time to change my plan, but I kept thinking of Duncan's anguished face when he told me about Albert. I could not retreat from my cause.

I watched the shadows of the evening stretch their talons longer and longer across the sky. At the bend in the road, I asked Dr. Nickles to drop me.

I would not need him to go out of his way; I lied. I told him once inside I would make sure I had some hot tea and took his recommendation to place a hot water bottle in my bed. Thanking him more than I needed, then worrying I raised his suspicions, I watched his wagon disappear down the lane as darkness descended like a slow-falling theater curtain.

I wanted to gain access inside without even those I trusted knowing I was there. My mind ran through the checklist I'd started on the train. It was Saturday. The majority of the servants were gone until Monday. With Duncan and Tim out of the house, Mr. and Mrs. Johnson would stay in their own cottage at the bottom of the hill.

Fellowes was the wild card. In all likelihood the valet would be the sole guardian of the house. And I had the house itself to fear.

The road was desolate, and I tried not to think of the tales of Washington Irving that scared me in a wonderful way when I was a child. Then, I could crawl under my blanket, secure it was just a tale. This deserted road that wound toward the sea with its crashing waves; the trees rubbing their branches above me, the increasing fog and dampness—this was all too real.

Slipping through the bronze gates, the cozy lights from the Johnson's home beamed through their windows. My attention turned to the house upon the hill. 'Nary a light gleamed from its windows. It was as formidable an opponent as the task before me.

Walking without a sound along the back drive, I passed the stables, shivering at the thought of James Middleground's body, undetected in the cold ground for five years. As I climbed the footpath to the house, the dense trees protected me from the cold air and fog, and, feeling winded, I was glad I left my bags behind. The pearl-handled revolver was my sole protection, and secure in my coat pocket.

As I grew closer, the absence of lights from the house began to affect the little bravado I had mustered. The face of Seacliff was dark and brooding, as defiant as Duncan had been last night at the town house. With the wind picking up, the thick fog nipped at my face and heels. The house defied me to unearth its secrets, and I would not buckle under its tricks to scare me off.

I circled the entire length of the house. Every room was without light or activity. I rounded the back and crept outside Fellowes' room. Like my own, it was on a level where the window butted up to the hedges and earth of the hill. This was the only room that offered light, and I knelt down and peered over the shrubs through the open curtains. His gramophone played and the valet sat in his rocking chair, his back to me. I could just make out the thinning top part of his gray hair, and saw his left arm sway in time to the melody. The music was quite loud, which pleased me, and with the gathering wind these sounds would combine to cloak my entrance into the house.

I wound my way back around and climbed the flagstone stairway to the terrace and rushed to the library door. Looking up, I prayed that the light I saw flicker in Duncan's bedroom window was my imagination. Out of the corner of my eye, the branches of the elm seemed to be telling me to flee. Finding the library door locked, which was unusual, I rued that I had never been given keys to the house. Walking along the terrace, I tried the dining room and morning room doors, with no success. With each locked door I peered through the glass panes into the lifeless rooms. Tonight, no logs burned a welcome in the fireplace; the deserted kitchen was dark, cold, and sterile. The house reserved all its energy to prevent me from coming inside. Rounding the corner by the reflecting pond, I jiggled the lock on the east wing door to no avail. There was no point in going to the front of the house, the main door was always locked—this I knew.

Perhaps Duncan had alerted Fellowes, told him to seal the doors, and that I had been dismissed and under no circumstances was to be allowed entrance. I entertained going down the hill to the Johnson's—but what if they had been warned of me also? I had come too far on my own to turn back. Breaking in was my single option.

I retraced my steps to the bedroom where Albert and Gordon died. The window was long, wide, and low with a series of individual panes. I imagined Gwendolyn and James, standing in this same spot, two lovers in the moonlight, hearing shouts that drew their attention to this window. The lovers were now dead, but neither death was as recorded. Because of what they witnessed, they were murdered. I could stop right now, run down the hill, steal Angel and ride back to town. There would be another train departing for Manhattan late tonight, perhaps the same train Steven had taken to escape.

But I could not leave Duncan. If he were innocent, I would be abandoning him. And I knew I loved him too much to do so, even if my discovery sealed my fate.

Without hesitation I picked up one of the round stones from underneath the shrubs and smashed the paned glass, praying opera music would be serenading Fellowes' ears at the opposite end of the house. Placing my hand through, I nicked my left hand as I undid the latch to open the window. Without difficulty, I climbed atop the low sill and swung inside. As I did, I swore the house gave a low growl and shook from its limestone walls to the slate roof.

Pushing the drapes aside, moonlight illuminated the room. I studied the space where two men had lost their lives with the same intensity as if I were to sketch it. I tried to recreate in my mind that awful night and what happened. The furniture remained shrouded, and the moon's rays gave the impression that a dozen ghosts surrounded me. I feared turning on the electric light by the door, for it would be distinguishable from the hallway and the bottom of the hill. Maybe I could locate a candle.

I pulled the first cloth away. It revealed a long mahogany bureau, and the reflection in the mirror almost unnerved me. My hair was windblown, my face pale, my white shirt open at the neck. Searching the drawers, I discovered that unlike Steven Charles, all traces of Albert Brown had been swept away. As I went around the room, uncovering small tables, two chairs, a gramophone, and the bed itself, I reasoned that this room would be the least plausible to retain a secret. If Duncan and his mother had killed Albert and Gordon, they would have removed the evidence eight years ago. I prayed that in the haste to seal the room a clue was missed. There were too many questions and hearing the grandfather clock down the hall begin to chime the hour, I knew I had little time.

I exposed everything save one final piece, and stared at the cloth before me. With a great swoop I pulled the covering away; exposing a clock. Atop it rested a pewter candlestick and I delved into my pocket, finding the souvenir matchbook from The Looking Glass. Lighting the candlestick, I studied the piece. It was the twin of Janina's upstairs. Saint Margaret's clock: the one that completed the symphony of chimes in the house. I noted the time frozen on its face: nine-twenty, a frowning face, my uncle would have said. I wondered if this were the exact time Albert and Gordon had been murdered.

I dropped to my knees, running my left hand alongside the shaft of the timepiece, as I went. The secret button was in the same place as its twin upstairs. The decorative panel at the base popped open and I used the candle to light the exposed hiding place.

It was empty, save the cobwebs festooned inside. Setting the candlestick down, my shoulders dropped. No clue lay inside. The house enjoyed a breath of triumph as I heard the wind rush through the empty hallways, and I thought a door might have opened. Crouching for a moment, I heard nothing more. I stood up and leaned my forehead on the face of the clock in defeat.

The door that covered the face of the clock was not quite secure. Holding the candle closer, I could see why. Paper had been wedged in the left corner. I tugged on it and the clock's face swung outward. Wedged between the gears was a yellowed envelope. I sat the candle back atop the clock, and with trembling fingers, pulled my discovery out. I saw no one, but had the distinct feeling I was being watched. The wind had stopped outside and the air was still. It was if the house was holding its breath at my discovery.

With the letter in hand, I sat upon the bed, the candle providing a clear light. Addressed to Duncan, the letter was in handwriting unfamiliar to me, but I knew in my heart to be Gordon Stewart's own.

> *My Dear Son,*
>
> *How proud I am of my grandchild, and I admit I was wrong to attempt to force you into an arranged marriage. You can thank Albert for softening this old Scot's heart. Now I realize I was hasty in my decision to send you away, and I know you blame my jealousy of your own relationship with Albert. I know he loves you only as a son, and nothing more. Forgive me for doubting both of you.*
>
> *The impending business scandal threatens the happiness Albert and I have had these thirty years, and we have chosen to leave Seacliff together than face separation. We depart for the West Indies tonight. You have proven yourself well prepared to take over our business interests, and I entrust them to you. This is how it must be.*
>
> *Farewell, my beloved son, and remember, as I have always taught you, to be true to yourself. Do not grieve, for Albert and I are together.*
> *Your Father*

A tear rolled down my cheek. The letter proved Albert did not kill Gordon. They were planning to leave, just as the steamship tickets inferred. Duncan's father must have expected him to discover the note when he synchronized the clocks. Destiny had intervened, and Duncan had carried an unnecessary guilt for eight years. He was completely innocent. My heart soared. I would count the seconds until I could give this to him.

I turned to go out the side door, when I saw a shadow coming toward me. A figure approached from outside. I had to hide within the house. Darting across the hall into Janina's office, I kept the door open a crack and held my breath. In less than a second, a loud rap came at the door. In moments, I heard Fellowes' quick stride, and he passed by the room where I hid. Hearing him open the door, I peeked into the darkness. A clap of thunder rolled through the house, and I could neither see who the caller was, nor hear what was said. With a catlike stealth I didn't know I owned, I slid out of the room. As another burst of thunder masked my footsteps, I raced up the stairs, ruing the design of a house built into a hillside that prevented a quick and direct escape. I hid behind the enormous potted palm at the top of the stairs. Fellowes' voice called out in a sing-song style into the darkness.

"Mister Andrew, Dr. Nickles wished to know if you made it home safely. I told him you had, and were sleeping soundly. He's quite concerned over your health, as am I! Come out now and let us have a nice chat."

Terror gripped me as never before. I stared through the wide fronds of the tree, down the stairs at the valet. He stood in the center of the unlit hallway, searching the air for me and cocking his head.

"I'll find you Mister Andrew! You cannot hide in this house! Mrs. Stewart will help me."

I looked behind me at her portrait. The oil figure's hand no longer pointed the way to her bedroom, but appeared to point toward the exact spot where I stood. Watching Fellowes walk over to the electric light switch by the front door, I knew I would be exposed. Perhaps if I bolted down the stairs I could catch Dr. Nickles before he left the grounds.

A tremendous bolt of lightening flashed, giving everything in the Great Hall a cold blue-gray tint. The thunder roared, and as Fellowes pressed the switch, the chandelier lights came on for an instant, then went out.

"Not to worry, Mister Andrew. I can find my way about the house without the electrical lights!" He picked up one of the ornate silver candlesticks on the refectory table and lit it. The flickering light cast a skeletal glow upon his long face.

At that moment, the distinct chime of Saint Margaret's clock echoed from the bedroom. My stomach churned: by removing the letter, I must have reactivated the mechanism.

Fellowes' reaction was one of questioning, then recognition. Turning, he disappeared down the hall. "No more hide-and-seek my little mouse! This cat will find you!" As he walked inside, I ran toward the one refuge I knew, Duncan's study. Trembling, I opened the door to this room and slid inside.

I could see the angry branches of the trees scraping at the air through the windows. The rain pounded down on the roof. The animal heads and weapons along the walls that frightened me once now seemed willing to protect me. To my surprise, a fire was roaring, and the smell of Duncan's lingering tobacco and the sturdy leather furniture had an effect of calm upon me. I scouted for a place to hide. The most logical place would be in one of the giant leather chairs; if Fellowes opened the door and surveyed the room, I would not be visible. I secured the revolver in my pocket; if I had to use it, I would.

Grabbing one of the large red tartan plaid blankets from the long sofa, I moved to hide under it, when I saw the red ball that was the tip of his cigar.

"Duncan?"

He turned around in his chair, and the reflection of the flames lit his face. He was as ragged as I; wild hair, shirt opened to the waist, his face tired. He wore the same clothing as last night. Resting his cigar in the ashtray, he opened the desk drawer.

"I thought you were on the grounds." The cold businessman, not the man I cared for, was talking to me just as he had on our first meeting.

"I love you, Duncan. I want to help you. What's wrong with that?"

He looked at me, emotionless. "Misery and unhappiness are all I can provide." He withdrew a ledger from the desk. "And money. That's your real reason, isn't it? How much do you want to go to Edgar or Leo and be out of my life?"

"Stop feeling sorry for yourself. I don't want to go to Edgar, I . . ."

Opening the book, he next removed a pen from its holder. "Ah yes. Paris, that's your ultimate destination." He began to write. "This check should be enough to buy your own art studio in Paris: your own gallery. Perhaps you will cross paths with Steven and have a bottle of fine champagne at my expense."

I walked over to the desk. "You are right Duncan Stewart, you are unlovable. You push everyone away. Your son, me, even your father. It's always about money; what you can buy, who you can buy. Never anything else."

"And with you, it's all about tormenting me with my past. Our accounts are settled." Taking a puff of his cigar he tossed the check at me and folded his hands. "Now will you leave? Johnson can take you to the station." He looked out the window at the torrential rain. "Probably tomorrow. Damned if I can't be rid of you!"

I threw the letter on his desk. "This will keep you company in your wealthy loneliness, Mr. Stewart." Walking to the door, I had no idea where I would go. In a flicker, the electric lights came back on in the room.

"Wait!" he barked. "Where did you get this?"

"It was in Saint Margaret's clock. Had you not been so vain to assume your father was killed because of you, it might have come to light eight years ago." I didn't care how mean I was. I would never see him again.

"This is my father's handwriting."

I watched him read it. I remembered the key around my neck. I took it off and tossed it on his desk. A tear was in the corner of his right eye. "Andrew—"

"You don't have all the answers, Duncan Stewart. This key belongs to a chest of Gwendolyn's. It's in this house, I'm certain, and it will reveal who murdered them. Perhaps in your isolation here, you will find it. If you care."

"Look in that cabinet on the wall."

"I've been discharged, remember? You no longer control me."

His voice remained calm. "It's what I'd forgotten . . . when you told me she and James witnessed the murder. Gwendolyn gave me the chest before she died. Look on the bottom shelf of that tall cabinet. Get it, and then get out of my house."

I walked over to a massive oak cabinet carved with intricate figures, and opened the double doors. Kneeling down and looking behind a stack of ledgers on the bottom shelf, there was indeed a medium-sized chest, decorated with shells and rope. As I pulled it out, he said, "And forgive me for refusing your offer to help."

Looking back at him, this giant bear of a man, I knew I could not resist my heart. As I brought the chest to his desk, he spoke as he inserted the key.

"When Gwennie gave me this, she had accepted the job and wanted me to hold it for safekeeping. I remember thinking she would send for it once she was settled at Oak Lawn."

"The sanitarium."

"Mother had been one of the trustees for years; it was a special cause for her. She had a sister who was not well. Gwennie wanted to get out of Seacliff, and this was a good chance. I'd arranged the job for her. It was good money—yes, I do think about money too much. I thought nothing more of it until now."

I put my hand on his left one, and he placed his other hand over mine. Looking into his eyes, I saw myself again reflected in them.

"This may tell us who killed your Father and Albert, Duncan."

He released his hand and pressed the buzzer on his desk. "I already know. One of the theories I had, but perhaps not as deviant as I thought."

A slight rap came and Fellowes walked inside. "I see you've found our intruder. I will have Johnson stop the search. Shall I telephone the sheriff?"

"Andrew brought this to me. Perhaps you'd like to read it." He handed it to the valet, who took a short breath when he recognized the handwriting. He folded it back into place and returned it to Duncan without registering emotion.

"I don't understand, sir."

"Mother killed them and you've covered up for her all these years."

It made complete sense. Fellowes protected Janina, even insinuating to me that Duncan committed the crime to save her reputation.

The valet gave an odd smile, and turned away. He walked toward the wall of weapons and clasped his hands together.

"You knew so little about her, sir. What a pity."

"Don't protect her any longer."

At that instant I realized the gun that had taken two lives was missing from its place on the wall. The valet removed the weapon from his jacket and smiling, pointed it at Duncan.

"Do you not remember your mother's teachings? No scandal must ever touch this house. Her fine name: her reputation was at stake. Yet, her husband was going to leave her for another man. We could tolerate their actions as long as they were confined to Seacliff. But no, they wanted to go off into the world. The shame."

Duncan's voice was calm. "Put down the gun."

"On her deathbed, she made me promise I would keep the reputation of this house intact. But you, sir, are no better than your father. An illegitimate son. That whorish Steven Charles, and now this . . . this child."

I pulled the revolver from my pocket and with an unsteady hand, pointed it at the valet. Duncan registered more surprise than Fellowes.

"Andrew! You'll hurt yourself. Let me handle this!"

The valet gave a deep laugh and his eyes were wide. "At least Mister Charles had the decency to leave. It will all work out perfectly. We made sure, Mister Andrew, that you would find Miss Janina's revolver. You see, it's the mate to this one. He looked down at the gun in his own hand, caressing the silver barrel with his long fingers. "I would have hoped you would have shot Mister Duncan by now. That would have made my job so much easier."

Duncan regarded him. "What do you mean?"

Fellowes gave us his crooked smile. "Mister Andrew broke into the house. He confronted you here in the study. Angry over his dismissal and suffering from disease—the same disease that made you want him— he murdered you with the gun he stole from Miss Janina's room." He smiled again. "I reported the theft to the sheriff earlier. I came in to this room, found your body, and to defend my own life, killed Mister Andrew." He dropped his voice. "There will be no tearful notes left behind this time."

Duncan's desk drawer was ajar, and I remembered the revolver he kept there. I held my breath wondering when he would use it. Instead, he removed a pale green envelope, and spoke with complete softness.

"Think of the scandal if you kill us. Mother would never have supported that. And . . ." he said, waving the envelope in the air, "you would have to return to Oak Lawn."

The valet's face drained of all its color.

Duncan smiled with the skill of a man who indeed, always won. "You see, when you gave me the contents of Mother's desk, you destroyed the steamship tickets." He turned the letter around. "But you overlooked this correspondence from Dr. Luckenbill, who wrote Mother inquiring of his former patient's health. Your health. A copy is on file at my attorney's; in the event of my death, you will be exposed."

The valet's hand began to tremble; I feared he would kill us both. He was deranged, answering to what he believed were his dead mistress's wishes.

"When Gwendolyn received a job offer from Oak Lawn, you thought she would learn about your past, and you wanted to protect yourself."

"Gwendolyn. Another tramp. Wouldn't get married first and then produce a child. And James, fornicating with anything that breathed, just like your father."

"You pushed her off the cliff. You didn't know James gave her the chest." He tapped the lid. "What's in here old boy, Mother's confession? You paid James to keep his mouth shut. Is that why the stipend Mother left you disappeared so quickly?"

The valet's entire body began shaking and the revolver tumbled to the floor. "Don't open that chest, Mister Duncan. Please."

Duncan turned the lock and the lid flung open. Fellowes turned, and scanning the wall behind him, selected one of the large daggers. He spoke in the direction of the hallway.

"She calls me. Do you not hear her lovely voice? Excuse me, gentlemen."

We watched him leave the study and walk down the corridor of Stewart portraits, illuminated by the moonlight, where the larger-than-life image of Janina Stewart waited at the top of the staircase. Facing the portrait of his beloved mistress, Fellowes spoke to her, words we could not hear, and then laughed.

I screamed as the servant plunged the dagger into his heart, burying my face in Duncan's chest. He held me as the rain continued to pound without end.

It was not until hours later, once Dr. Nickles arrived and the body removed, after Mr. and Mrs. Johnson had been told of the circumstances of Gwendolyn's death and weeping anew with them over the loss, that Duncan and I examined the chest. It was indeed filled with money and a signed confession from Edward Fellowes, but the shocking part was the thirty-six letters inside. They were from Fellowes to Gordon Stewart, professing his eternal love and, in the final correspondence dated the day he murdered the two men, begging Gordon to take him to Barbados instead of Albert. From what we could determine, Gordon Stewart toyed with the valet's affections with the promise that if he took care of Janina, Fellowes might become fortunate enough to periodically land in his employer's bed. Unaware that the valet's self-loathing over his own sexual desires had been the root of his mental problems, Gordon Stewart's virile pride sealed his destiny.

What was important to us was that the dark shadow hanging over Seacliff was vanquished, and the promise of a new dawn was on the horizon.

Chapter Thirteen

Sunlight streamed through the large paned windows casting criss-cross shadows onto the black and white marble floor of the Great Hall. I descended the stairs, doubtful I could ever erase the image of Fellowes' body from my mind. But I no longer felt the internal hatred that had hung in the air.

The soft tinkling of the piano reached my ears. The player was moving through a quite complicated piece. I thought of Steven Charles. It could not be. Perhaps Elena or Leo had dropped by. In the five days since Fellowes' suicide, Leo had been conspicuously absent; this morning I had seen Elena running across the terrace. I called to her yet she ran away without speaking. It appeared she had been crying. I could almost excuse Leo's distance, after all his long-held theory that Duncan had killed two men had been shattered, but I wondered what was wrong with Elena. I knew she called upon Duncan this morning; perhaps he had made a cruel remark to her about Leo. I hoped the revelation of the murder would heal all the old wounds, but the now-serene house had become a lonely oasis.

The music continued, but on opening the door to the drawing room, I stopped short. No one was seated at the piano. Remembering the night of the séance, I wondered if the house was indeed haunted. I approached the mahogany instrument, which continued to serenade what sounded like a Liszt composition.

"Ash!"

The child stopped, looking up at me with his wide gray eyes. He was so small I couldn't see him from the doorway.

"I didn't mean to frighten you. I had no idea you played so well." With Fellowes gone, I thought the house's secrets had been brought to light. Yet here was a new one.

In silence, the child presented me with a piece of sheet music. It was titled 'Asher.' Its composer: Steven Charles.

"Would you play this for me?"

The Master of Seacliff
Published by The Haworth Press, Inc., 2007. All rights reserved.
doi:10.1300/5778_13

Ash nodded and from memory began the piece. It was a haunting tune, and although my knowledge of music was limited, I admitted Steven Charles was quite talented. As was Ash. The child played the melody with an agility I expected professionals to possess. I pulled some other pieces, and he played each of them with ease. When he finished the last, I squeezed him.

"That was wonderful! Steven taught you, didn't he?"

The child jumped off the bench as if he had been scalded and began pulling me to the door. I noticed the time; it was clear Ash was headed to the cemetery for his afternoon rendezvous.

"Let's stay here where it's warm. Play some more for me."

He dropped my hand, and frowning, raced out of the room. I heard the gates at the top of the stairs clang shut, and knew he was gone. Instead of following him, I went to the kitchen to find Mrs. Johnson. She sang an Irish hymn as she fashioned dough into a piecrust with her stout fingers.

"Why didn't you tell me Ash plays the piano?"

"Oh, 'tis nothin', Mister Andrew. Mister Steven taught him a few little things. But he can't play 'Nearer My God to Thee' at all."

"That may be true, but he can play some of the most difficult pieces ever composed. I think you may have a child prodigy on your hands."

The woman shook her head.

"Mozart began playing when he was four. Ash is five, Mrs. Johnson. We should not dismiss this as inconsequential."

The look in her eyes told me she was not fathoming what I had said. Instead she cut off a corner of the dough and plopped it in my mouth. Wiping her hands on her apron, she smiled. "You've brought such goodness into this house, Mister Andrew, I don't know how much more happiness my old heart can take."

"I will investigate getting a music teacher for him."

"We can't afford that, Mister Andrew."

I thought of the money in the chest. Mr. and Mrs. Johnson had refused it, claiming it was tainted by the devil. Unbeknownst to them, Duncan had set up a trust for Ash with the funds.

"Duncan will provide for him, I'm certain."

"Clearing the heartache over me Gwennie was providence enough." She then lowered her voice, and the creases across her face deepened. "But there's somethin' I must confess." She beckoned me closer, although I was only a few feet from her.

"I heard Mister Duncan speaking to the sheriff about the night his father was killed. Oh, I'm so ashamed!"

I looked at her, waiting. Her protracted manner of giving information was familiar. "Please go on."

"Mister Duncan said he was hit on the head the night his father was killed. I'm afraid it was poor James that did that."

I laughed out loud, remembering my own disbelief at that alibi. Indeed, it was true.

"Shh! James knew Mister Duncan didn't approve of his courtin' Gwendolyn, and was fearful they'd been seen on the terrace together. I never said nothin' about it to no one before."

"It doesn't matter." I looked at the stove laden with kettles. "Remember, Tim returns tomorrow, so don't outdo yourself tonight."

I insisted Tim come back to Seacliff for the weekend. When he would refuse to go back to the boarding school Duncan placed him in after I left, I intended to plead his case. Then I would insist I remain at Seacliff as well—despite Duncan's continued insistence I go to Edgar LaVina's.

The housekeeper picked up a rolling pin. "Master Tim I'll be glad to see. But as for that Oriental—"

"Lu is only coming to assume some duties until a replacement for—"

"Don't speak his evil name! That crazy loon. All these years, workin' next to a maniac and never knowin'." She wrinkled her mouth. "And I suppose 'some duties' include me being turned out of me own kitchen so those awful concoctions he calls 'food' can be prepared. Why, I wouldn't feed that slop to me pigs."

"Chinese food is really quite delicious, Mrs. Johnson."

"Laced with opium! Read the newspapers like I do and you'll know. Too much of that and you'll be sold off into white slavery before you know what's hit you."

I gave up. "I will speak to Duncan about Ash."

The housekeeper gave me a curious look, a broad smile, and her plump cheeks turned pink. "I'll worry about tomorrow's supper tomorrow. Tonight it's quite a special meal I'm preparing for just you and him. Mister Duncan planned the menu himself." I saw a thought cross her mind. "He probably knows that he won't be eating so well while that 'Louie' is here."

"Duncan planning supper? That's a first."

"I understand you're leavin' Seacliff, Mister Andrew. We'll be sorry to see you go. You've done so much for us—" Her voice faded as she wrung her apron.

"Nothing has been finalized yet."

Rolling her eyes up to the ceiling, she continued, "And poor Mister Duncan, all alone in this big old house. He'll be mighty lonesome, and most disagreeable."

I would not take the blame for Duncan's isolation. "It is his decision that I leave. Have you ever known him to change his opinion?"

"There's a first time for everything and everyone," she said in a light tone, turning and strolling across the room.

I blushed, but rather than excuse myself, I followed the housekeeper over to the enormous stove where she inspected simmering apples for a pie. Her behavior was unusual. Again acting oblivious to my presence, she lifted the lid and continued with her singing, this time a cheerful folk song.

"Mrs. Johnson, what do you remember about Duncan and Steven Charles?"

"Mister Charles wasn't one to mix downstairs with the servants, unless he needed something." She held up a spoonful of apple and I took it in my mouth. "Not at all like you, love. Why I think if you were the master of Seacliff, you'd be just as kind as you are now. How's me apples?"

"Delicious. What I mean to say is—" I started to stammer. "Were Duncan and Steven— were they happy together?" I knew of Lu's confession, but I wanted another opinion.

"People act different with different people. I guess you could say Mister Duncan and Mister Steven were quite happy in their way. But you make Mister Duncan happy too, child."

Tonight at supper Duncan would insist I leave Seacliff, forever. He had avoided me since the night Fellowes died, and although I knew he was relieved of the anguish of his father's death, Steven Charles would remain a silent wall between us. This morning I received a terse note asking me to join him at supper. Unlike our wonderful evening at The Looking Glass, this would be a final goodbye. As I reached the swinging door into the hall, Mrs. Johnson called after me.

"But I never saw so much broken bric-a-brac as I did those last few days before Mister Steven left. You know, as much as a person can love, they can hate someone just as much."

"What do you mean?"

She waved her ladle at me. "Run along Mister Andrew! If you're so curious, ask Mister Duncan tonight, while the two of you are alone, eatin' off the china we only use on special occasions. And I had one of the girls press your black suit to wear this evening. Can't let fancy clothes like that go to waste."

She started singing at the top of her voice and ignored me despite my attempts to question her. The more I spoke, the louder she became. I would indeed have to wait until tonight to see what she was talking about.

Just before eight o'clock I walked to the Great Hall. I heard the door chimes earlier, and wondered if perhaps Elena and Leo would join us. It would be easier to say goodbye with others around. I checked my pressed suit for imaginary wrinkles and twisted the curls of my hair. How different my life had become. On the outside, I never looked better, yet inside I felt empty. My dream was just a train ride away; on my life would go, to study art, and Edgar LaVina and I would travel to Paris in late autumn.

The clocks ushered in the hour: Saints Margaret and Mary's voices had been added back into the chorus and now the sound of violins and a harp floated from the ballroom at the end of the hall. There was no time to investigate, and taking a deep breath, I walked into the dining room.

The room was ablaze with the glow of dozens of candles. Duncan stood by his chair; dressed in formal wear, and had never looked so handsome. It would be how I wanted to remember him.

"Would it be possible for you to manage a smile, Andrew? You look as though you've lost your favorite toy."

I wanted to slap him. After confessing my love to him, he still regarded me as a child. "Where is that music coming from?"

"I hired some entertainers from The Looking Glass to play while we dine. Madame Marcella is most generous. Since we can't be in Manhattan, I thought I'd bring the city to us. I've sent the other servants away for the night as well."

He held the chair for me, then sat down. "You look quite charming, Andrew. Especially your eyes. They say candlelight brings out the true soul of a person."

We ate our lobster bisque and I watched Duncan carve the roast beef. Aside from the grand setting, it was how life existed in the town house. Duncan refilled his wineglass. Offering some to me, I shook my head. This would not be as before.

"It is nice being alone here, isn't it, Andrew?"

I nodded.

"Almost like being at the town house."

"I want to apologize about that night, Duncan. Presenting you with Steven's portrait was obviously wrong."

Waving the carving knife, which startled me, he said, "Let's not discuss him."

He would not change. I should jump at this opportunity to leave and see the world. Instead I felt as if I were being sent off to boarding school along with Tim.

We finished supper within the next hour. Duncan excused himself to the kitchen, returning with two dessert plates under gleaming silver covers.

"That's a fancy way to serve apple pie," I said.

"If there was an apple pie, I know nothing of it. Mrs. Johnson must have spirited that away to her own home. This is a special treat." He sat the covered dish before me, and lifted the cover of his. A huge slice of chocolate cake, enough for two people, with thick frosting and a wedge of white chocolate like a fin stuck from the top. "I prepared this myself, you know."

I gave him a weak laugh. When would he tell me to leave?

"Lift the cover of yours, and see that I speak the truth."

I raised the silver cover. On the china plate was not pastry, but a velvet box the color of chocolate, topped with an ivory bow. I looked at him.

"I wanted to give you this at the town house, Andrew."

"Duncan, you have already given me so much. Look at me."

"I am," he said, but his tone was not the same as mine. It was a darker, earthier one. "Open it."

I untied the bow, but my fingers were not functioning as I wanted. Nestled on ivory satin identical to the bow was a silver medal on a long delicate chain. On the front, in an engraved script was my first initial. On the back, in tinier block letters, the inscription: *Forever*. It was the most precious item I had ever seen.

"It is beautiful, Duncan. It looks so old, is it antique—" The realization came clear. This was his way of saying goodbye. His eyes concentrated on the medal.

"My father gave it to Albert. I kept it, ashamed of their deaths. But you have shown me the truth. My father loved Albert very much."

I looked up from the small box: Duncan's black eyes were as soft as I had ever seen them.

"But not as much as I love you, Andrew."

I expected I would awaken from this dream. As if we were inside The Looking Glass again. Duncan Stewart loved me. He said he did.

"Duncan, I—don't know what to say. I—"

"Perhaps you could say you love me too."

Tears welled up and I grabbed the napkin from my lap. "I do love you," I removed the chain from the box and opened the clasp. Duncan stood up and took the medal from my hands. Standing behind me, he undid my cravat and placed the chain around my neck. The medal rested just above the center of my chest.

"You will move into my room upstairs. Perhaps this invitation is a little more decorous than my previous offer." He stroked my shoulder and bent down, kissing the top of my head, and sat beside me.

"Steven's room?"

The minute I spoke his name I regretted it. Duncan's eyes darkened, but only for a moment. He extended his hand and on instinct I knew to place mine in his. My hand was so different compared to his, so large, dark, and with a hirsute backside. He lifted my hand to his mouth and kissed it.

"Our room. Please share my life with me Andrew. Forever."

I could not go forward without hearing his love for Steven would never die. Perhaps it was all right for me to love him more than he could me. "But Steven—"

Duncan rolled his eyes.

"Please let me finish. I know you cared for him very much. Wouldn't you like to find him and apologize?"

"Apologize? Why?"

"Reconcile, then. A disagreement came between you two."

"There is to be no reconciliation."

"But you went overseas to find him just before I was engaged here."

"That is what I told everyone, but in fact I was tracking George Upshaw, who kept eluding me. It was a mere business trip, and one of my few failed ones."

Coming behind me, he put his hands on my hair and rubbed my earlobes. The familiar tingle of blood raced up from my toes to my thighs and then straight to the apex of my legs.

"Andrew, Steven is never coming back."

I could not face him, so I talked to his reflection in the mirror above the sideboard. "Don't you want to see him again?"

"Frankly, no. I asked him to leave. Our association was over. We came to an irrevocable parting of the ways."

"What?"

"It's not an easy thing to talk about. Come, let's have a Scotch."

The musicians were still hidden from view, but their beautiful melodies echoed through the house, making it more peaceful than I had ever known it. Duncan poured us both a drink and sat beside me.

"Steven was quite indiscreet. Not only was he involved with Leo—"

The appointment book in the jacket. Leo's obsession with Steven. I nodded.

"—but just about anything male between here and Manhattan. I surprised Edgar and him one day."

I took his hand.

"Can't you see how humiliating that was for me? Everyone knew this except me. The laughing stock of the East! We had a tremendous argument, and I ordered him out. I had no idea it would be so sudden, but I imagine he did that to throw suspicion on me."

"And he succeeded," I said.

"For a while, I decided I would never be involved with another man again." He clasped both my hands. "Then, you came to Seacliff, with your brightness, your innocence, and your blind faith. I tried to fight it, but I fell in love with you." Holding me snug against him, he whispered in my ear. "May I sweep you off your feet and carry you to our bedroom?"

Winking at him, I replied, "I can walk. I'm not the helpless heroine of some medieval romance."

He extended his hand. I took it and he led me out, while the musicians continued their serenade to an empty first floor.

At the top of the stairs, he opened the door to his room but before I could walk in, he scooped me up in his arms and carried me inside. At last I would see his bedroom, and I didn't have to sneak in. I had been invited by the master; I was being carried in his arms. The room was large; his bed covered in thick purple velvet with gigantic saffron pillows that faced the windows to the sea. One window was open, and the sound of the ocean came in. Soft light from the gas jets also gave the room a sense of quiet splendor. I laughed out loud.

"What's so funny?" Duncan said, dropping me onto his massive bed. I said nothing and rolled atop it, mingling his smell with my own.

Walking over to the bureau, he opened a drawer and tossed two night-shirts beside me. Next, he removed my clothing with the gentlest of touches. The excitement coursing through my veins was so overpowering I surrendered to my emotions and allowed him to see the repercussions of his masculine touch. A glance at his waist showed I had the same effect on him.

In silence he disrobed; my breath grew shallower and shorter as I watched him, bathed in the light from the gas lamps. Naked, Duncan Stewart embodied the physical that I had dreamed of being. He looked even better than the day I spied on him in the gymnasium. He crawled in beside me and the silk coverlet wrapped us in its cocoon. He guided my hands over his body. It seemed every inch of his chest and belly were covered with hair, thick on his torso, and to a lesser extent, on his upper arms and shoulders. His mouth traveled over my face and neck and I let his tongue and teeth probe my neck. He kissed me, soft and tender: the second kiss I had received in this house. But Leo's kiss was nothing compared to Duncan Stewart's.

He extinguished the lamps but the moonlight streamed in the window, making everything shadowy and sensual. I marveled at his body, so muscular, so dark, and I examined his powerful arms and back. Pulling me close and then atop him, his arms enveloped me. I nuzzled him, resting my head on his massive chest. I could hear his heart beating, calm and measured, while mine pounded. He stroked my hair and massaged the outside of my ears. This made me tingle and I crowded in tighter. His fingers explored my neck and upper back, but they would return to twist my hair and rub my temples. My own fingers entwined themselves in his thick black mane and traveled to his beard and moustache. His strong hands traveled down my back and cupped my bottom, kneading the muscles and sending what seemed like electrical charges up my spine. I rubbed my legs against his, again thrilling in the feeling of his hirsute frame against my smooth one. He made soft sounds: low and throaty and I responded to them.

His exploration of my body continued as we rolled in one gentle movement and I was now on my back. He looked down at me with a tender expression, and smiled.

"Uncross your arms from your chest, Andrew. I'm not going to hurt you. I promise."

Trusting him, I outstretched my arms, watching him poised above me.

He lifted my right foot, placing it over his shoulder. He rubbed the back of my thigh and sensations rushed to my brain in such a rapid manner that I expected to explode from the overload. I appraised his body, felt the warm weight of his generous erection against my left leg. His face grew serious and whispering in my ear to breathe deep and low, I closed my eyes and let him possess me as he wished. I felt a gentle push between my legs and the warm feeling of complete penetration. Anchoring himself, he began his exploration of my insides and with gentleness began to thrust against me, groaning in pleasure. We were as one; and I surrendered to passion, calling his name loud into the night, no longer caring who heard me.

The light of dawn awakened me, and I opened my eyes to see Duncan staring out the window. His gold silk robe was tied loose about him. In the rays of the morning sun he looked even more magnificent. I watched how the light played off his muscles, his powerful legs, and the hair on his body, which seemed to be a gift from Zeus. He heard me stir and turned, smiling.

"Good morning, Andrew. You were asleep in an instant last night."

He walked to the bed, discarding the robe as he moved in a languid fashion toward me. Seeing him in a full state of aroused manhood made me want him again. I reached toward his center, feeling my wrist brush against the medal and chain around my neck. It had all been real.

Duncan crawled under the coverlet and silk sheets and held me in his arms again. I gave in to his will again but soon became his equal in discovering his most sensitive points of release. Feelings I had read in his letters to Steven coursed through my own veins and I experienced incredible joy, sadness, release, and pleasurable pain all at once. Duncan alternated between tenderness and rougher, more primitive actions. Our needs and desires were similar and I seized his body as I wished, satisfying our urges together. We fell asleep after this intense session of lovemaking, drenched in each other's sweat as I lay atop him.

Waking again, I watched him sleeping and noticed how at peace he was. I found myself examining the curves of his powerful back and legs; he awoke and we made love again. Afterward, he opened the door to the bedroom; breakfast for two sat on a mahogany cart. Mrs. Johnson! Duncan saw me blushing at the realization and laughed loud enough that I was certain the housekeeper would hear, even if she were in her cottage at the bottom of the hill.

We bathed together and dressed for it was time to collect Tim at the station. I fingered the medal he gave me over and over.

"I shall never remove this medal, Duncan. And I pledge to love you forever."

"And you will do this by avoiding Leo Van Horne, forever."

"Leo is my friend." I remembered what Leo said about the gilded cage Duncan placed Steven in. Was that the price of loving the master of Seacliff? "He is no one to be jealous of, Duncan."

"I told you before, Leo equals trouble. Obey me, Andrew."

"Obey you?"

"That is final. I have new business to attend to, and cannot accompany you to the station."

This distracted me from arguing about Leo. "But it's your son!"

He walked away to his study. I shook my head after him. I was not going to end my friendship with Leo just because Duncan ordered me.

Chapter Fourteen

Searching the windows of the train as it pulled into the station, I spied a small head bounding through the car and out the door before it had come to a complete stop.

"Tim!" I called. "Please be careful!"

The child jumped into my arms and I held him fast. "Andrew! I'm so glad to see you." He wriggled from my grasp. "Where is my father?"

"At his desk. Lu! It is good to see you." The Chinese man stood on the platform, frowning at his surroundings, with an oversized piece of baggage. He bowed and shook my hand with such fervency I thought it might become dislodged from my shoulder.

I turned to Tim. "I'm so sorry you were in that awful place. I—"

"What place? You mean school? I like it. But I'm glad to be home. I want to ride my horse."

I should have predicted the unpredictable response from Tim. He had only been gone less than a week, but to me it was an eternity. I realized I missed him more than he had me.

Lu was to fill the gap left by Fellowes' suicide until a new valet or butler could be engaged. I hoped that the tranquility that resonated through the town house would transfer to the house by the sea. Things were already looking up. On this afternoon the sun had broken through the clouds and the fog had been held off shore all day.

When we got back to the house, Tim flew up to his father's study. In less time than I expected, he ran to his room, grabbed Ash, and pulled him toward the stable. How much had changed! John and Fellowes were dead, and I wondered how to approach the subject once Tim sensed no one wanted to discuss it.

I walked into Duncan's study and he tossed his cigar aside, smiling at me.

"My son seems none the less worse for wear."

"He told me he likes school."

The Master of Seacliff
Published by The Haworth Press, Inc., 2007. All rights reserved.
doi:10.1300/5778_14

"You've read too many books where the main character lives a dismal childhood in a rat-infested school. I assure you, Wolverton Hall is nothing like that."

"I overreacted, I'm sorry."

"Don't be sorry, Andrew. Your devotion to my son—I've seen nothing quite like it, and I thank you. I've made a decision."

I flopped into the leather chair, hoping he had changed his mind about Leo. "Yes?"

"Being in Manhattan I have greater control over business, and Tim could attend school but be home with us on the weekends, if he wanted. You could work for Edgar during the day. I'm closing Seacliff. Indefinitely."

The house shuddered, and for once there was no storm outside.

"Seacliff is your home. Your memories—"

"Memories of unhappiness. I'd like us to start off the new century fresh, Andrew. You are fond of the town house; hell, if you're not, I'll build us another one."

"If it makes sense to close Seacliff, then so we shall. Perhaps we can return here in the spring."

The house groaned again, and my skin tingled as a draft filled the study. I was afraid to discuss leaving Seacliff aloud. I sensed the house would plot revenge to prevent us from ever leaving.

"Excellent," he said, slamming his ledger closed. "Come Monday, we shall be back in Manhattan." He grabbed the telephone receiver beside him. "Run along now, there are some preparatory things I must do."

Walking to the stairs, I saw Lu's arrival had another purpose; Steven Charles' bedroom was denuded of all traces of the former occupant. Crates were stacked as high as my head outside the door, and a glance at the mirrored closet showed it to be bare. The crates were labeled with an address in Buenos Aires. I questioned Lu, who offered no details, other than these were Duncan's instructions. I had a sudden urge to run to Duncan and insist we leave Seacliff tonight, but I dismissed the thought as foolishness. A walk through the grounds would clear my head. It might be my last one until springtime.

I was below the terrace when Leo emerged from the trail leading to Whispering Hill.

"Congratulations," he smirked. "I understand you're moving upstairs."

I laughed at his way of wording things. "You're ordinarily more direct than that."

"I'd prefer not to think of Duncan sharing your bed. In fact, I've come to say goodbye."

"Where are you going?"

"To Cuba: for a start. The family has some languishing investments there and the weather is extraordinary. I have to try and prime the family fortune, you know."

"When will you return?"

"In time, I suppose, but there is really nothing to keep me here. After Havana, I'm traveling onward to South America. I... have a friend there."

I thought of the trunks upstairs, marked for Buenos Aires. And Edgar LaVina mentioned Steven and South America.

"You'll be pleased to know I'll be seeking out Duncan to say my farewells. And apologize."

"That is very good of you, Leo."

"Not really. True, I was wrong about his involvement in Gordon's death. He'll be suspicious regardless of what I say. But the thought of you and him—" His voice trailed off, and I felt a twinge of sadness. I had not meant to hurt Leo, and I don't think I realized the depth of his feelings for me until that moment. He had always been so frank, I didn't know when he was bluffing or not. But now, there was a mocking tone in his voice.

"Will you write me Leo? I'd be most interested to read of life in Cuba."

"That I shall Andrew. And perhaps you, and Duncan if he must, will visit me there. Elena has already promised. It is paradise."

He acted happy with this decision. It wasn't just an impetuous reaction to my and Duncan's news. Leo Van Horne would never be lonesome. Perhaps he would find Steven. They seemed well suited to each other.

Before I knew it, he clasped me to his chest. "Come with me, Andrew. The *Cara Mia* is a beautiful ship. After Havana, she sails on, eventually to Hong Kong."

I pushed him away, as he threw back his head and laughed. "Plus one depressed Van Horne is enough for Glendower Hall. Two of us would be unbearable."

I thought about Elena and how I had not seen her. "What do you mean?"

"I think my sister hoped Duncan would have finally broken down and asked her to marry him."

"Elena? And Duncan?"

"Our fathers betrothed my sister and your lover practically before we were born. But Duncan refused and ran off to Europe. He met that gypsy tramp and came back with Tim. Then there was Steven. And Miss Upshaw.

And now you. I told my sister she couldn't continue to expect to catch Duncan between his romances."

"I had no idea. What about Richard Lawrence?"

"What about him? I hope old Richard finally woos Elena into marriage. He's due on the train tomorrow."

Leo embraced me again and I smelled the sea. I started to move away, but he held me fast. "How about one final kiss, until we meet again?"

He gave me no time to agree or refuse, plunging in and touching my lips to his. I closed my eyes and compared his delicate kiss to Duncan's warm and powerful control: I felt nothing. He broke away, and I opened my eyes to see him looking away, smiling.

"Uh-oh, dear boy. I'm afraid we've attracted an audience."

I followed his gaze, up the path, to the house, to the window above the terrace. Duncan watched us, with Elena at his side. I broke from Leo.

"Duncan will be furious. We must go to him— Leo?"

Leo Van Horne had disappeared. I called, but heard only the sea. I wouldn't be surprised if he hadn't planned this kiss as a final jab to his former friend.

I ran up the path two steps at a time and into the house. Elena floated down the stairs and clasped my hands.

"Duncan is enraged. I've never seen him so angry." The look on her face, always serene, even in the worst of Duncan's moods, concerned me more, for she looked terrified.

"I have to go and explain, Elena. It was nothing, Leo was—"

"Let Duncan calm down. He would never believe you in his current state of mind. Or me. I told him Leo is leaving, but he wouldn't listen." She led me to the large table. "I had come looking for you. I thought it would be lovely if we went together to the cemetery and lay fresh flowers at Gordon and Albert's graves. So much has happened; I think we should remember who the real victims were in Fellowes' scheme."

A large arrangement of flowers rested on the table. Foxgloves: the flowers Elena stood among in the painting Edgar LaVina had in his studio. Remembering its size, I knew the painting had been commissioned to hang in Seacliff's hallway. Elena and Duncan. The arranged marriage he had escaped. Because he was not in love.

I picked up the flowers and followed Elena to the door. On our way out, she pulled a heavy cloak from dozens on the rack.

"I think this old thing is Leo's, but I find it quite warming."

I took my lighter jacket; it was not that cool, and we would not be gone for long.

"My brother is quite fond of you, will you miss him?" she asked as we strolled through the woods, which were becoming mistier with the fog. Like Leo's, her green eyes seemed more intense than usual today.

"I am sorry to see him leave. Duncan will be angry at what he saw." I thought of his order to avoid Leo. He assumed I defied him on purpose. "Will you come with me to explain?" I regretted saying this. Elena no doubt suffered herself and it was selfish of me to ask her help this time.

"I've known Duncan all his life, Andrew. He seems strong, but he is actually weak. He needs a stronger person to guide him." Her comments were sharp and brisk, so different from her usual placid demeanor.

I had never seen any display of affection between her and Duncan that was different from that of Elena and her brother. But I could not ask. I wanted to turn back and rush to the house, to the study, to Duncan. I had faced his anger before, but now I knew of the wounds in his heart.

She looked around. "The woods today remind of the ghost stories Duncan, Leo, and I would tell each other when we were children. It seems autumn is upon us."

The woods did indeed seem eerie this afternoon, and the shadows were growing longer. By the time we had paid our respects at Gordon's crypt and returned to the house, it would be close to darkness.

She placed her finger to her chin. "I understand Duncan plans to abandon Seacliff and go to Manhattan."

"Abandon? Oh, only for the winter. I'm sure we shall all return in the spring. But you must come and visit us there."

"It will be the first time Seacliff shall be empty since it was built."

The house, furious at our plans used Elena to verbalize its dislike. I admitted in my heart that I hated Seacliff and would be thrilled if I never saw it again.

I avoided looking at the two fresh graves near the entrance. Inside the grounds, we laid an offering of flowers at the headstone of Albert Brown. I reached through my shirt to finger the medallion Duncan had given me. Under different circumstances, I would have shared my happiness with Elena, but today was not one for such confidences.

We walked up the stone steps of the mausoleum and turned down the west corridor to Gordon's crypt. Elena placed the flowers in the copper vase, smiling.

"It still seems to be a place of unrest," I said. When we got back, I would march upstairs alone, and explain to Duncan what I was doing with Leo.

Elena laughed. "You're letting your imagination run away from you, Andrew. As children, we terrified ourselves with little effort. Duncan and I would lie in wait to scare Leo, or he and I would frighten Duncan. Let me show you our secret hiding place." Her eyes were bright with excitement. "As a permanent part of life at Seacliff, you should know where everything is."

She moved in a swift manner down the corridor, the slightest rustling of Leo's cloak over her dark blue gown. An unmarked marble wall stood beside a stained-glass window of Saint Anthony and two angels. Standing on her tiptoes, Elena reached toward a marble lion's head with an iron ring through its nose, similar to the pin Ash showed me in Steven Charles' jewelry chest. With a tug on the ring, the wall moved, opening a few feet. Beyond the narrow opening lay three steps downward into blackness, and the smell of dank air made me cough.

"This was a storage room for weapons during the Revolutionary War."

"Miss Jones mentioned this, I believe."

"You saw her? When?" Elena perked up and narrowed her eyes.

"In New York. Apparently there is a similar room at the Vernon estate."

"Had she seen this room?"

"I think she guessed it was in the same location. She said you discussed American History at length."

Elena gave a small laugh and I was relieved she was becoming her old self. "Poor Miss Jones and those sapphire earrings. It was easy to suggest to Fellowes she had stolen them."

"You?"

"Duncan was charmed by her innocence, much like he is with you. Fellowes hated her from the start. And had she not been discharged, you would have never met Duncan. Let's go back to him, shall we?" As she raised her arm to close the room, her enameled bracelet slipped from her wrist and rolled into the void.

"Oh, bother. I've needed to have that clasp repaired for weeks. Can you retrieve it for me? It's difficult to do anything but stand straight up in this dress."

I knelt down and looked into the darkness, seeing nothing but a forgotten candle inside, by the steps, and breathing only foul air.

She stood behind me. "The room has been closed up for years. No one remembers it is here. Do you see my bracelet? There it is, below."

Indeed it was, at the foot of the steps. A flash of silver beckoned as I leaned further in, reaching toward it.

A swift and sudden shove against my lower back caused me to tumble forward into the empty space and with a yelp I landed on my side, my head hitting the stone floor. Looking up, I could not see Elena's face, only her silhouette within the coat that framed her. A gray cloak I had seen twice before. Her hand pulled the iron ring downward with deftness. With utter calm, her voice echoed into the chamber, "You should have gone with Leo."

The wall of marble closed, sealing me from her, and the outside world.

I tried to get up, but a sharp pain in my right ankle and left wrist told me I could not support my own weight. Reaching out, I found the steps and pulled myself up. I called to Elena, but she was gone. I pounded against the stones, until I felt my palms become raw. Using the wall for guidance, I fumbled for the candle I had seen. As I bent over, wetness trickled into my mouth and I probed my face. I had cut my forehead when I fell, and a small stream of blood dribbled down my left side. Finding my handkerchief in my pocket, I pressed it to where the wound was stickiest. The pain in my ankle grew.

Locating the candle, I took a match and lit it. There was a little wax left. My eyes traveled to Elena's bracelet, and the fact that she tricked me settled in.

Shoving the candle against the wall, I could discern the slightest trace of the outline of the door. Perhaps there was an exit lever at the foot of the stairs. I backed onto the floor and finding my left hand could not hold the candle firm, I sat it on the step and felt along the bottom with my right hand.

I became aware of another pair of eyes watching me. I wondered if Elena viewed me from another passage, one that might provide an escape. Grabbing the candle and extending it high in the air, I swung around. Indeed, I was not alone. What remained of Steven Charles rested against the back wall. My search for him had ended.

Panic set in. I dropped the candle the moment it shined upon the lock of dried blond hair that fell over the remnants of his face and on the golden rings that adorned the outstretched mummified fingers. I pounded on the wall, screaming until I no longer recognized my own voice.

In the darkness, Elena's evil plan was becoming clearer. She stated she saw Steven at the train station, and she would tell Duncan I left with Leo. We had been fooled by her gentleness, her friendliness. It was her cloaked figure I saw that first day, and she had thrown the rock at me on the cliff.

No doubt it was also she who turned the gas on in my room that night. She was as cold as the house itself. The house! Another thought came clear: Elena did not really love Duncan—it was Seacliff she wanted. She would commit murder to get it.

I fainted, or so I thought, for it seemed a gap in time occurred from pounding on the wall to when I found myself slumped against the stairs, awakened by a noise. I called out to the darkness.

I was cold, and my handkerchief was moist with my own blood. Duncan would not believe I had left with Leo, despite what he saw in the garden. He would find me if I called for him. I pummeled the wall again. I rebelled for hours, though perhaps it was only minutes. Then, I heard a voice. Steven's remains spoke to me from across the secret room.

It's no use. Stay with me.

I hit the wall again. Duncan had to find me. He would not believe Elena's lies. Steven's voice called out again, much as the sirens do to sailors at sea.

We belong together. Rest. You are tired.

He could not speak: he had been dead for months. It was my nerves. The room was empty, except for Steven and me.

Sleep, Andrew. Take a short nap. I will call for help.

After awhile, I could no longer ignore Steven's voice. I decided I would rest. I had no idea how long I had been in the tomb, four hours or four weeks. I only knew it had grown colder; I was hungry and my head, hands, and ankle ached, but I was not alone. Steven was there. I called out to him.

"Steven, are we dead?"

I was talking nonsense. I must conserve my strength. All I needed was just a few minutes rest—.

A light that grew larger made me squint. I must be at the gates of Heaven.

"Holy Mother of God!"

I floated through the air. To Heaven.

"Steven? Am I dead, Steven?"

From far away, a familiar voice carried to my ears. "You are safe."

It sounded like Duncan, and it felt like his arms were around me.

"Steven, can we dream in death?" I mumbled, as the bright light faded, and went out.

I was looking up at the angels: the ones in Steven's old bedroom. Turning my head, I saw sunlight shining on white hair. From above, another voice spoke, like the warm tones of Mrs. Johnson.

"Asher brought Duncan to ye. He saw her—"

I focused my eyes, and indeed Ash was beside me. I was in the bedroom that once had been Steven's, and I was not dead. I had been saved from sharing his fate. A glance over to the mushroom-colored chair revealed Duncan, his head buried in his hands, thanking God for my rescue. When I next awoke, Ash had gone, and I was screaming. But Duncan was beside me this time, his voice tender, soothing. "I'm here, Andrew. And I shall be, always."

I did not remember much of what happened and years later I can only wonder what horrific thoughts tortured my mind that cold afternoon in the Stewart mausoleum.

Ash saved my life. A child born of sorrow led the way to my salvation. He had been in the cemetery, his usual playground, and saw us enter the mausoleum. Seeing only Elena leave, he assumed I would come out soon. He had witnessed Steven disappear the same way twelve months earlier and returned to the cemetery every afternoon waiting for him.

That evening, Ash returned to Seacliff, which was in chaos over my disappearance. Elena told Duncan I departed with Leo; the kiss they witnessed from the second floor was a validation of my falseness.

Duncan listened to her claim, but Elena had not counted on one variable in her ideal scheme. While she and I walked to the mausoleum, Leo visited Duncan as he promised, apologizing and wishing us well in our life together. When Duncan confronted Elena with this, she branded her brother as a liar and Duncan as a fool for believing him. Although Duncan could see this as plausible, he reiterated I would not leave, and demanded a search of the estate and beachfront.

This infuriated Elena, and her cool demeanor began to crumble. As Duncan paced back and forth between the study windows, Ash tugged on his sleeve to come with him. Mr. and Mrs. Johnson, not understanding what their grandchild wanted, tried to remove him, but the child refused to budge. Duncan, knowing of Ash's deep affection for me, realized he was trying to help search, and it was through the child's halting speech that Duncan pieced together my whereabouts.

Elena, now at wit's end, tried to discredit the child, but Duncan brushed her aside and let Ash lead him and Mr. Johnson to the mausoleum.

I do not remember Duncan and Mr. Johnson opening the secret door, but both swore it was my voice that led them to the wall, where Duncan recalled his childhood hideout. To this day, I believe Steven Charles summoned the two men to our dark tomb. Perhaps Steven realized it was not my destiny to remain with him, but to join Duncan in life. And so, the iron ring was pulled, and they found us: Steven and I.

Elena followed Duncan to the mausoleum, pleading with him to believe her. When they found us, she fled, her once-perfect hair blowing about her in a wild manner. The sheriff and his deputies, who joined the search party at the mausoleum, trailed after, but she headed directly to the edge of Whispering Hill and plummeted to the rocks below.

My first clear memory after waking up in the bedroom at Seacliff was the throbbing pain throughout my body. Second, I remember Ash's shy smile as I opened my eyes and looked into his. Third, a haggard-looking Duncan Stewart asleep in the chair by the window.

"Duncan," I called, my voice raspy from having screamed.

Duncan Stewart jumped up and came to my side, collapsing on his knees and sobbing across me. Only one of a handful of times I have seen him so emotional in our forty-five-year relationship.

I reached out to stroke his hair, but found both my hands bandaged. The damage done to me by my imprisonment in the mausoleum was extensive. I had lost much blood from the wound on my forehead. The flesh on my fingers had been scraped raw as I tried to claw my way out. I had broken my right ankle and sprained my left wrist. I had been in a delirium for four days.

Within two weeks I was out of bed and navigating the second floor. My progress was slow, though everyone opined to the contrary. And over Duncan's objections, I hobbled back up the path to Whispering Hill, with Ash at my side, and we placed flowers at a new grave: that of Steven Charles. At that moment I knew he was at peace, and the scent of sandalwood greeted my senses, never returning.

One month later, Duncan, Tim, Ash, and I sailed to France, where we remained for a year. Duncan found a little cottage outside Paris and I realized my dream of becoming a professional artist. Imagine my surprise when a small gallery near the Left Bank hosted a showing of my work alongside those of Monsieur Monet.

But the real reward remains the look of love in Duncan Stewart's eyes when he pulls me close to him and whispers the words engraved on the medal I still wear around my neck. *"Forever."*

ABOUT THE AUTHOR

Max Pierce's love of mystery and horror began with a childhood subscription to Famous Monsters of Filmland and watching countless hours of late-night movies without adult supervision. He explored the world of the vampire as a contributor to the 2005 anthology *Blood Lust*. As a journalist, he writes on Hollywood history and pop culture. An active member of PEN West, Max led a writing group based out of the landmark A Different Light bookstore in West Hollywood.

The Master of Seacliff
Published by The Haworth Press, Inc., 2007. All rights reserved.
doi:10.1300/5778_15

Order a copy of this book with this form or online at:
http://www.haworthpress.com/store/product.asp?sku=5778

THE MASTER OF SEACLIFF

_____in softbound at $16.95 (ISBN-13: 978-1-56023-636-8; ISBN-10: 1-56023-636-1)

200 pages

Or order online and use special offer code HEC25 in the shopping cart.

COST OF BOOKS_____

POSTAGE & HANDLING_____
(US: $4.00 for first book & $1.50
for each additional book)
(Outside US: $5.00 for first book
& $2.00 for each additional book)

SUBTOTAL_____

IN CANADA: ADD 6% GST_____

STATE TAX_____
(NJ, NY, OH, MN, CA, IL, IN, PA, & SD
residents, add appropriate local sales tax)

FINAL TOTAL_____
(If paying in Canadian funds,
convert using the current
exchange rate, UNESCO
coupons welcome)

☐ **BILL ME LATER:** (Bill-me option is good on
US/Canada/Mexico orders only; not good to
jobbers, wholesalers, or subscription agencies.)
☐ Check here if billing address is different from
shipping address and attach purchase order and
billing address information.

Signature_____

☐ **PAYMENT ENCLOSED: $**_____

☐ **PLEASE CHARGE TO MY CREDIT CARD.**

☐ Visa ☐ MasterCard ☐ AmEx ☐ Discover
☐ Diner's Club ☐ Eurocard ☐ JCB

Account #_____

Exp. Date_____

Signature_____

Prices in US dollars and subject to change without notice.

NAME_____

INSTITUTION_____

ADDRESS_____

CITY_____

STATE/ZIP_____

COUNTRY_____ COUNTY (NY residents only)_____

TEL_____ FAX_____

E-MAIL_____

May we use your e-mail address for confirmations and other types of information? ☐ Yes ☐ No
We appreciate receiving your e-mail address and fax number. Haworth would like to e-mail or fax special
discount offers to you, as a preferred customer. **We will never share, rent, or exchange your e-mail address
or fax number.** We regard such actions as an invasion of your privacy.

Order From Your Local Bookstore or Directly From
The Haworth Press, Inc.
10 Alice Street, Binghamton, New York 13904-1580 • USA
TELEPHONE: 1-800-HAWORTH (1-800-429-6784) / Outside US/Canada: (607) 722-5857
FAX: 1-800-895-0582 / Outside US/Canada: (607) 771-0012
E-mail to: orders@haworthpress.com

For orders outside US and Canada, you may wish to order through your local
sales representative, distributor, or bookseller.
For information, see http://haworthpress.com/distributors

(Discounts are available for individual orders in US and Canada only, not booksellers/distributors.)

PLEASE PHOTOCOPY THIS FORM FOR YOUR PERSONAL USE.
http://www.HaworthPress.com   BOF07

Dear Customer:

Please fill out & return this form to receive special deals & publishing opportunities for you! These include:
- availability of new books in your local bookstore or online
- one-time prepublication discounts
- free or heavily discounted related titles
- free samples of related Haworth Press periodicals
- publishing opportunities in our periodicals or Book Division

❑ OK! Please keep me on your regular mailing list and/or e-mailing list for new announcements!

Name _____

Address _____

_____

STAPLE OR TAPE YOUR BUSINESS CARD HERE!

*E-mail address _____
*Your e-mail address will never be rented, shared, exchanged, sold, or divested. You may "opt-out" at any time.
May we use your e-mail address for confirmations and other types of information? ❑ Yes   ❑ No

Special needs:

Describe below any special information you would like:
- Forthcoming professional/textbooks
- New popular books
- Publishing opportunities in academic periodicals
- Free samples of periodicals in my area(s)

Special needs/Special areas of interest:

_____

_____

_____

_____

Please contact me as soon as possible. I have a special requirement/project:

_____

_____

_____

The Haworth Press Inc.

PLEASE COMPLETE THE FORM ABOVE AND MAIL TO:
Donna Barnes, Marketing Dept., The Haworth Press, Inc.
10 Alice Street, Binghamton, NY 13904-1580 USA
Tel: 1-800-429-6784 • Outside US/Canada Tel: (607) 722-5857
Fax: 1-800-895-0582 • Outside US/Canada Fax: (607) 771-0012
E-mail: orders@HaworthPress.com

GBIC06

Visit our Web site: www.HaworthPress.com